what they always tell us

what they always tell us

martin wilson

delacorte press

Published by Delacorte Press
an imprint of Random House Children's Books
a division of Random House, Inc.
New York

Chapter 1 was first published in slightly different form under the title "Alone for the Weekend"
by *Rush Hour* in the Summer 2006 issue #4 ("Reckless").

Visit us on the Web! www.randomhouse.com/teens
Educators and librarians, for a variety of teaching tools, visit us at
www.randomhouse.com/teachers

Library of Congress Cataloging-in-Publication Data
Wilson, Martin.
    What they always tell us / Martin Wilson.—1st ed.
        p. cm.
    Summary: Sixteen-year-old Alex feels so disconnected from his friends that he starts his junior year at
a Tuscaloosa, Alabama, high school by attempting suicide, but soon, a friend of his older brother draws
him into cross-country running and a new understanding of himself.
    ISBN 978-0-385-73507-0 (trade hardcover)—ISBN 978-0-385-90500-8 (Gibraltar lib. bdg.)
    [1. Social isolation—Fiction. 2. Brothers—Fiction. 3. Self-actualization (Psychology)—Fiction.
4. High schools—Fiction. 5. Schools—Fiction. 6. Homosexuality—Fiction. 7. Family life—
Alabama—Fiction. 8. Tuscaloosa (Ala.)—Fiction.]   I. Title.
    PZ7.W6972Wha 2008   [Fic]—dc22   2007030269

The text of this book is set in 12-point Adobe Garamond.
Printed in the United States of America
10 9 8 7 6 5 4 3 2 1
First Edition

To Mom and Dad—for everything

And in loving memory of
Eleanore Hubbard "Lolly" Wilson (1904–1992),
author, artist, and grandmother

what they always tell us

1

Alex

On a Saturday morning in November, Alex finds himself alone for the weekend, so he decides to break a few rules. First, he wears his father's worn-out, blue terry-cloth robe around the house and turns the thermostat up. He doesn't flush the toilet right away or put the seat down, nor does he take the trash out, just lets all the debris—balled-up napkins, fast-food bags and wax-paper cups, a clunky box of stale cereal—pile and cling close to the edges of the trash can. Last night he ate a cheeseburger and an order of fries with ketchup on his parents' wedding china, and he didn't even wash the plate afterward, just let it sit on the counter, the crumbs and salt caking on the grease. He also drank three Heinekens from the refrigerator, and some of his older brother's stash of cheap vodka from a large, green-tinted plastic bottle, which James hides in his old toy chest under his tennis gear.

The weekend isn't supposed to be a solitary one, but James has also broken rules: after their mother and father left for a wedding in Nashville—leaving numbers to call in case of an emergency, and money for meals and groceries—James went to stay with his girlfriend at the La Quinta hotel by the interstate. He told Alex that he had planned this La Quinta weekend for a while. *"Don't screw it up for me,"* he said. James's girlfriend is named Alice, but the name doesn't suit her, Alex thinks, because Alices are usually maids or Sunday school teachers or sweet-faced TV weather girls. He has seen this Alice at school—she's a senior, like James—and Alex knows that she always wears tight jeans and too much makeup, she swears a lot, and she smokes Virginia Slims cigarettes in the parking lot both before and after school. Alex is certain that she's had plenty of other boyfriends before; James isn't so special.

So, a whole day alone, and Alex doesn't feel like doing much of anything. No homework, no exercising, no pleasure reading, nothing. His parents had almost made him go to the wedding—a family friend's son is getting married, someone Alex doesn't even really know because the guy is so much older—but they finally relented, allowing him to stay home under the watchful eye of James. Ha.

When he gets tired of sitting around, Alex walks around the house, peering out the windows like he's examining some strange world. The front lawn is beige and brittle, and the limbs of the slouchy oak tree are an exposed and pocked pale gray. The backyard butts up to a small thatch of forest of mostly pine trees that are tall and thin and almost menacing-looking. Alex and James used to play in that forest, but neither of them has ventured back there in years.

Alex ends up in the kitchen and picks at a powdered dough-nut he has plucked from a plastic package. When he looks out the bay window at the house across the street, he sees the small boy who lives there with his mother. The boy and his mother are quiet and have kept to themselves, mostly, since they moved in this past summer. Alex's mother said they must be renting the place, because as far as she knew, Mr. Pembroke still owned that house. Mom has done all the neighborly things—made them cookies and stuff—but, still, the two of them remain mysterious. The little boy has red hair, extremely red, the unnatural color of a Coke can. Today, he lies in his driveway without a coat on and reads a heavy book. Alex often sees the boy outside, lurking, talk-ing to himself, moving his hands about like a conductor, always alone.

The phone rings—an angry, intrusive noise—and Alex thinks about not answering it. The little boy, as if he can hear it ringing, picks up his head and stares at Alex's yard. Before his parents left, they instructed Alex to tell anyone who calls for them that they are busy or out running errands, not out of town. In case a potential robber or kidnapper or killer calls and gets some ideas. Yeah right. Before the answering machine can pick up, Alex answers quietly.

"May I speak to Mr. Joseph Donaldson, please?" A female voice, overly formal, practiced.

"He's out of town." Another broken rule, but it doesn't matter—it's just a woman from the phone company and she says she'll call back at a more convenient time.

He hadn't thought the phone would be for him anyway, be-cause no one has called Alex for a couple of months, ever since he swallowed Pine-Sol at Marty Miller's lake house party and had to be rushed to the hospital. The party took place in early September, the weekend after Labor Day, and served as the annual welcome-back-to-school drunk fest for the junior and senior class. Because of Alex the party had been ruined. And after that night, everyone thought Alex was mentally disturbed. Fucked in the head.

After the incident, Alex was out of school for three weeks. He sat at home, mostly in his bed, waiting for the phone to ring, waiting for his friends Kirk and Tyler—his musketeers, his mother always said—and the others to call him, maybe with some gesture of concern. He expected that, at least from the girls like Beth or Lang. Girls are supposed to be sweet and caring, aren't they? But they never called, either. Instead of sympathy he was greeted with silence. And that's not all—they avoid him at school, too. All of them, all of his classmates. They walk by without meeting his eyes, and he can almost hear their thoughts about him as he continues down the halls: *Freak, loser, stay away from us.*

James thinks Alex is crazy and has said as much. At the hospital, while their parents talked to the doctor in the hall, James said, "Why would anyone do that? Why?"

Alex had wanted to answer him, but he just fingered his identification bracelet and watched the empty gray-green screen of the TV that was perched on a ledge in the corner of the room. If only he could have transported himself into the TV, into some after-school special, where a boy like him, after an event like this, could return home, return to school triumphantly in the fiftieth minute of the show, all forgiven, all misunderstandings cleared by the time the credits started rolling.

After the party, Alex's mother locked all the cleaning supplies in her bathroom cabinet, using an actual padlock, even though Alex swore that they didn't need to worry about him doing something like that anymore. It was ridiculous, locking it away. After all, couldn't Alex just buy more on his own if he really wanted to do it again? Now the lock is gone, but his mother still hides all toxic supplies behind boxes of Kleenex and rolls of Charmin.

On this Saturday, Alex has taken a bottle of Mr. Clean (as if, somehow, a different brand would be enough of a deterrent) out from under the dusty cabinet and placed it on the kitchen counter next to the blender. He has no plans to use it, but he gets a rare bold charge from placing it in plain sight.

Outside, the little redheaded boy is throwing pebbles at the neighbors' iron mailbox, which is painted to look like a cozy, two-story lime green house, complete with a shingled roof and a flagstone walkway. Alex's own house is redbrick, two-story, rectangular, pretty, but not an architectural wonder. The backyard has a swing set that hasn't been used for some time now but that is still rooted in the ground with concrete. Alex's mother wants to build a gazebo where the swing set is, but his father is dragging his feet about it, complaining that it's too expensive. Alex thinks about all this now, the particulars of his home. He has lived in this house his whole life. And yet it doesn't feel like it used to, it doesn't feel familiar—something is different, and the silence only reminds him of this. He even smells his house—the way a stranger would upon entering an unfamiliar dwelling. It is a sour smell, like a lemony sweat, maybe from the dried-fruit potpourri his mother places out in cut-glass dishes all over the place.

The phone rings again and he grabs it immediately. He doesn't say hello, but holds his mouth there, as if waiting to kiss it.

"Hello?" a voice says. Maybe the same woman as earlier.

"No one's home," he says, and hangs up.

At noon Alex showers and changes his clothes but continues to wear the robe over a pair of jeans and a purple T-shirt that his eighth-grade class made a few years ago. The T-shirt shows everyone's signatures under white stenciled lettering that says MRS. JOHNSON'S BEST-EVER 8TH GRADE CLASS! It's cheesy, he should throw it away. But it still fits, and its worn cotton feels comfy.

Outside the sun tries to slip through the stubborn clouds, and he sits on his bed like he is waiting for something to happen. He eyes a stack of books on the floor next to his desk, school textbooks covered with brown grocery bag paper that he has doodled on. His wire-bound notebooks are also filled with doodles and a few scribbled sentences, often incomplete. Alex opens the yellow notebook, the one for American government class, and sees a page that is dated October 1, the day he returned to school—just over a month ago. On the page, in his neat print, he reads WEEKEND PLANS. But no plans are listed. He used to make lists all the time, lists that outlined what he needed to do, what he wanted to do, what his parents wanted him to do, what he would like to buy, what books he should read to better himself. So many lists, so much plotting out. And for what? Every day feels the same now. The only time he experiences quick spurts of excited happiness is right when he wakes up in the morning, but that's before he's fully awake, before he realizes a whole day like all the others stretches in front of him.

He leaves his room and heads downstairs, restless. In the living room he looks outside once again and sees that the boy is still out there, walking on the curb as if negotiating a balance beam. Alex wants to go outside to check the mail. But he doesn't want to have to look at the kid, doesn't want to nod or say hello as neighbors should. That requires too much energy. He wishes the boy would go inside to eat lunch or something. He suddenly remembers that the kid's name is Henry. A few weeks ago the child's mother—a pretty woman with wispy, dirty blond hair who likes to wear short skirts with ankle boots and other flashy but stylish clothes—hung a large white banner across the garage that read HAPPY 10TH B-DAY HENRY! The day after, Alex saw the kid on a ladder taking it down, while the mother, wineglass in hand, watched from the front door.

Alex decides to check the mail anyway—he will just have to keep his eyes glued to the walkway until he is safely inside again. He walks to the foyer and pulls open the door, and it sticks a moment, then squeaks open. The air is a little nippy and smells of wood burning in fireplaces. The sun is still trapped behind the clouds—it might as well give up. He walks to the mailbox self-consciously because he knows he's being watched. And just as he feared, Henry talks to him.

"Hey there."

Alex nods without looking at him.

"Why you wearing a robe?" the boy asks.

Alex looks at Henry, who stands on the opposite curb. He is wearing black church pants and a yellow sweatshirt with no logo and is holding the large book against his chest. The book is cloth-bound red, and even from a few feet away Alex can see that it is heavily dog-eared. Henry's mouth is open like he is preparing to swallow something, and he is scratching behind one of his ears.

"Because I feel like it," Alex says, reaching and opening the mailbox, which is empty.

"I could've told you the mailman hasn't come yet."

"Well, now I know," he says. In a sudden fit of irritation that surprises him, Alex asks, "Why have you been outside all day long?" He turns to face the kid only briefly, then looks back inside the mailbox, as if a letter will appear out of thin air to prove the kid wrong.

"I just want to," Henry answers. "I get sick of being inside."

"It's not even a nice day. And what's with the book?"

"Oh. I'm reading the dictionary. My mom says it's never too early to sharpen my vocabulary. She gave me the dictionary for my birthday."

"That's nice," Alex says, but what it really is, he thinks, is weird. He turns to walk inside.

"You're going in?" Henry says.

"What?" Alex says, turning and tightening his eyes.

"Do you know what *smalto* is?"

"What? No," Alex says.

"It's colored glass. Like they have in churches. I just learned that."

"You shouldn't be reading the dictionary. You should be playing or something. Whatever you kids do nowadays." Like he is so old himself, a hardened adult, though he is only sixteen and a half.

"Who would I play with?" Henry asks. "I don't know any kids in this neighborhood. I don't even know if there are any."

It's true—the neighborhood is old now, full of doctors and lawyers (like Alex's father) with kids in high school or away at college, professors from the university, and retirees. When Alex was little, there seemed to be a lot of kids to play with, but everyone has grown up and remained in the same houses. Henry and his mother are rarities—new people. And really, no one knows much about them. The house they live in belongs to the president of the local paper mill, Jack Pembroke, who lives in a big mansion on the grounds of River Crest Country Club, which he also owns. He has never even lived in the house across the street. Alex remembers that the man's son used to live there, but he moved out or away, and for many years it had been empty, as if forgotten, until Henry and his mother moved in.

Alex stares at Henry, shakes his head. "We have a swing in our backyard," he says, almost not believing his own words. "You can come use it if you want." Henry nods as if mulling it over, then steps across the street, already accepting the offer. For a moment Alex is uncertain what to do, but then he walks up to the front door, and out of the corner of his eye he sees the flash of red hair beside him.

Alex must lift his legs because he's too tall and gangly for the swing. The blue plastic seat strains underneath him, pulls into a tight U, pinches his hips. Henry sits in the swing next to his, a perfect fit. They both cut through the air, and because of the combined weight, the back end of the swing set sometimes lurches out of the ground. Alex imagines swinging high enough so that the swing set gets completely yanked out, sending the two of them sprawling onto the grass.

"You have very red hair. It's not natural," Alex says in flight.

"I like it. My mother did it. I told her I wanted red hair, not orange hair. Everyone said I had red hair, but that wasn't really true. Mom said she could make my hair really red if I wanted."

"Well, it looks funny," Alex says.

"I like it," Henry says again, tossing his head back as he rises into the air.

"I do too, in a weird way," Alex says. Besides the hair, Henry is normal-looking, though his nose is lightly freckled and his eyes are a deep, almost black brown. He is probably small for his age, too—not short, but slight.

Alex's own hair is light brown and short, trimmed close to his scalp so that he hardly ever needs to brush it. James tells him he looks like a dying sick person with such a haircut. But he likes it this way—it sets him apart from James. Since there is only a year between them, people always used to think they were twins, especially when they were younger and less developed, with their big brown eyes and thin but wavy chocolate brown hair, their long legs and arms, their fair skin and prominent brows. But now, Alex thinks, they don't really look much alike—James is a little taller and a lot more muscled, and his hair is cut at a normal, short length, wavy but always in place.

"Where are your parents?" Henry asks.

"They went to some dumb wedding. In Tennessee."

Alex slows down and hops out of the swing, and Henry follows him onto the back deck. Alex wants to tell him to go away, that their time together—twenty minutes of swinging—is over, but then he remembers the smell of the house, the electric silences of it, and decides that company would be okay for a while, but just for a while.

Alex is hungry for a snack, but the things he sees in the fridge and pantry don't really appeal to him. He settles for crackers and butter, which is what he ate a lot when he was younger. He sets these delicacies on a plate—a plain blue one, not the wedding china this time—and shares with Henry. They sit on the blue couch in the front living room, which his mother calls "the parlor" and where food of any kind is usually forbidden, especially something like crackers. From their adjacent seats they can see Henry's house across the street. It's a nice but unkempt house, two stories of painted-gray brick, with a gray-tiled roof. Overgrown and dying boysenberry bushes cover many of the front downstairs windows. It used to be a well-kept place, when Mr. Pembroke's son lived there, but not anymore. Henry's mother doesn't bother to cut the lawn, doesn't bother to repaint the cracking paint of the trim. She leaves the garbage can on the curbside even after the trash has been picked up. The house is large, and Alex wonders what Henry and his mother do with so much unneeded space.

Henry presses his knife, which holds one square of butter, down too hard on the cracker, causing it to fracture like a sheet of ice. A chunk of cracker topples to the floor.

"Oops," Henry says, picking it up and popping it into his mouth.

"Where does your father live?" Alex asks.

Henry places the cracker into his mouth and doesn't speak again until he has chewed and swallowed. "Mom says that I don't have one," he says.

"You have to have one."

Henry shrugs. "I don't know. She never talks about him. She doesn't like it when I ask her. So I don't."

Alex stares out at the house. Henry's mother drives a yellow Volkswagen Beetle, but it's not there at the moment. Alex tries to remember if he has ever seen any other cars parked there, early in the morning, or late at night, and he is sure he has. Boyfriends, maybe.

"You must be happy to have a brother," Henry says.

"I guess." But the truth is Alex hasn't felt comfortable around James for some time now. He remembers when they were younger, how even though they fought they seemed closer, more at ease with each other. They used to walk back into the woods together, constructing forts made out of downed tree limbs and pine needles, which they would hide in and pretend they were escaping dangerous bad guys. But that was when they were kids, really. When he was Henry's age and younger. He could laugh with James back then, when James still looked him in the eyes and Alex could return such a look without feeling like he was being intrusive. Without feeling the need to apologize for something. That seems like so long ago. When did it all change between them?

"Does your brother tell you dirty jokes?" Henry asks.

"Sometimes. He has a girlfriend named Alice. He's with her right now."

"I read this book about two brothers and one was always telling the other one dirty jokes. I thought if I had a brother we could do that."

Alex closes his eyes and leans back in his seat, resting his head. He doesn't know why, but what Henry has just said makes him feel overwhelmingly sad. The same feeling of sadness he got when he saw one of the janitors outside in the back parking lot after school one day. It had been a windy day in the spring, and the janitor, overweight in a huff-and-puff-breathing and doughy way, had his hat blown off by the wind and he chased it across the lot, bending just in time for the wind to carry it away again. Alex's friends, sitting on their car trunks, had laughed at the man and said, "Fat fucker." Then they had yelled it so the janitor could hear, though he pretended he hadn't. Alex hadn't joined in, but he didn't tell them to leave the man alone, either. He just sat there and got a sinking, gloomy feeling in his gut. "You're no fun," Kirk had said.

"Have you ever had vodka?" Alex asks.

Henry laughs and says, "No, I'm a kid."

"Oh yeah."

Later, on the back deck, Alex sits on a lawn chair, holding James's bottle of vodka. James was always good about sharing his booze at least, and that seemed to be the only activity that could bridge their silences. On Alex's sixteenth birthday in April, James had shown him how to mix drinks that tasted good—whiskey and Coke, or vanilla-flavored vodka and Sprite, screwdrivers with just the right amount of orange juice. When he had thrown up later from drinking too much, James was there to give him a hot towel to wipe his face with. He had thrown up after the Pine-Sol incident, too, burning his throat so bad he couldn't open his eyes. And then, at the hospital, they had pumped his stomach, shoved a tube down his nose and throat. He had kept his eyes closed then, too—because he was ashamed, but also because the tube felt like some monster trying to strangle him, and Alex didn't dare look at it.

Henry sits down on a wrought-iron chair and drinks from a small glass of Coke. "That stuff smells," Henry says, pointing with his glass to the vodka bottle. "My mother doesn't drink it anymore. She used to, though. It gave her bad headaches in the morning."

"Vodka doesn't smell," Alex says, remembering that he heard that somewhere. But Henry is right, it does stink, like a powerful medicine. "Anyway, one day you'll learn that it makes you feel good."

"My mother likes to drink wine."

Alex thinks of his own parents. They are probably dressed up now, sitting in the church. They are watching the bride and groom exchange vows, trying to enjoy themselves. After, they'll go to the reception. They will both have wine, maybe cocktails. Dad will eat too much from the buffet. Maybe they will dance, but probably not, and then eat pieces of icing-heavy cake. All that time, Alex figures, they will be wondering if he is okay and if they should have brought him along. Then they will remember James is keeping an eye on him, and they will remain calm.

In September, right after he checked out of the hospital, Alex and his parents spent a weekend at the family beach house. His father wanted him to get some rest—and to get away from Tuscaloosa, the scene of the crime. Alex still had his full head of hair then. Lang had told him that he had beautiful hair. For four months he had let it grow. His bangs covered his eyes, and the sides hung over his ears like tassels. But that night on the deck of the beach house, Alex cut his hair with some scissors he found in the kitchen drawer.

"I just don't know what's wrong with him," he heard his mother tell his father the next morning, after she had seen his unevenly shorn head. "I just don't."

Alex had walked along the beach the next day, the still-strong September sun burning his once-hidden forehead.

"My mother didn't come home last night," Henry says.

Alex takes a swig from the bottle, closing his eyes as he swallows.

"I stayed up for her, but she didn't come home. She stays out on Friday night a lot. At her boyfriend's place. But she usually comes home by now. Or calls me."

Alex looks at Henry, this ten-year-old boy with red hair who wears a yellow sweatshirt and black pants. "You look like the German flag," he says.

Henry looks at him as if he hasn't heard a word. "I hate my house when it gets dark outside."

"I'm still hungry," Alex says. "Want to go somewhere? We could go for a ride."

Henry nods, then looks up into the darkening sky, like something awful is floating his way.

Alex drives his mother's Volvo, not his own Honda Accord. It's a bigger car, smooth and fast. He drives to the mall but decides not to stop because it's crowded.

"I hate the mall," Henry says.

"Me too," Alex says, but he doesn't hate it as much as he hates all the people there and the easy chance of running into someone he knows. Tuscaloosa's like that—you'll run into people everywhere. When he eats out with his parents, they can't make it through the restaurant without having to stop to talk with some acquaintances. His mother always introduces him to people he's met ten times already, people he used to see at church every Sunday or at James's soccer games or tennis matches.

Alex drives past other strips of shops, past a string of chain restaurants whose lots are half full, past the hospital where he was born—and where he went the night after Marty's party. The hospital is modernized now, with a new, glassy wing. A big but undecorated Christmas tree is perched in front of the new wing, in the patch of grass before the circular drive to the main doors. It's not even Thanksgiving yet, but already this early holiday decoration. Alex can't even remember what he got for Christmas last year, and he hasn't asked for anything this year. His mother has talked about spending the holiday at the beach house, for a change of scenery, but no one else seems enthused about it.

He drives into neighborhoods off the main streets, narrow lanes of dull ranch tract houses with yards of natty yellowed grass, tucked cozily away from the busier roads. A few men rake leaves in their front yards, but mostly the streets and houses seem devoid of life.

"Are we ever going to stop?" Henry asks. Alex sees the clock—it is now 4:12—and realizes he has been driving for almost thirty minutes.

He turns around and goes back the way they came, past the same shops and landmarks, then over the bridge that stretches across the muddy Black Warrior River. Soon he sees Burger King up ahead. It's the same Burger King where, months ago, he hung out with his friends. It was such a lame thing to do, but it was a good place to collect before going to parties. They'd park their cars, turn up their stereos, buy big paper cups of Coke or Sprite and then mix alcohol into them.

He was there the night he swallowed Pine-Sol. *That night.* They had all hung out in the parking lot, tying on a buzz before the big party. That whole night, starting at Burger King, Alex had felt a bit off. Like he didn't belong. He sipped his drink as his friends talked around him, barely noticing his presence. When they did notice him, it seemed to Alex like they were mocking him, knocking him back and forth like a piñata. Still, he laughed along with them and kept drinking and pretended that everything was okay.

From Burger King they went to Marty Miller's party, out on the winding roads by the lake, down a curvy hill where they had to park on a muddy shoulder. Walking down the hill, he could hear the lake waters slap against the wood of the docks, a peaceful sound that hadn't matched his uneasy mood. The lake house was big and made of dark wood, and inside, it was decorated with mix-and-match furniture—pea-green couches, wicker side tables, lamps made from logs. Alex remembers a musty smell, the crowd, the blaring stereo that kept being turned on and off while people fought over which music to play. His friends quickly broke away from him. He drank cups of beer from the keg, walked around the house. He felt invisible, like he had wandered into the party by mistake.

He continued to drink beer that night, but he also took a few more shots of rum. Then things get foggy in his mind. He was in one of the back bathrooms, he had just peed, and in the medicine cabinet, instead of finding pills or Band-Aids, he found the Pine-Sol. It looked so safe—the liquid was the color of apple juice, housed in a simple plastic bottle with a green and yellow label. He twisted off the yellow cap, paused, and then took a swallow. His throat burned after he took the swig. He took another and then another, though each swallow was hard—much harder—than taking a shot of the cheap rum. The burn felt like little needle pricks down his throat. He felt like he needed to vomit, and he did manage to puke out a little bit. But his throat felt scalded, so he held the rest in and started coughing. He remembers someone finally opening the door to the bathroom—he hadn't locked it. He remembers a lot of cussing from some of his classmates and a blond girl he didn't know who kept calling him Alan and asking what his last name was: "Last name, I need your last name!" Commotion, the awed faces of those who had ignored him, jolted out of flirting and boozing into something surreal. He doesn't remember seeing Kirk or Tyler or the girls, though they must have been there. He remembers the paramedics, and then the bizarre stares of anguish he got from his parents at the hospital. Oh, and James, the look on his face—pure disgust. The hospital psychiatrist, a pinched-looking man trying so hard to be kind, even he seemed baffled.

The psychiatrist he ended up seeing was a different doctor named Tim Richardson. He specialized in dealing with adolescents, supposedly. His office was in the shaded front room of a house he shared with his wife and young child, whose pictures Alex saw on his desk, framed portraits of familial bliss. At first Dr. Richardson—he said to call him Tim, but Alex felt weird calling an adult by his first name—would mostly chat with him about school and stuff and then slowly work his way to questions about the incident: "Why did you want to end your life, Alex? Is this something you'd thought about a lot? What made you feel like you wanted to die? Do you still want to die, Alex?"

The questions exhausted Alex, because he didn't think he knew the answers. He just remembered how he felt that awful night, and the days and nights leading up to it. One day he'd felt as if he fit into the world, and the next he felt badly out of place. Still, even though therapy and all the talking seem pointless to him, Alex shows up each Wednesday after school, right on schedule, to sit there and talk with Dr. Richardson, trying to convince the doctor—and everyone else—that he'll never hurt himself again.

Coming up on Burger King, Alex almost drives right by, but at the last second he slows and turns into the parking lot. "Is this okay?" he asks Henry.

"I don't have any money."

"I'll spot you."

Henry nods.

Alex sits in the car a moment before shutting it off. He scans the lot for familiar cars—Lang's bumper-stickered (MEAN PEOPLE SUCK) Mercedes, Tyler's maroon Explorer, Kirk's gray Bronco. But none of their cars are here—the coast is clear.

They get out and enter the heat and fried smell of the place. Mostly solitary diners on this Saturday night, maybe some travelers, though this franchise is miles from I-59. Alex takes a closer look around only after he has ordered his chicken sandwich and onion rings, Henry's fries and chicken tenders. There are no teenagers, only two kids who look Henry's age, maybe a bit older, throwing fries at each other in a booth.

"To go," he tells the cashier, an older woman with a pleasant and effortless smile that reassures Alex.

"To go?" Henry asks.

"I don't want to eat here."

Henry accepts this with a shrug, and Alex fidgets while he waits for his order to be bagged and handed over.

And then they come in: Tyler and Kirk. He knew this would happen eventually, maybe he even hoped for it to happen: to run into his old friends, to see them away from school, and for them to see him. *Them*—they have become a collective unit in his mind.

With these two here, Alex thinks that the girls can't be far behind, some of the other guys, too. Alex watches as they walk in, their eyes looking up at the glowing menu. They haven't noticed him yet. Alex looks away, anywhere but where his old friends are. The cashier scoops his onion rings. The drive-through alert beeps, and one of the cooks shouts something to someone farther back in the kitchen.

Alex can sense their eyes on him now, like the shine of a flashlight in a dark room. Alex turns and Kirk lets out a tiny wave, almost just a hand raise, nothing more.

"Oh, hey," Alex says.

Tyler just jerks his chin up, ever so slightly. Tyler has dirty blond hair that is long on the top, parted to the left, but short on the sides. Kirk is shorter than Tyler, but his dark hair—almost black—is styled in exactly the same way. They both wear T-shirts over long-sleeved shirts, and ratty ankle boots. Alex, luckily, took off his robe at home, but he's sure he looks absurd to them anyway, in his jogging shoes and loose jeans, his thin and corny eighth-grade T-shirt, especially when it's cold outside.

"How's it going?" Kirk asks.

"Fine." Alex looks down at Henry. "Just grabbing some food."

"Cool."

The woman hands Alex his bag, smiles at him, and moves to take Tyler's and Kirk's orders. Alex pauses before moving, thinking that Kirk is about to say something more, ask him to stay, sit down, join them, call him later, something. But Kirk just looks at Tyler and says, "You ready to order?"

Alex motions for Henry, whom Kirk and Tyler seem not to have noticed. "Bye," Alex says.

"Bye," Kirk says, giving him one last quick glance as Tyler scrutinizes the menu like he hasn't eaten there a million times before.

At the door Alex pauses and hears Kirk snicker and say something under his breath, and Tyler joins in and snorts out a laugh. Right then Alex pushes open the door and enters the coldness and the twilight.

In the car Henry munches on a French fry and asks, "Who were those boys?"

"Nobody."

"Okay."

After a few minutes, Alex says, "They were my friends."

*   *   *

Back home, after eating his food straight from the bag, Alex stretches out on the couch in the parlor, still wearing his jogging shoes. Henry stands by the window. It's dark outside now, and lights are popping on in the neighboring homes.

"Your mom home yet?" Alex asks.

Henry just shakes his head side to side and sniffles.

Alex sits up and looks at Henry. He listens as Henry begins to sob, his body shaking, his hands held over his ears as if he is trying to block out the sound of a loud siren. The vodka—which Alex resumed drinking once he got home—has made Alex feel tired, but he stands up and walks over to the window. "Don't," he pleads. "Henry," Alex says, touching him on the shoulder. He takes a deep breath. "Stop." But Henry keeps going, a near-silent cry. "Henry? I think it would be kind of okay if you stayed here tonight. If you want. Until your mom gets back."

Henry, like a windup toy slowing down, stops shaking and looks up at Alex. Although it's dark in the house, Alex can see his wet, blank face, the tears streaking it like little inlets of salt water. Henry rubs his eyes with his fingers, sniffles, and, struggling to catch his breath, says, "Okay."

"Okay," Alex says. "I'll be right back."

Alex leaves Henry in the living room and walks into the kitchen. He carries the bottle of Mr. Clean back upstairs to his parents' bathroom. He opens the cap and sniffs around the edges of the bottle and the ammonia smell tickles his nostrils.

He thinks back to a few weeks earlier, in late October. James had come home from some party drunk, very drunk, drunker than Alex had ever seen him. He burst into Alex's room, where he was lying in bed but not asleep.

"Alex, are you awake?" he said, his words slightly slurred. James sat down on his bed and grabbed Alex's wrist, like he was half pinning him down.

"I'm awake."

"Good." In the greenish glow from the digital clock by his bed, Alex could barely make out James's face. "Because I've got something to tell you, okay?"

Alex said nothing.

"I just want to say, that . . . you better not do anything fucking stupid again." He paused as if waiting for Alex to protest. But he didn't. He was shocked into silence. "I mean, I could . . . I couldn't care less what you do. If you want to fucking hurt yourself and throw your life away, fine. Fuck you." Alex could tell James was about to cry, but that he was fighting it. "But . . . but, Mom and Dad would . . . If you do something like that again, and if this time you succeeded . . . well, you'd ruin our lives. You'd ruin their lives. You do realize that, don't you?"

Alex heard James start to cry, and it was weird, because James never cried.

"Fuck," James said, like he was pissed at himself for bawling in front of Alex. After all, Alex was the one who cried, the weak one. "Just remember that," he managed to mutter. Then James left, leaving Alex where he'd found him, sleepless in bed, his heart pounding, his mouth growing dry.

Now in the bathroom, he pours the bottle of Mr. Clean out into the sink and runs his fingers over the sticky remains on the ceramic basin, listening to the liquid escape down the drain. He puts the bottle back under the sink, knowing that his mother will eventually discover that it is empty and probably suffer a moment of fear. But then she'll find Alex sitting reading a book or watching TV, not passed out on the floor, and her fear will subside, though it might never disappear, at least not for a while. Alex knows he may never be trusted again, but here he is alone—well, mostly alone—and he's fine. A little vodka-buzzed but fine. They'll see that, they all will, eventually.

Back in the living room he finds Henry sitting on the couch, still staring outside.

"You want to watch a movie or something?" Alex asks.

Henry nods.

"Cool."

"Alex?" Henry says.

"Yeah?" he says.

"I'm not a baby."

"Oh, I know that."

"I didn't mean to cry."

"It's okay. I cry a lot."

"You do?"

"Sure. All the time."

Henry looks at him, like he can't imagine Alex crying.

"And so does James, my brother. So do lots of people. It's normal."

Henry sniffles and nods and then breaks into a relieved grin.

At midnight they sit at the kitchen table drinking hot milk, because Henry said it's what people in the movies drink to help them sleep. The curtains of the bay window are pulled. Alex has put sleeping bags on the floor in the den, but they aren't tired yet.

The dictionary lies open on the table and Henry thumbs through the thin, tissuelike pages, reading definitions aloud.

Soon Alex hears a car pull up outside, and then the engine stops, but it's hard to tell where the sound of the car is coming from. It could be James, or Henry's mother, or just a neighbor returning home late from a party. Maybe even Alex's parents, returned early. When the car's engine starts up again, Alex looks over at Henry, but neither of them rushes to the window to see who it is. Then he hears the car drive away.

For a moment Alex wonders what James is doing. Is he even thinking about him? Or is his mind focused solely on Alice? Then he thinks about Tyler and Kirk. Alice. Henry's mom. Everyone's out there, living, and here he is, at home with a kid.

He should feel sad, like he's missing out on something. But he doesn't, not really. He's not alone, after all, and tonight that feels very good.

James

Everything is boring, James thinks. This town. This day. This night. Even this girl, Alice. He's known all this for a while, but tonight it hits him even harder. Hits him like a punch to the gut.

It's a Saturday night, and he's in a hotel room with Alice, whom you might call his girlfriend, though he's not so sure. She's pretty but in that cheap sort of way—big boobs, fleshy body, dyed-blond hair. She goes heavy on the makeup, heavy on the perfume she always wears. Today, since they checked in, they have fooled around twice, and as far as that goes, she is good at it. And yet James is still bored.

Since the Alabama football team isn't playing this weekend, he doesn't really care about the other games on TV. The movies on cable are stupid, or else they've seen them before. They ran out of beer—kept cool in the small ice bucket provided by the hotel—an hour ago. Why he only brought a six-pack, he has no idea. And he forgot his stash of vodka.

Now what?

That is what Alice is asking. "What should we do?" she says, drawing out the "do" like it has three syllables or something.

"I dunno," James says, pretending to watch the movie on TV. It's a comedy with teens, though James knows that all the actors in this movie aren't his age at all, but twentysomethings, probably living fabulous lives in Hollywood, not stuck in high school hell.

Alice lies next to him, on her back, wearing just her bra and panties—both lacy and a pink color that she probably thinks looks classy but doesn't. James is just in his boxers, though he sort of wants to put his clothes back on. Alice is not touching him, but any minute now he is sure she will start rubbing his body— his mostly smooth chest, tight tummy, then down farther, to try to get him excited. She's very touchy-feely. "We could go somewhere," Alice says.

James doesn't respond. He wishes *she* would go somewhere: home. He thinks he'd rather be bored on his own. But the hotel is paid for, and Alice paid half, and he knows they are both here at least until the morning. Besides, they'd planned this night weeks ago, when James found out his parents were going to be away at a wedding. At the time, the idea excited him, the "badness" of it all. At the time, he liked this Alice a lot more than he does now.

"I know a girl from Hillcrest, and she's having a party in Northport somewhere," Alice says.

Alice, James knows, doesn't have many girlfriends at Central High. It's probably because she stole some girl's boyfriend during freshman year, and the girls all turned on her in an act of female solidarity. Alice mostly just hangs out with the guy she happens to be dating. So he's surprised to hear about this other girl at Hillcrest. Maybe girls at other schools don't know about her reputation. "I'm not going to some hick's party," James says.

"She's not a hick. Don't be such an asshole."

"Hillcrest?" James says. "Yeah right." Hillcrest is a county school, about six miles south of the city limits off Highway 69, and everyone knows all the kids who go there are hicks and rednecks. Alice isn't a hick. But James knows that people—even his own friends—think she's sort of trashy. Low class. She's not like the other girls he has dated—Helen, Mary Margaret, and Clare—all girls from good families, with good taste, nice things, outwardly good manners. This is why he is with Alice now. He was bored with those girls, with their fake primness and shallow vanity. But now he is bored with Alice. He can't win.

"Why can't I just come over to your house?" she'd asked when James had told her that his parents were going to be out of town all weekend.

"My brother will be there," he'd said.

"So, won't he stay out of your hair?"

"Yeah, I guess. But he'll still be there, hanging around. He gets on my nerves. Just his presence." He couldn't really describe this, not to Alice, at least. She doesn't have siblings, and she barely knows a thing about Alex—except what everyone else at school knows. Alex the nutcase. That's how everyone thinks of him now, though they'd never say so to James's face. Because James knows he's considered "popular." He plays soccer and tennis, though he gave up soccer last year after making varsity tennis, because he's better at tennis anyway. He knows he is good-looking—not because he's full of himself or anything, but because girls and other people tell him so. He makes really good grades. People laugh at what he says. They think he's cool.

And so here they are, at the hotel. Maybe it's not even a hotel. Maybe it's a motel. What's the difference? It's called La Quinta Inn, but James has never taken Spanish and he doesn't know what *la quinta* means. The building is all off-white stucco with a red-slate roof. A little touch of the Southwest right here in Alabama.

James is spent, irritated, and just as he'd predicted, Alice starts touching him. And of all the things in the world he wants right now, her touching him is *not* one of them.

He shuffles away from her on the bed, toward the phone. He picks up the receiver.

"Who you calling?" she asks, sounding annoyed but not angry.

James shakes his head. He is calling Greer, one of his best friends. But the phone rings and rings, and he figures Greer is out with Julie, the college girl he met at a frat party a few weeks back. Everyone thinks Greer is this big stud for scoring a college girl, but she's not that hot—James has met her. What kind of girl would date a high school senior anyway? James wonders.

It's a different story for college guys. Lots of girls in his class have college-age boyfriends. For instance, his ex Clare—she's now one of these girls, dating some guy from Cullman who is a sophomore Phi Delt at Alabama. She probably thinks she's hot shit now. Sure, she acts as nice as she always did, but James can sense the smugness underneath.

"I knew I should have brought some of my mom's booze," Alice says.

"I wish you had, too." He scoots back onto the bed and flips the channel, hoping against hope that something new is on.

"We could go get your stash at your house," she says. James guesses she is bored, too, desperate for the energy in the room—or lack of energy—to change.

"I'm not going there."

"Because of your brother?" she asks.

James doesn't reply. He stops the remote on a sports channel. Football is on, two schools he doesn't give a shit about. Still, it's better than a stupid movie or an infomercial. And at least it's noisy.

"Seriously," Alice says, nuzzling closer to him, her clammy hands on him again, her long fingernails scratching his shoulder. "What's the deal with you and your brother?"

James doesn't want to answer. He doesn't know *how* to answer. So he grabs Alice closer to him and starts kissing her. He can feel her relax now, and even if he's not in the mood, at least this will keep her quiet.

The night of the incident with Alex at the party—James can't call it an accident, though that is how his parents sometimes refer to it—James had been hanging out with Nathen Rao and Preston Atkins. They are his other best buds. Greer had had a date that night or something. Greer always has dates, always has a girlfriend—he's one of those guys.

They were all seniors, newly minted, and refused to stoop to showing up at Marty Miller's party. Marty was a junior, and most of the kids at his party would be, too. Or younger. James knew that

Alex was going with his own friends, and that was just one more reason for him to skip it. To be honest, Alex put him on edge. At home he was quiet and closed off, like he was hoarding misery. Not that he had ever been loud or rambunctious, but he used to be good-natured and outgoing, fun to be around. People had liked him. But in the spring, soon after he turned sixteen, something in Alex seemed to shift. He became morose, even lazy—his usually tidy room was littered with dirty clothes and stray sheets of paper, magazines, and dog-eared books. He seemed awkward, too, like he was unable to function in social situations. After school ended James dragged Alex with him to Greer's house for a small gathering, and he didn't say a word the entire night, just drank like a fish and stared off into space. "Dude, your brother is a drag," Greer had told him before they left. He *was* a drag.

"Is something wrong with Alex?" his parents asked James a few times.

James shrugged. "How should I know?"

"Maybe he's going through the whole sullen teenager phase," Mom had said, sounding reassured.

All summer Alex kept mostly to himself, closed up in his room. He never seemed to go out with his friends, nor did they ever call him. It was like, all of a sudden, Alex had turned into a new person, and not in a good way.

So that night, instead of going to the party, they smoked pot at Preston's house, drank Maker's Mark on ice, watched a movie, talked about girls, smoked more pot, thought about crashing Marty's party after all, and then thought better of it.

Really, it was a boring, do-nothing night—unavoidable and constant in this city—but because James was with his friends, it felt comforting and fun in a low-key way. They had all year for parties and football games and dates. Plus, the pot had been good stuff—"really nice shit," as Preston called it. Preston's older stepbrother had given it to him before heading back to college.

They smoked it in Preston's pipe, which was a ceramic replica of a cigarette, hollowed out for the weed. Preston said he liked this pipe because you could drive around getting high and no one would know you were smoking anything worse than a Camel. James was mostly new to pot, and he still had trouble lighting and inhaling at once. Sometimes he'd inhale too quickly and burn his lungs, coughing out any good puffs and looking like an all-around idiot. But that night, he'd sucked down hit after hit like he was breathing sea air. It made him feel euphoric and profound and silly, not paranoid and woozy like it had on past occasions. They started watching episodes of *Three's Company* on cable and it was more hilarious than ever.

"Dude, I'd love to lick those tits," Preston had said, about Suzanne Somers. Nathen and James cracked up. *Everything* cracked them up—Mr. Furley, the bad 1970s haircuts and too-tight pants, Chrissy's airheaded brilliance. James had made a mental note to watch this show more often. It ruled!

Preston lived in the garage apartment of his parents' house on the lake—on the opposite side of the lake from Marty Miller's place, the more developed side. His garage apartment was a big, nice space, with a little kitchen, like he had his own apartment already. His dad and his stepmom never seemed to be around or to care what he was up to. James envied this freedom to a degree—Preston could do what he wanted, when he wanted. James's mom, meanwhile, always wanted to know what he was doing, where he was going, and who with. She said she could never truly fall asleep until he was safe at home in bed. The woman either never slept or was an insanely light sleeper. His dad slept like a rock; James could have blasted his stereo all night and never woken *him* up. But it's not like James was invisible to him, either. Quite the opposite. He always grilled James about school, his girlfriends, tennis, everything in his life. James kept few things from him—except for the pot, his sex life, and, really, how much he drank and how often. Some secrets parents can never know. They wouldn't want to know, probably.

At some point that night, James had fallen asleep on Preston's couch. The jarring ring of the phone woke him up. He opened his eyes quickly. The lights were still on in the room, but Nathen had gone home and Preston was zonked out, lying on the floor with his head on a pillow. The phone rang again and again and then the machine picked up, but no one left a message. James checked his watch: it was only 12:03. His curfew was 12:30 on weekends, though he had said he was sleeping over here. But now that he was up, he wanted his own bed.

He let Preston sleep and laced up his sneakers.

Then the phone rang again. This time Preston stirred and mumbled something. James smiled and grabbed the cordless and passed it to him. "Here ya go, buddy."

"What the fuck?" Preston said before answering with a half-assed "Hello."

After a few seconds, Preston said, "Yes, ma'am, he's here." Preston passed him the phone, giving him a look of stoned indifference.

And so, half-stoned, a little drunk, and for sure tired, standing in his friend's garage apartment, James found out from his hysterical mother that Alex had swallowed something poisonous while at Marty Miller's party and was in the hospital and would he meet them there as soon as he could? Mom was a worrier, but he'd never heard her voice like this—scared and panicked, maybe anger mixed with shock.

James doesn't remember how he responded on the phone, nor does he recall hanging up and driving the curvy roads from the lake back to town, to Druid City Hospital's emergency room, somehow arriving without wrecking the car or killing someone. He only remembers thinking, at some point, *I should have been at that party.*

After a few minutes of kissing and groping, Alice says, "What's wrong?"

James pulls away from her. "What do you mean?"

"You don't seem into it."

Oh God, here we go. Alice is no different from all the other girls—a total head case, always analyzing and sensing stuff. Of course, James *isn't* that into it, so Alice is no dummy. But can't she just let it go? "I'm just tired," he says.

And the feelings he's had all day—boredom and disinterest and mild annoyance—come together as he stares at Alice across the bed. He's filled with a strong desire to be rid of her, for good. It always happens with these girls. Sometimes it takes months, like with Clare. Sometimes weeks, which is the case with Alice. But eventually it happens—his interest, even sexually, goes kaput. It's sad, really. He wishes those initial feelings of attraction and excitement would last. Wouldn't a steady girlfriend sort of be great? Someone to rely on, someone to think about at night?

He feels bad for Alice, too. He can tell she likes him—a lot. And he never likes to hurt girls' feelings. He doesn't take pleasure in being a heartbreaker. For real, he doesn't. But he also knows Alice likes him for the same dumb reasons he thought he liked her—because he's a new flavor, something she's never tried before. Vanilla. A nice, good boy. Smart, jockish, a rich kid, though James doesn't consider himself rich. Maybe upper middle class. Maybe just middle class. *So,* he thinks, *she only likes this idea of me. She doesn't like me.*

"Why are you so tired?" she asks. "It's not even that late."

"I dunno."

She laughs, not because he has said something funny. Probably because she's exasperated.

"Do you even . . . ," she starts. "Do you even, well, like me?"

His knee-jerk response would normally be "Yes, of course." But not this time. This time he is quiet, doesn't say a word for a few seconds. He is on his back and stares up at the ceiling, then closes his eyes. "I'm just tired."

"So you keep saying. Jesus. You didn't answer the question," she says.

If he's totally honest and tells her he doesn't like her, that he wishes she would leave—then what will happen? Will she start crying? Or worse, maybe start swinging at him?

So he decides one thing: no more girls after tonight. For now, anyway. He just can't take it. With Alice, he thought it would be laid back, more about hooking up than romance. He wasn't her first, and she wasn't his. She'd had a lot of boyfriends, he knew, and he figured he'd be just another one for her to add to her list. But now she's like the others—the doubts, the expectations, the big ideas of romance. Sure, he wants love, he wants sex, he wants all that stuff—but not all the crap that goes along with it. Not right now.

And so he decides one more thing: to be honest. "Alice," he says, still on his back, but with his eyes now open. "I'm just . . . I'm just not looking for a girlfriend right now." It's the best he can do.

He can feel her looking at him. She mutters something like "hmm" or "uhh." Some verbal hiccup of realization.

"I'm sorry," he says.

"So . . . you . . . you get me all the way to a hotel and . . ." Her voice is cracking now. She wants to cry, he can tell, but her anger is winning out. "Oh my God. I just . . . I don't even know what to say."

She hops off the bed and James just continues to lie there. He can hear her putting on her clothes. He wants to say something, maybe even explain himself. But he knows that if he does try to say something, he will just interrupt and delay what she is doing—preparing to leave. So he keeps his mouth shut. He listens but doesn't hear any sobs or crying noises, thank God.

He hears her rustle around on the dresser for her keys and her watch. He finally steals a glance at her and sees that she is dressed now in her sweatshirt and jeans, with her earrings back on. He sees her face—she has brushed her hair out of her eyes—and it is a mask of stony rage. He keeps expecting her to look at him, but she doesn't.

Finally, he hears the sound of shoes being laced up. Tennis shoes. Neither of them dressed up for the occasion. They were meeting at a cheap hotel, after all. So he's thankful for that, at least—that Alice can quickly slip on her casual clothes without much fuss.

He sees her look around the room, as if checking to see if she left anything. Then she looks right at him and says, "Well, asshole. I'm leaving. I'm out of your hair. Now you can fucking go to sleep since you're so fucking tired." She turns and opens the door and then slams it behind her.

At last she is gone.

He's relieved, but he doesn't relax for a few minutes, until he hears her car rev up and then drive off.

After the doctors pumped Alex's stomach, James sat with his brother in his hospital room while their parents were outside consulting with the doctors. James was still fuzzy on the details— He swallowed *what*? How come?—and he was also a bit groggy. It was almost light outside. He had pulled an all-nighter.

His parents knew a lot of the doctors at Druid City, though not the one who was treating Alex. Luckily. James knew his parents didn't want word to get around that their son had swallowed Pine-Sol in some crack-headed attempt to—to what? Off himself? Grab attention?

This fact was not only upsetting, of course, but also, well, embarrassing. Tuscaloosa was not a large city. Maybe sixty thousand people, which seems like a lot but isn't. People know things about people, word gets around. Hell, when his parents had friends over, James heard their gossip and stories. He knew who was cheating and with whom, whose business was failing. He knew who had health problems, who drank too much at the country club, who'd had boob jobs or face-lifts. Kids were fair game, too—whose kid flunked out of college, whose kid got a

DUI, whose kid totaled the car. It all seemed so boring and clichéd to James, just like the similar gossip at school.

James knew his parents worried about Alex, about his well-being. First and foremost they would want to make sure he was okay. But then they'd also wonder if Alex's stunt would become just another juicy morsel. Would it be confined within the walls and mouths of students at Central High? Or would it seep out into the adult world? They'd want to keep this little affair as private as possible, wouldn't they? And maybe they could contain it. Their friends, at least, would have manners enough not to bring it up.

But kids were mean little bastards. What Alex had done would seem like a pitiful joke in their classmates' eyes. No one had any mercy.

Poor, poor Alex, James thought, staring at him. Alex was awake, but his eyes were closed. His hair was wet at the bangs, pasted to his forehead. His usually rosy cheeks—both he and Alex were blessed and cursed with fair, sensitive skin—looked almost yellowish orange. People always thought they were twins, but James thought this was ridiculous. There were so many differences between them. For one thing James would never have pulled this Pine-Sol stunt. James was bored, yes, and sometimes moody. But overall he was happy.

Alex wasn't supposed to talk, even if he could. But James could talk, and he did: "What the fuck were you thinking?"

Alex kept his eyes shut, but James knew he had heard him.

"I mean, Pine-Sol? Wasn't there beer at the party? Why couldn't you drink that?" James regretted saying that the minute it came out. But he was mad. For so many reasons. Mainly because Alex had done something stupid, something reckless. Something that James couldn't begin to understand.

"Why did you do it?" James asked. He knew Alex wouldn't answer. But what James had really wanted to ask was, *Who are you and what have you done with my brother?*

Outside the La Quinta room, it is dark and cold, but not freezing. James has slipped on his jeans and a T-shirt, but not his sweatshirt and jacket. In the distance, beyond the sparsely populated parking lot, and past a wide lot of dead grass and a kudzu-covered chain-link fence, he sees the interstate, cars zooming by, heading west toward Mississippi.

It is only nine-thirty. What is he going to do the rest of the night? Now that Alice is gone, he feels relieved, but also a little bummed. Not because she is gone, but that he is alone now. He could go home, just shut himself in his room. But avoiding Alex seems like too much work. And he doesn't want to go back inside the hotel room, either. He's in fucking limbo.

He looks down from the railing—he's on the second floor of the hotel—and notices his Jeep. The navy blue Jeep his dad bought him for his sixteenth birthday, exactly the car he'd wanted. He loves this car like it's his private traveling refuge. Some good times in that car, with girls and his friends, speeding around town, heading to this party or that one.

Then he notices the front tire, passenger side. It's flat. *Son of a bitch.* James walks down to the stairwell, races down the stairs, and then makes his way to the Jeep. The light outside Room 104 sheds enough illumination for him to see that the tire is not only flat, but also punctured.

"God dammit!" he shouts, then kicks the tire, which looks droopy and violated. "That stupid bitch!" He's had girls call and

39

hang up on him in the middle of the night, had nasty notes shoved in his locker. But none of them have done something this violent.

He checks the rest of the car for damage, and though it is hard to see the back and the driver's side in the darkness, he thinks everything else looks okay.

Now what do I do? Shit. Double shit. He has to change the tire, which he knows how to do, but not in the dark, and not when he's tired and had a few beers and not wearing his shoes or his jacket. He'll also have to buy a new tire, and that's going to cost a pretty penny. Unless he tells his parents what happened and they buy him the new one. But then he'd have to lie and say his tire blew out or something—not that his latest ex-girlfriend slashed it in an act of payback.

His head suddenly hurts, so he goes back to the hotel room and lies down on the bed. After a few minutes, he picks up the phone. He thinks about calling Nathen, but he doubts his college professor parents will let him out this late. Nathen's dad was born in India, but he grew up in England, where he met Nathen's mother, who is white. They both have these great British accents, though Nathen—and his college-age sister, Sarita—sound as southern as everyone else. Sure, they stand out in Alabama, but Tuscaloosa is a college town with a lot of foreign students and teachers. Plus, Nathen and Sarita are good-looking and athletic and smart, and people in school have always cared more about that than their heritage.

Instead of Nathen, he calls Preston. When Preston answers after a few rings, James says, "What are you doing home?"

"Me? Aren't you supposed to be with Alice? Boinking at the Motel Six?" he says, then laughs.

"The La Quinta."

"Big difference. So what's going on?"

"Man, this weekend hasn't gone so well."

"Uh-oh. What happened?" he says, still chuckling. He must be stoned, James thinks.

"Alice got mad and left."

"Nice," Preston says, drawing it out like a hiss.

"Yeah, and get this. Before she left, she managed to slash one of my tires."

"No way!" he shouts, drawing in his breath, then laughing again. "Man, that's fucked up!"

"Tell me about it. I just went out there and noticed it. What was she thinking? Does she fucking carry a knife around or something?"

"Man. . . . I always told you that chick was messed up. Something about her, man."

"Yeah, I know."

"Damn, I can't believe she did that. What a crazy bitch!"

Preston himself doesn't have a girlfriend, though plenty of girls are hot for him. He's got shaggy strawberry blond hair that makes him look like a surfer boy, though he's never surfed in his life as far as James knows. He seems more into his pot than dating girls. He's perpetually single, which is how James plans to be from now on.

"Yeah, so I'm stuck here till tomorrow, when I can change my tire."

"I'm not good with cars, but I can come help."

"I'll be okay."

"You want some company? I'll bring some pot."

41

"Okay. Sure," James says. He doesn't really want to get stoned, but he also doesn't want to be alone in this depressing hotel room. "It's Room 204."

James's friends have largely avoided talking about Alex and the incident and anything surrounding it. They—Preston, Nathen, Greer, a few others—have been like his personal sanctuary from having to deal with that. The subject hovers out there in the air and is swatted away if it ever gets too close.

Tonight James is glad not to talk about Alex. He is lying on one of the motel beds, and Preston is on the other. The glow of TV provides the only light in the dark hotel room. It is late now, two in the morning, and they have been smoking since Preston got there. They talk every now and then, but James easily loses his train of thought. He feels like he is levitating.

Some horror movie is on TV—a rip-off of a rip-off about one of those masked psycho killers. The ones where stupid and horny teenagers are always the victims. Preston laughs each time someone gets it. James just smiles. Sometimes these movies scare him—after all, there *are* nutcase killers out there; this kind of awful stuff could happen. But tonight he is unafraid. Maybe it's the pot, maybe it's the fatigue. Maybe it's the relief he feels to be rid of Alice.

"Want another hit?" Preston says. James hears the lighter flick.

"Sure," he says, and reaches for the ceramic joint, from which he inhales in a quick, short burst, then hands it back to Preston. "You finish it, I'm done," James says.

"No worries there, man."

James doesn't want this relaxed, calm feeling to end. Because under the haze, he thinks of Alex at home and wonders what he's doing. Is he watching this movie by himself? These movies *really* scare Alex—he refuses to watch them, usually. James remembers seeing *Salem's Lot* years ago when they were kids. The babysitter had fallen asleep downstairs, and Alex and James had snuck into their parents' bedroom to watch it on their TV. Alex had spent most of the time with his face buried under the covers, while James had watched and told him when it was safe to look again. James can feel the worry and sadness trying to poke through the protective shell he feels around him. But oddly enough, he doesn't feel the anger. Anger is exhausting, and he is tired of it.

On-screen, a guy wearing just his underpants is creeping out of a tent to go take a piss in the woods. If James was at home now with Alex—and shouldn't he be, rather than here in this awful hotel room?—he would tell Alex to start covering his eyes, because a half-naked boy creeping out in the woods when a masked killer is on the loose, well, anyone with a brain knew what was coming next.

"He's toast," Preston says.

Preston is good company. He knows to let James lie there in peace. And lie there he does, until his eyelids feel too heavy to remain open. With his eyes closed, it's only a matter of time before he falls into a dreamless sleep.

Both he and Preston wake up sometime after nine—too early. But James feels surprisingly alert and refreshed, while Preston groans and moans.

Outside, in the nippy morning air, Preston is worthless when it comes to changing the tire—James basically does it by himself.

"What you gonna do today?" Preston asks, once James has finally secured the spare tire onto the Jeep. "Call the cops on that crazy bitch?" He is smoking—a cigarette this time—and he takes a drag and then busts into a big grin.

"Nah," James says, wiping his dirtied hands on his jeans. "I guess I'll just go home and chill out. Do some homework. I just hope my parents don't get home till late, so they won't see the tire." He's still torn about what to tell them.

"Well, call me if you want to throw the football or come over or some shit like that."

"Yeah, I will," James says. "Thanks for, you know, coming here."

"Sure thing." They knock fists and then Preston pops into his BMW and zooms out of the parking lot. Probably going home to sleep some more, James thinks.

After turning in his key at the front desk to a sallow-faced older man wearing a maroon vest over a white shirt, James drives home, the roads mostly empty except for churchgoers. He stopped going to church regularly about a year ago. Alex stopped, too, and their parents have given up nagging them to come along on Sundays. Not that they're religious freaks or anything. James thinks they just go because all their friends do, or maybe just out of habit.

The calm he felt the night before has vanished, and when he turns into his neighborhood—loftily called Woodland Heights—his belly clenches. It hits him then—the thought that Alex may have done something to himself. That, in his absence, Alex may have succeeded this time. And that James would be to blame and that his parents would never forgive him and that their worlds would fall apart.

But as he rounds a corner and heads to their house, he sees Alex in the yard, wearing jeans and a purple T-shirt. And he sees that Alex is not alone. That kid who lives across the street is talking with him, the weird one with crazy red hair. They both turn and stare at James and his Jeep, and the little boy says something to Alex and then darts across the street.

James pulls into the driveway and parks. Before he gets out of the car, he looks over to see if Alex is looking at him. That's when Alex holds up his hand in a slight wave and smiles. Not a big smile, not a huge grin. It's more tentative than that. But it's a smile, something he hasn't seen Alex do for a long, long time.

3

Alex

"I'm glad to see you boys didn't burn the house down while we were away," Dad jokes when he and Mom get back from the wedding that Sunday afternoon. Alex is in the den, watching TV, but he gets up to greet and hug them. Alex is glad to see them in good spirits; his dad is a jokester at heart, but lately he hasn't been making his usual jokes and comments, at least not around Alex, as if jokes are inappropriate now, after what happened.

"Yeah," Alex says. "We didn't trash the house too much." He smiles. *See,* he thinks, *I can make jokes, too. Everything doesn't have to be all doom and gloom,* he wants to say.

"Where's James?" Mom asks.

"Upstairs," he says. That's where James has been ever since he got home from the La Quinta, in a seemingly bad mood.

At dinner, a few hours later, Mom and Dad talk about the wedding—Dad says it must have cost a fortune, and Mom says the flowers were a little tacky for her taste but that overall it was nice. Alex and James just sit there and listen, really.

"And you guys had a good weekend?" Dad asks.

"Yeah," James says.

Alex nods in agreement, before glancing briefly at James, who looks guilty and nervous.

"But I ran over a nail or something, because my tire got busted," James says.

"Oh, no," Mom says. "How did that happen?"

"I don't know," James says. "On the way back from Preston's last night? I made it home okay. But I put on the spare this morning."

Dad says tomorrow he'll go with him to the tire store to get a new one. "Tires are expensive," he adds.

"I *know*, Dad," James says. "If you want me to pay—"

"Don't be silly," Mom says. "It was an accident."

Alex looks over at James, and he knows he is lying about something. Not that he cares. But it's funny, he thinks, how he can just *tell* such things about James—the way his face gets slightly flushed, how his eyes flutter, how his mouth tightens.

"And you had an okay weekend, honey?" Mom asks Alex.

"Yeah," he says. "I mean, it was boring, but fine."

Both his parents look at him and nod, like they're relieved he didn't have something awful to report. "Boring is good sometimes," Dad says.

The next week passes slowly for Alex—five days of school, therapy on Wednesday, a lazy Saturday spent reading and daydreaming in his room, and now this dull Sunday. The weather has been a roller coaster, mild one day, cold the next, then wet and cold, then sunny again. It's like fall and winter are duking it out for control; winter will likely win out after Thanksgiving, which is still about a week and a half away.

This Sunday evening it is chilly but not frigid, and just as the sun is setting and the streetlights around the neighborhood flicker on, Alex decides to go for a run. He puts on his sweats and laces up his jogging shoes. He hasn't jogged for many months—he just hasn't felt up to it—but he used to jog all the time, to clear his head. Tonight, after being trapped in the house all day, his legs tingle with nervous energy, demanding to be used.

He passes his mom in the kitchen as he heads toward the garage door. "I'm gonna go for a jog."

"This late?" she says, stopping the onion chopping and glancing at her watch. "Okay, but be back within the hour for supper."

He heads off on what once was his usual route—down the street, left on Country Club Way, then straight ahead to the golf course. The country club borders the neighborhood, so anyone can jog along the golf cart trails, at least after the golfers have finished for the day. Alex's breathing is pinched in the cold evening air, but still, the coldness feels good on his face, and soon he starts to feel that once-familiar clearheadedness.

The grass along the course is brittle and brown, but the putting greens are still a bright, emerald green. The country club groundsmen dye the grass during the winter so golfers can still see where to hit the ball. It's a goofy-looking landscape, little green islands floating in a sea of yellow-brown. Tall pine trees line the fairways, and the dropped brown pine needles litter the edges of the asphalt pathway. The trail snakes this way and that, up hills, down hills, dictated by the layout of the golf course.

Up ahead, Alex sees a jogger coming toward him. It's a guy wearing white sweats and a crimson sweatshirt with a hood. Could be anyone. It's not like Alex is the only jogger who lives near the course. He usually runs into middle-aged men who are out trying to lose a few pounds. But this person moves like he is young, someone lean and crisp.

Alex is hell-bent on passing with nothing more than a nod, whoever it is. Plus, the guy's face is shrouded, and it's getting dark. But just as Alex passes, the guy calls out his name.

Alex stops and turns back, and the mystery person peels back his hood and reveals himself to be Nathen Rao. James's buddy.

"Hey, man. I *thought* that was you," Nathen says.

Nathen has always been nice to Alex, even after the incident. Some of James's friends make Alex feel awkward, nervous. Like Greer, who always talks about the girls he gets with, like it's a sport and Greer is the best at it in the world. Or Preston, who sneers at Alex and looks at him like he's defective. Or else they ignore him—which is fine by Alex. But Nathen is different—friendly, comfortable to talk to. Nice. Whenever Alex saw him after the incident, he didn't avoid the topic like so many others. He asked how he was doing, did he feel better? Alex has always liked him—and felt shy around him.

"Yeah," Alex says. "Just thought I'd go for a jog."

"I didn't know you jogged."

"I used to, all the time. This is my first time in a while. I'm out of shape."

"Ah, well, you'll get back into it." Nathen wipes his brow with his sleeve. He's breathing heavily. His black hair—usually combed back and styled—is flat and matted.

Alex nods, doesn't know what to say, really. He wants to get back to running, before it gets too dark, while he has momentum, but it also feels nice talking with Nathen, even if it is just stupid, meaningless small talk. Then he remembers that Nathen is on the cross-country team at school. "You training?"

"I guess you could call it that. Our meets are over, for the most part, until spring. But coach keeps us in shape."

"Yeah," Alex says. "I bet."

Nathen smiles at him like Alex just said something funny. His big white teeth, set against his creamy brown skin, seem to glow in the dusk. "Well, I better get going. But I'll see you at school tomorrow!" He taps Alex's shoulder with his fist, like play boxing, and darts off again. Alex watches him run off at a pretty fast pace before he resumes his own jog.

His breathing is labored, and his legs get tired and stiff, but he keeps going, jogging for over half an hour. In a way, seeing Nathen has given him a weird sort of energy. As he continues his route, an idea sets in his mind: *If I jog every night this week, I will get better. Faster. It will become easier.* It's a goal. Something to strive toward.

He exits the golf course and picks up speed. He rounds the corner and sees his house up ahead, the lights blazing through the windows. There is dinner to eat, homework to tackle, but it doesn't seem nearly as dreary to Alex as it did just an hour earlier.

* * *

The next morning, Alex wakes up, showers, dresses, and eats a bowl of Cheerios in the den, watching the *Today* show as his mother busies herself in the kitchen before heading to her job at the historical commission. His father reads the paper while eating his grapefruit and boiled egg in the breakfast room. James usually grabs a banana on the way out. They drive separately to school—James in his Jeep, Alex in his white Honda Accord. His mother says driving to the same building in two cars is a waste of gas. And it is. But James usually stays late for extra tennis practice, and Alex comes home right on time. Plus, it would probably kill James to be stuck in the car with Alex, forced to chat with him.

Central High is a big school—so big that it is divided into two campuses. The freshmen and sophomores go to Central West, on the run-down side of town, while the juniors and seniors go to Central East, which isn't that far from the university. It's the nicer-looking school, newer, but it still looks like a prison.

And in many ways, it *is* a prison, to Alex at least, trapped there all day, inside its pale walls with linoleum floors. It's a two-story, U-shaped building, made of dark red brick. Big black screens cover the windows—to conserve energy, the school board says—and the back parking lot is surrounded by a high chain-link fence. Alex pulls into a spot farther back, away from where other students have parked and clustered. Inside, the school smells of bad cafeteria food and cleaning supplies.

First period is American government with grumpy Mr. Wiley, then it's chemistry with Mrs. Alexander, followed by trig with Mrs. Summers, who is young and surprisingly pretty for a math teacher. Nothing unusual happens today. Alex sits in his uncomfortable seats and pays attention and feels just like another student. None of his friends—well, his ex-friends—are in his early classes. This used to disappoint him, but now, he knows, it's a blessing.

Advanced English is fourth period, his favorite class. He likes the work (the reading, writing, analyzing), and the teacher, Mrs. Winters, who's sarcastic and no-nonsense and funny. She doesn't treat Alex like some fragile head case, like some of the other teachers. After English, it's time for lunch, and Alex heads for the library, where he sneaks nibbles from a package of peanut-butter crackers he buys from the vending machine, does his homework, and daydreams. Luckily James has a different lunch period, or else he might comment on his absence from the cafeteria or, worse, feel obligated to have Alex sit at his table. When Alex returned to school after the incident at the beginning of October, his old lunchroom pals would set their bags and books on the empty seats to discourage him from even *thinking* about sitting with them. At first he sat alone, on the other side of the cafeteria, where most of the black kids sat, in an odd habit of mutually agreed-upon segregation. Some of the black kids gave him funny looks, but most just ignored him. None of them, at least, prevented him from sitting near them. Eventually Alex figured out that he could sit in the library, where his solitude wasn't so obviously on display.

The librarian is a fortyish woman with short, curly brown hair. She always wears long pleated skirts and buttoned-up white blouses, like it's her librarian uniform. She never smiles at Alex. She probably hates him because he never checks out any of the books. The only other people in the library are Valerie Towson, a quiet, mousy black girl who's a senior, and a boy named Jess Blankenship, a math geek with no personality. Great company he's in. They all sit alone, at separate wooden tables, their faces buried in homework.

Today Alex pulls out a notebook and maps out a jogging plan for himself. This week, he decides, he'll keep to the same path and the same distance. But next week he'll need to go farther, longer. He figures the golf course runs about three miles, give or take. So he could always run the course twice, to increase the distance. Or he could run through the neighborhoods—his and a few others—that border the course. Nathen Rao lives in one of those neighborhoods—Pinehurst—with his parents, professors at the university. He maps out two weeks' worth of jogging regimens, and after that he will see how his body is holding up.

The bell rings—time for Spanish class. As he trudges up the south stairwell, he sees James and Nathen.

"Hey, buddy," Nathen says, passing and, just like last night, play-punching him on the shoulder. Alex tries to say something back, but he feels like he has twenty pieces of bubble gum in his mouth, so he just nods and smiles. He continues up the stairs and he wonders what James—who only looked at him, not even nodding—is thinking, what expression he wears. It makes Alex smile to think about.

In Spanish it is "conversation day." Mr. Ramos, who is actually *from* a Spanish-speaking country, unlike Alex's southern-twanged tenth-grade teacher, assigns him to chat with Patty McPherson. He notices that Tyler and Kirk, who sit in the back, are conversation buddies today. Lang is also in this class. It's like a minefield. But when they do have to talk to each other, at least it's in a foreign tongue.

Mr. Ramos tells them to talk about the weather, but Alex can barely concentrate. He wants to be outside, back in his sweats, running in the fall air.

"Alejandro?" Patty asks, using his Spanish-class name. Patty's Spanish-class name is Patricia. Pa-TREE-see-ah. Their names are prettier in Spanish.

"*Sí?*" he says, breaking out of his spell. Patty frowns and continues droning on, her accent mangling the language. "*El* weather *esta nublado y frío, uh, hoy,*" she says. The classroom is filled with such manglings, all about the autumn air and cloudy sky, the orange and yellow leaves, whatever else they can manage to say with their limited vocabularies. When the bell rings later, he dawdles so that Kirk, Tyler, and Lang leave before him.

The next and final class of the day is study hall. Each week a new teacher fills in as the class babysitter. This week it's Mr. Wiley. He mostly ignores them and grades a stack of papers.

Alex received special permission to skip gym this semester, which he is thankful for. Still, it's not like the incident made him an invalid or anything. And starting in January he will have to join the gym class throng again—the people not good enough to qualify for a varsity sport. Varsity athletes practice during sixth period—so right this very moment James is at tennis and Nathen is at cross-country, enjoying the air outside. Alex barrels through some chemistry reading and gets a jump on a set of trig problems. His work is sloppy, lackluster. Mostly he stops, puts down his pencil, and stares outside, waiting for the jolt of the bell to announce yet another end to a school day.

When he gets home, Henry is sitting on the curb in front of his house, wearing jeans and an oversized green sweater.

"Hi, Alex! How was school?" he shouts the second Alex gets out of his car.

Alex lumbers over to him, his school satchel on his shoulder. "The usual."

"I like school."

"Just wait till you're my age. Then you won't."

Henry squints up at him and smiles. "Whatcha doing now?"

"Some homework. I may go jogging later."

"Mom is taking me to a movie tonight."

"Oh yeah?"

"And pizza after."

"That's nice," Alex says. Henry's mother had finally come home that Sunday after Henry had stayed over. Alex had watched her with Henry, from the living room window, as she got out of her car, acting as carefree as if she'd just come home from a haircut. He'd walked outside with Henry, and when she saw them she just waved at them and shouted, "Hi, sweetie!" Alex had wanted to say something—but what? It wasn't his place.

"Yeah, it should be fun. Mom doesn't let me eat pizza much—she says it's junk food. But she knows I like it."

He should ask what movie. But he just wants to go inside. "Well, I better get started on my homework."

"Oh, okay," Henry says.

An hour later, while grabbing a Coke from the fridge, Alex spies Henry outside, still on the curb, staring off into space.

James walks into the kitchen and grabs an apple from the fruit bowl. He follows Alex's gaze out the window. "What's the deal with that kid?"

Alex shrugs. All of a sudden he feels protective of Henry. "I dunno." He wants to say, *What's the deal with* you?

James is still in his tennis clothes—black, shimmery nylon sweats and a long-sleeve T-shirt that all the players got for playing in the state finals last spring. "Nate said he ran into you jogging last night."

"Yep. I'm going tonight, too. Need to get back into it."

James takes another crunch out of his apple. "Good," he says, before climbing the stairs and shutting himself in his room again.

Alex guesses that was James's attempt at brotherly conversation. It's better than nothing.

When he turns to look out the window, Henry is gone.

Alex takes the same route tonight, starting at the same time. His muscles are a little sore from yesterday's jog, but his lungs feel stronger. He focuses on breathing, on keeping his stride nice and steady, while also watching for Nathen. Running by the later golf holes, Alex can see the houses of Pinehurst, their lit windows, beautifully landscaped yards, driveways full of nice cars. The Rao house is on a street a few blocks away from the course, one story, flat-roofed and modern-looking. But he doesn't see any sign of Nathen. And as he loops around the course, down and up and down mini hills, past the mucky pond by the fifteenth hole, closing in on the end of his jog, he feels a stupid clunk of disappointment. Why should he care if Nathen isn't out jogging? And just then, Nathen zooms by him from behind, as if summoned by his thoughts. "Come on, slow ass!" he says, glancing back and shouting, barely breaking his pace.

For the next ten minutes—ten minutes longer than Alex meant to jog—he follows Nathen, who glances back every now and then, checking to see if he is still following. It's a struggle, his lungs start to burn, his legs want to give out, but he keeps on. Nathen follows the course at first, but then he veers off across a fairway and onto a makeshift trail through a small thicket of forest, then out onto a street Alex doesn't recognize. It might be a part of Pinehurst, but who knows—it's like Nathen has led him to a new world.

"To the river!" Nathen shouts, continuing down the street, past more big houses.

They run down a small slope and finally Alex realizes where they are—at the back entrance to Pinehurst, right on Rice Mine Road. Across Rice Mine is another small band of forest that borders the north bank of the river. When there are no cars coming, Nathen dashes across the road and starts running along the shoulder. Alex doesn't care that it is late, that it is getting darker, and that he is now a good twenty-minute jog from home. He just follows Nathen, who has finally slowed a bit, allowing Alex to run alongside him.

"Where are we going?" he says between breaths.

Nathen smiles and finally veers left into a new, unfinished subdivision that has sprung up along the river. There are only a few half-built houses set on dirt lots, but all with views of the river. The exposed dirt here is orange-brown, fresh and wet-looking. Nathen jogs up to one of these skeletal houses and finally stops. "Good job, Alex." He is breathing heavily, but not as heavily as Alex is. Now that they've stopped, Alex feels ready to collapse.

"Thanks, I guess. But I may drop dead in a sec."

"You did good. I thought I would have left you in the dust by now, but you kept on."

Alex sits down on the curb, not caring if his sweats get muddy. Nathen sits down next to him.

"You should consider joining the team," Nathen says.

"You mean cross-country?"

"Yeah. Matt Jones sprained his ankle real bad, so he's out for the rest of the year. There's an opening now."

"I doubt I'm good enough," he says.

"You kept up with me, and we all know what a stud I am." Nathen laughs like he is joking, but also like he means what he says. "Plus, I guarantee you that you're better than some of the other guys on the team."

This doesn't seem possible to Alex, but he says, "Maybe."

"I bet you can outrun your brother, even," Nathen adds.

"I doubt that."

"No, seriously. I bet you can."

"Maybe." Maybe, maybe, maybe—can't he say anything else? It's like he has bubble-gum mouth again.

Nathen leans back into the orangey dirt lot and clasps his hands under his head. Alex can see a peak of his underwear—black Calvins—and then his flat stomach, where his sweatshirt rises up from his hips. He veers his eyes away and stares straight ahead.

"I can talk to Coach Runyon if you want," Nathen says. "I mean, you need to train more and get better, for sure. But I bet he'd want you on the team next semester. We need a full team to be competitive."

"Really?"

"Yeah."

"I guess it would beat gym class."

"Hell, yeah—sixth-period athletics rocks. Seriously. Plus, we get to go to meets in Birmingham and Mobile and other places. It's fun. It's a good group of guys. You'd like them."

"So you'll really talk to your coach?"

"I said I would. Unless you don't want me to."

"No, that would be cool." Alex suddenly envisions himself running triumphantly across a finish line, bursting that red tape, his arms raised in glory. "But Mom will be mad if I'm not home for dinner."

"Yeah, I guess we should get back." He propels himself up and stands and shakes his limbs. Nathen is Alex's height, lean-limbed, but muscular up top, with broad shoulders and a defined chest that pokes out a little, just like James's.

Alex stands, dreading the walk home—and it will be a walk, because he can't possibly run anymore. But when Nathen starts to jog off, shouting for him to get moving, he somehow summons the energy to follow him back down Rice Mine Road, up through Pinehurst.

"Okay, I'm headed this way," Nathen says, jogging in place before hanging a left down his street. "But I'll talk to Coach Runyon, like I said. Wait for me in the parking lot after school tomorrow. I should know something by then, okay?"

"Okay," Alex says, "that's great."

"Cool. Okay, buddy, see you later." Nathen winks at him and

makes a clicking sound and then runs off, turning once to hold up his hand in a wave.

Without Nathen to spur him on, Alex walks—back to the course, back along the trails, all the way home. He has been away for over an hour, it is dark now, and he knows his parents will be worried, wondering where he is. He smiles thinking about his very real explanation—that he was running with Nathen.

The halls and walls of Central High seem a little less depressing the next day. Maybe it's because the sun is shining outside, after days of a gray November funk. Or maybe it's because Alex has something to look forward to. He cautions himself not to get too excited—maybe the coach won't even let him try out—but he can't help feeling, like it's lodged in the pit of his stomach, a tiny kernel of hope.

The day is a chore to get through: a government quiz on the judiciary branch. An experiment in chemistry, which beats listening to Mrs. Alexander lecture. During lunch Alex tries to study for his Spanish quiz, but he can't focus. He thinks only of Nathen and running and the coach who holds his fate in his hands. At least Coach Runyon isn't like the other coaches Alex knows—meatheads who teach shop and health ed, flirt creepily with the pretty girls in class, and treat the jocks like their best buddies and everyone else like negligibles who are taking up too much space. Coach Runyon teaches calculus, so Alex thinks he's probably smart.

On his way to Spanish Alex doesn't see Nathen or his brother, as he usually does. Bad timing. It's not like Nathen would have anything to report anyway. They both won't know anything until after school, which makes study hall torturous. All day he has been a space cadet, staring out the windows, imagining himself as an actual team member, running alongside Nathen through the city streets, on running trails, around the golf course, wearing the crimson school colors.

Finally, the bell rings and Alex gathers his stuff and heads to his car. All around him his classmates drive off or else linger at their cars, sneaking puffs of cigarettes, talking shit to each other, making plans for that night or the weekend or whenever—plans that don't include Alex. Not that he cares.

A few cars over, he sees Kirk chatting with Beth. Beth is petite and has wavy dark brown hair that rests on her shoulders. Alex wonders if the two of them are finally a couple now, after months of flirting and claiming to be "just friends." The thought of them as a couple makes him feel a little queasy. Tyler and Kirk have never had serious girlfriends, and neither has Alex, and this seemed to bond them together. But after the summer, both of them started acting like they were girl magnets. They talked about the things they had done with girls—more than kissing and groping—but Alex had no stories of his own to tell. And it made him feel panicked and uneasy, because he knew this was loosening his ties to them.

As he stands there, Alex tries to keep his eyes away from Kirk and Beth, but the more he avoids looking at them the more he can feel their presence. In a flicker, he sees Kirk staring straight at him, mouthing something to Beth, who is holding in a laugh. He wants to shout, *What's so funny?*

He waits and waits, maybe ten minutes, which feels like eternity, and there is still no Nathen in sight. He has his appointment with Dr. Richardson in fifteen minutes, and if he doesn't leave soon, he will be late. He starts to have an odd feeling about the whole situation, like the delay means bad news. And wouldn't it suck to get the bad news right here, in this lot, under the eyes of Kirk and Beth? His heart starts to race, so he gets in his car and drives off, both disappointed and relieved.

Later, in his room at home, Alex sits on his bed and starts reading *Uncle Tom's Cabin* for English class. Mrs. Winters says it's one of the great American novels. He'll have to take her word for it, because so far it just seems like homework. But at least this homework—reading—is more enjoyable than translating some Spanish sentences or, worse, the set of trig problems due tomorrow. The sine function, the cosine function, the tangent function. And even more functions. All of it pointless. His parents took math all through high school and college and they both admit to not remembering any of it. So why should he even bother with it? Because he has to. It's what you do. He sighs, letting out frustrated air.

When the doorbell rings, he stays on his bed and waits for James to answer the door. He hears the door open and then voices—James's and someone else's. Then the voices get clearer and he realizes it is Nathen, now inside his house, come to see *him,* not James.

Alex's heart pounds and he lurches off the bed. He leaves his room and moves to the head of the stairs. Nathen, in the foyer with James, glances up and nods. "Hey, buddy," he says, not even pausing for a response. "Good news: Coach Runyon gave us the go-ahead. He says he wants to see you run tomorrow. After school."

"Really?" Alex starts moving down the stairs. "You're not kidding or anything?"

"Nope. So get your running shoes on. I figure you might need one last training session, me and you."

James just stands there silently, blank-faced.

"Okay," Alex says. "I'll be right down."

As he changes, Alex can hear them talking downstairs, but he can't really make out any of the words. He puts on his gray sweatpants and a navy blue sweatshirt, laces up his worn-down jogging shoes, and finds Nathen where he left him.

"Let's go," Nathen says.

"Have a good run," James says. "See you at school tomorrow."

The two knock fists and then Nathen and Alex head out.

"Let's run to the river and back again," Nathen shouts as they take off. Alex nods. Talking while running is bad for his lungs, so they run in silence for a while, at a fast clip. Alex wonders if he can keep it up, but it's easier with Nathen next to him. When they get to the river in the new subdivision, Nathen jogs in place on the freshly laid asphalt, while Alex catches his breath.

"We gotta keep going, buddy. Only a brief rest!"

Despite being beat, Alex smiles at Nathen's bossy tone.

"You're doing great. Just keep it up," he says, before darting off again. When he looks back, flashing his big smile, Alex summons his legs to get moving. They run together all the way back to Alex's house. His parents' cars are in the garage now, and the lights of the house burn in the twilight.

"That was good," Nathen says. They both walk in circles around the front yard, catching their breath and keeping their legs moving.

"I'll meet you after school tomorrow at the track field? You can change in our locker room." Nathen lifts his shirt and wipes his brow.

"I'll be nervous," Alex says, his hands clasped behind his head, opening his mouth wide to gulp in extra air.

"Don't be. You'll do great. I'll be there to root you on."

Alex nods, and when he looks at Nathen looking at him, he almost asks him why he is being so nice to him. Why he has *always* been nice to him. The night air is chilly, and soon winter will arrive in full force. Standing there, it almost seems like Nathen is the only warm and kind presence that exists on the entire planet.

During dinner later Alex waits for James to say something about Nathen and cross-country, but he barely speaks, just shovels the baked chicken and new potatoes and salad into his mouth. His parents ask their usual questions—how was the doctor and school and so on—but Alex doesn't dare tell them about tomorrow. Because what if he fails? Why get their hopes up? Alex knows *he* can handle the disappointment, but his parents? Haven't they had enough to deal with when it comes to him?

"Nothing big going on at school?" his mom asks.

"No, just the usual," Alex says. Across the table, he and James trade knowing glances. And Alex realizes James won't say a word because he's thinking the same thing: why set them up for more disappointment? For this, Alex is grateful.

Later, just as Alex is about to turn off his light and go to bed, James taps on the door and pokes his head in. "Hey, good luck tomorrow," he says, and before Alex can even thank him or anything, James pulls the door shut and is gone.

After the school bell rings and most kids clear out, Alex takes his book bag and the duffel with his jogging clothes in it to one of the bathrooms and changes in a stall. He wants to show up ready to run. Plus, he doesn't want to change in the locker room with all the other athletes, all of them likely wondering what the hell *he* is doing there.

Thankfully the track field isn't crowded when Alex shows up. Most kids have gone home for the day. The track is the usual size—about 400 meters of bright red surface, recently refurbished, surrounding a field of grass. This used to be the football field, too, but two years ago they built a new one on the other side of the school campus, with stadium-size seating and custom-designed locker and weight rooms just beyond the north end zone. Football rules the roost in this city, in this state. Track is an afterthought, really. Cross-country especially, which lacks the glamour of the sprints.

Alex sees Nathen in the grass along the track, stretching his long, toned arms toward the tips of his blue and white jogging shoes. Alex walks to him and plunks his bags on the ground. Nathen looks up from his stretch. "Hey, buddy. You ready?"

"Yeah. As ready as I'll ever be."

"Here, sit next to me and stretch. Coach R will be over in a minute."

Coach Runyon is across the field, talking to another runner, a tall black guy Alex recognizes as Joseph Ewusi-Mensah, the star of the team. Coach Runyon is short and lean, probably in his midthirties, with receding red hair and a gaunt face.

"You're gonna kick some ass today," Nathen says.

"If you say so." Alex is so nervous that he can barely complete a stretch. His limbs feel heavy and rubbery, and his belly feels like it wants to explode. And now he sees Coach Runyon pat Joseph on the shoulder, sending him toward the locker rooms. He starts crossing the field, heading right toward them.

"Alex?" the coach says, pausing in front of him.

"Yes, sir." He stands and, for lack of anything else to do, shakes his hand. "Uh, thanks for letting me try out today."

Coach Runyon is all business. "We have a solid team here. Not the best in the state, but pretty darn good. But we're short one man, which I guess Nathen told you about. And we need a full roster to be competitive in the team competition. So I'm looking for someone to fill in this coming spring season. We'll be doing some track events, but we also have some road races."

"Great," he says, even though he knows this already.

"I've tried out a few other guys already, but no one has really impressed me. Nathen says you've got talent."

Alex lets out a shy smile and shrugs. He's never been able to take a compliment or praise.

"So," Coach says, "I'm going to have you run a mile, just to get a look. That's basically four laps around the track. You about ready?"

"Yes, sir."

With Nathen watching and with Coach Runyon's hand on his stopwatch, Alex takes his place behind the fat line that marks the starting point in the innermost lane. Coach counts down from five and then Alex takes off. His rubbery legs suddenly kick to life and he lets loose, as if racing next to actual opponents. He hears Nathen shouting encouragement as he passes them after the first lap, and then the second. By the third lap he is sucking for air. He probably started out too fast, but he feels good—nice, even strides, pumping his fists, his legs feeling bouncy on the track, like they could keep going for hours. When he passes them for the last lap, he sees Coach Runyon scrutinizing the stop-watch, Nathen hovering at his shoulder.

Approaching the end of the run, Alex knows that in a few minutes his fate will be sealed. Coach will want him or not. He'll either return to gym next semester or be part of this team. Both prospects are scary. And how will he face Nathen if he fails, not to mention James? Will Nathen drop away, back to being James's friend and on the periphery of Alex's existence? He almost doesn't want to finish running, afraid of what comes next. But he crosses the finish line anyway, slowing down, breathing heavily but evenly. He walks ahead and soon Nathen is at his side, slap-ping him on the back, saying, "Great job, bud!"

Nathen is proud of him, at least. Alex turns back and heads toward Coach Runyon, whose opinion is the only one that matters.

Coach Runyon walks toward him, still eyeballing his stop-watch. "Five minutes, forty-three seconds. Not bad for a novice with no training," he says. "You've never run competitively before?"

"No, sir."

"Doesn't matter. Nathen's right—you've got talent. A nice stride, though you need to shorten it. And you definitely need to learn about pacing. But it's a good start."

"Thanks."

"Now, I want you to work on cutting your time before Janu-ary. I'll give you a chart with times to aim for, and splits. And I want you to come see me after school a few days a week, to work on your form. You'll need to do some training on weekends, too."

Alex nods, then says, "So . . ." He looks at Nathen and then back at the coach. "Does this mean, well, that I'm on the team?"

Coach, ever stone-faced and earnest, extends his hand. "You're on the team. Congrats."

Alex is speechless for a moment, but he manages to squeak out a thanks.

"I knew you'd do it," Nathen says, walking Alex to his car. He has his arm draped lightly around Alex's shoulder, and this only adds to his stunned euphoria.

"I still can't believe it," Alex says. But he edits himself from saying what he's really thinking—I can't believe I'm an athlete now; I can't believe I belong to a team; I can't believe your arm is around me.

Almost everyone from school is long gone, so there's nobody in the parking lot, save for a few cars here and there, sprinkled about like the misplaced toys of some giant. No one is there to witness his moment of glory. But it's okay. He doesn't need an audience. He's almost embarrassed about how good he feels.

"Take the night off, and we'll go running tomorrow, and this weekend if you want," Nathen says, finally pulling away and stationing himself in front of Alex.

"Sounds awesome," he says. "Thanks, you know, for all this. For making this happen."

Nathen just smiles and gives a thumbs-up sign and walks off. It's as if he's shy, too, all of a sudden.

*   *   *

At home, Alex waits in his car before going inside to face James, who is probably expecting bad news, and his father and mother, who have no idea he's just made the cross-country team, have no idea that Alex is even a decent runner. He wants to savor the moment, alone, for a few more minutes.

It's been so long since he has felt, well, happy. Or this happy.

He's not foolish—he knows it won't last, this euphoria. It will be replaced by the realities of the hard training on top of the daily grind of school and homework. And he can still fail, can't he? He's on the team, but what if, after all this, he really *isn't* a good runner? He could go on and on with these negative thoughts, but he shuts them out through sheer will. Because it's not even the jogging or making the team that is making him feel so ecstatic. It's the charge he feels with Nathen. The charge of having a friend again.

He finally gets out of the car and heads toward the side door. That's when he sees Henry across the street, sitting on his porch with his dictionary.

Henry waves, like he's been waiting for Alex to notice him. It's a wave that Alex can't just brush off with a wave of his own, even if he wants to. He drops his bags in the driveway and crosses the street.

"Learn any new words today?" Alex says. He sits next to Henry on the brick stairs.

"Not really. So many of them are stupid words no one ever uses." Henry's tone sounds down, like he's pouting about something.

"Yeah, I guess you're right," Alex says.

"But I guess we need them sometimes, to describe stuff."

"I guess so."

"This kid at school called me a 'redheaded bastard' today."

"That's horrible," Alex says.

"I didn't really know what 'bastard' meant, not really. But now I do. Most kids just ignore me. I don't care, either. I just listen to the teachers. They're the ones who are nice to me. But this kid, he won't stop calling me stuff."

"What a creep." It dawns on Alex that Henry is sort of a younger version of himself—an outcast, a misfit. A weirdo. And he's not even in middle school yet.

"Yeah, I guess so. Mom says just ignore him. She said, 'Sticks and stones may break your bones, but words can never hurt you.' "

"Yeah, that's what they always tell us."

"But it's not really true, is it?"

"Not really. Lots of things they tell us aren't true. A lot of what they tell us is garbage."

"Then why do they tell us stuff like that?"

Alex says, "I don't know." Maybe he could think of a few reasons, but he still feels wrapped in his little bubble of happiness, and none of the ugly things can get to him now. He feels happy and light, as if at any moment the cool breeze of this November night will lift him high into the air.

4

James

It is the Wednesday before Thanksgiving holiday, and James doesn't see much point in practicing, but that's what Coach Whitley makes them do for the last school hour before the four-day reprieve. Coach is not usually such a hard-ass, but he's in a grumpy mood for some reason and seems to be taking it out on the team. The girls' team members got to sneak home early, because their coach, Ms. Bettany, is cool. They all honked their horns as they drove off, rubbing it in.

"Well, they're not defending regional tennis champs," Coach Whitley says, before pairing the boys up in six groups of two. Like being regional tennis champs in this region is some big achievement.

James is paired with Tyler today. Tyler plays the number five position in singles, versus James's number three. Ron Hogue and George Thirkell, both seniors like James, play numbers one and

71

two, and they are (and always have been, since freshman year) doubles partners. Rudy Skyler, a sophomore prodigy, plays number four, and Dewayne Jackson, the fourth senior, rounds out the varsity singles team at number six. Lurking just out of varsity spots are two juniors, Mac Freeman and Paul Hansford, and then the rest of the team is sophomores and freshmen—guys whose varsity days lie ahead of them. It's a solid team, and for the most part everyone likes each other.

Tyler and James take the last court on the first row—as far away from Coach Whitley as possible.

"What an asshole," Tyler says, bouncing a ball with his racquet as he waits while James does some perfunctory stretches.

"Seriously. We should be on our way home."

But, truth be told, what would James do at home besides take a nap or watch TV or avoid writing his advanced placement English paper? His mom would be home from work early, cooking her sweet potatoes and green bean casserole and baking cheese biscuits. This year, like every year, they are celebrating Thanksgiving with the Ashfords and the Watsons, family friends. (Their relatives—aunts, uncles, cousins, and their two living grandparents—live all over the place, so large family holiday gatherings have mostly stopped because geography makes it a pain in the ass for everyone.) Tomorrow, they'll walk down the street to the Watsons' house—it is their turn to host. It is a tradition, this trifamily celebration, dating back to when all the kids were in elementary or middle school. Now they are all in high school or college, respectively: Clare Ashford, a fellow senior and James's onetime girlfriend; Steven and Michelle Watson, freshman and junior at college; and he and Alex. They are all grown up but still get stuck at the kids' table.

"You got big plans?" Tyler shouts, feeding him a ball, beginning their endless warm-up rally.

"Nah, just eating and writing a damn paper. Watching the Bama game." Alabama is playing Auburn on Saturday, always a huge deal. James gets into it, but not insanely into it, like the entire fucking city. If Alabama loses, some people in town and all over the state—grown adults—will be sent into a long period of depression and resentment. Ridiculous.

"We should hang out," Tyler says.

"Yeah, that'd be cool," James says, more as a reflex. They've never really hung out much before, outside of the tennis gang. Of course, he used to see Tyler all the time, when Tyler was best friends with Alex, before everything changed.

"My folks are heading to my grandparents' place in Savannah on Friday, and they're taking my little sister, so I'll be home alone," Tyler says.

"Cool."

"I'm gonna have a small party after the game is over. Nothing big. I'll call you."

"Okay," he says. But it all feels weird, wrong even. Wouldn't it be, well, disloyal to hang out with Tyler, a guy who has openly shunned his brother? Not that James blamed him at the time—and, besides, Alex didn't act much like he even wanted friends anymore, after the incident. Still, this promised invitation from Tyler makes him feel squeamish. Obviously, Alex isn't invited.

They rally back and forth, then play a few practice games, which James takes handily. Tyler is a big hitter, with a big serve, but so far he lacks patience and consistency. All James has to do is keep the ball in play. The weather is cool, so he barely builds up a sweat.

Finally, Coach Whitley blows his whistle, calling them in for the day.

"Okay, boys, have a good holiday. I'll see you Monday."

James says his good-byes, and he overhears Tyler talking up his party to Ron and George. This makes him less squeamish—if he's mostly inviting the team, it will remain a tennis-only sort of thing. And excluding Alex would be natural.

He piles his racquets and book bag into the backseat of his Jeep. Before taking off, he glances toward the front of the school. Most students with cars leave through the back parking lot. But during sixth period the tennis team gets to park in the side lot, right by the tennis courts. Today he sees Alice out in front of the school, clutching a few books against her chest. She's wearing tight jeans, as usual, and a peach-colored sweater, no jacket. He wonders why she is there—she has a car, after all, a dark blue Taurus. Then he sees a metallic gray Camaro pull up to the curb in front of her. She leans over and looks through the passenger window. He can't really make out her face from this far away, but he can tell she is probably smiling, flirting. Then she gets in and the driver zooms off. He gets into his car, feeling a mixture of jealousy and flat-out relief.

On the way home, he stops at Buddy's, the local convenience store, for a Gatorade and maybe a candy bar. Inside, in the candy aisle, he sees the redheaded kid, Henry, perusing packets of gum, a rainbow of choices.

James stares at the candy bars, trying to decide which one to get. He likes the crunchiness of Twix, the flaky buttery richness of Butterfinger. Hell, there aren't many candy bars he doesn't like. Except the ones with coconut in them. He decides on a Twix and then turns and sees Henry pick up a packet of Bubble Yum and shove it in the pocket of his baggy pants, then jam another one in the other pocket. Then Henry looks over at him. "Oh, hey," Henry says, acting as if he has done nothing wrong. "You're Alex's brother, right?"

"Yep."

In a lower voice, he says, "You're not going to tell on me, are you?"

"Nah. I did that kinda stuff when I was your age."

"You did?" The kid stares at him with an odd intensity that makes him nervous.

"A few times." James stares back at the candy bar selection. Really, he remembers, it happened only once, at Food World while in the checkout line, and mainly he did it because he was mad at his mother.

"I'm not a thief, I promise. I just don't have any money."

James looks back at him. "I can buy those for you if you want."

"Really?"

"Sure, why not?"

"I can pay you back. Once Mom gives me my allowance. She gets her check next week."

"It's only two packs of gum," James says, wondering what kind of check the mother gets. Surely not welfare, not in their neighborhood. But he *has* noticed that she doesn't really work, either. Henry and his mother are weirdos, like puzzle pieces that don't fit.

Henry pulls the gum from his pockets and hands it over and follows James while he chooses a bottle of orange Gatorade, then hovers to the side as James pays up front. The cashier is a sweet-faced middle-aged man, always friendly and chatty, like he's trying to be the actual buddy of the store's name. Would he have caught Henry? And if so, what would have happened? Do people call the cops on a little kid?

Outside, James hands the gum to Henry.

"Thanks."

"You need a ride home?"

"Okay," he says.

In the car, they are both quiet until James pulls into the entrance of their neighborhood. Henry says, "You're nice, just like Alex."

"Thanks, I guess." James knows he *can* be nice, but it's never a quality he'd use to describe himself. Sometimes he feels downright mean.

"I think it would be great to have a brother."

"It's okay." He wants to say that it must be nice to be an only child, but he's not sure if he means it.

"All I have is Mom."

James hesitates, then asks, "Where's your father?"

"I don't have one."

"Of course you do."

"Well, I guess so. But Mom always says I don't. And she doesn't like it when I ask about it. So I don't. That's what I told Alex. I guess it makes Mom sound bad. But she's not, if that's what you're thinking."

James shakes his head. "I'm not thinking anything."

"I mean, I'm not dumb," he says. "I know I have to have a father. But he's not around for some reason."

James pulls into the driveway, happy to be home so this conversation can end. He thinks Henry is probably one of those usually quiet kids who, once he has someone to talk to, can never shut up.

"Well, thanks for the gum and stuff. Happy Thanksgiving," Henry says, jumping out of the passenger seat and slamming the door. James watches in the rearview mirror as he dashes across the street, his bright red head bobbing up and down till he disappears inside the house.

"Nothing from Duke," his mother says before he can even ask. She is kneading dough for biscuits, and the kitchen smells of roasting vegetables.

James has applied for early admission at Duke, so he should hear something soon. Each day he checks the mailbox, half hoping for and half dreading an envelope. Some of his classmates are still taking the SAT, filling out applications, but his work is mostly done. He took the SAT once, was pleased with his score—1480—and has been able to relax. Well, not relax. He still has to hear from Duke. He has about six backup universities, and those applications have been sent in as well. He's on top of things. He didn't apply to the University of Alabama, where he figures most of his classmates will end up. He can't imagine wanting to stay in Tuscaloosa, like Preston and Greer. Their parents could afford to send them to most places, even though their grades aren't terrific. But it's like they think Bama is the greatest and only worthy college on earth. Nathen, meanwhile, is deciding between a few schools up north. Greer has taken to calling them both Yankees, even though North Carolina is part of the South.

"Oh, well," James says. "Maybe next week."

"Hope so," she says. She's told him a million times that early admission is great, but even if they say no, it doesn't mean he won't eventually get in. "You have to be patient," she always tells him.

"Dinner's just going to be sandwiches tonight, okay?" she says.

"Fine with me." He heads upstairs to his room with his Twix and Gatorade. He passes by Alex's room, sees that he's not there, and then wonders where he is. Probably running with Nathen again. Or staying after school, practicing. James is happy about this new thing—running cross-country—in Alex's life.

He knows he should do some homework or start work on his paper. But he doesn't feel like doing anything right now. He just lies on his bed and tries to doze off. His eyes start to feel heavy, but he never falls into a nap. Instead, he wonders who Alice was with. And why he even fucking cares.

The next day is Thanksgiving, and that morning his mother does some last-minute baking while his father reads a book in front of the TV. The Macy's parade is on. James sits with his cereal and watches the gigantic, inflated cartoon characters glide down the New York streets as a pop singer he hates belts out some holiday tune on top of a float. Mom always used to talk about how she wanted to go up to New York for Thanksgiving one year, but they always stay here, always dining with the Watsons and the Ashfords. Which is fine with James. He's not so sure about New York.

Alex, of course, is out running. "I have to get in a jog before we eat," he said in defense of dashing off on this fairly chilly November morning. James feels lazy in comparison, but it's a holiday, for Christ's sake, you're *supposed* to be lazy.

"I like Nathen," his father says, without any logical lead-up. "He's a good kid."

"Yeah, he is." The pop singer finally finishes her damn song, and everyone claps as if it's the best performance ever.

"Alex is really taking this jogging seriously. And I think it's all Nathen's doing. Well, a lot of it. It's good for him."

James, his father, and his mother have rarely chatted about the incident. Afterward, of course, they grilled him about whether he knew Alex was depressed and stuff like that. *No more than anyone else,* he'd wanted to say, but hadn't. They all knew Alex had started acting like a loner, shutting himself in his room. But it's not like he had started wearing all black or cutting himself or anything like that.

Since those initial weeks, the subject has been the elephant in the room, looming large but not spoken of. He sometimes hears his parents whispering behind their bedroom door, or talking in low voices, but they leave him out of it. Besides, Alex is seeing that shrink each Wednesday.

"Alex could use a friend," his father says.

James hasn't really thought about Nathen as Alex's friend before this. Nathen is *his* friend. Nathen is a senior, not a junior like Alex. And besides the running, what do they have in common?

"Yeah," James finally says, agreeing with his father. After all, it is true; Alex needs a friend. And James doesn't see the harm in his brother latching on to one of his.

Later, around four, the whole family walks down a few houses to the Watsons', armed with covered dishes and a few bottles of wine. The bright sky is fading and cloudless—it could be a summer afternoon, save for the nip in the air. James can smell burning wood, so people are already opening their fireplaces.

"If it isn't the lovely Donaldson family," Dr. Watson booms, opening the front door. Dr. Watson is James's and Alex's dermatologist, when they need one. Luckily, their pimples have never been too bad, the usual flare-ups here and there. Not like Preston, who takes a pill to keep him from being a total pizza face. Once inside, they're greeted with hugs and hellos, and then they set the food and wine in the kitchen. Mrs. Watson shoos the boys away, but Mom sticks around to help prepare the feast. The house smells heavy with food, the smoky scent of turkey blending with baking bread and cooking vegetables. James feels extremely hungry all of a sudden.

"Steven and Michelle are in the TV room—why don't you boys go join them?" Dr. Watson says, while James's father pours some bourbon at the bar in the living room.

Alex saunters ahead of James to the TV room, his hands in his jeans. This will be the first time they have seen Steven and Michelle since the incident, and James wonders if Alex is nervous. As greetings are made, James can't detect any trace of awkwardness. But he does notice Steven eyeing Alex more closely, as if looking for an outward sign of a defect. Steven is only a year ahead of James, a freshman at Vanderbilt, and Michelle is a junior at Colorado. They're both dark-haired and average-looking, more like their father than their mother, who's blond and pretty for an older lady. Actually, Michelle looks a little hippyish now, her hair long and stringy, her tissuelike long yellow shirt over baggy, bell-bottomy jeans and sandals. She's a pot smoker, James bets.

"How's C-High treating you?" Steven asks both of them.

"It's okay," James says.

Steven asks about his teachers and tennis, and James asks about Vanderbilt. "It's awesome," Steven says, not really explaining why it's so awesome, which makes James wonder if it really is awesome after all.

Snacks are laid out on the coffee table—cheese straws, cubes of cheese and little wheat crackers, bowls of almonds and spicy peanuts—and they all sit on the couch and surrounding chairs and start munching. An NFL game is on the TV.

Alex and Michelle start chatting, and occasionally James can hear snippets about Boulder and classes and how Alex likes her shirt.

"Mom says you applied to Vandy," Steven says to him.

"Yeah, I did. And a few other schools. But my first choice is Duke."

"Uh-huh," he says, laughing. "Yeah, everyone says that. But not everyone can get in."

James shrugs. "I guess."

Right after that the Ashfords arrive. Everyone goes to the foyer to say hello, then settles back to their respective domains.

Clare sits next to Michelle on the love seat and the two of them play catch-up, leaving Alex the odd man out. Clare is wearing a jean skirt with a satiny white blouse, her blond hair swept under a headband, making her look very prim and proper. Their breakup is ancient history—they dated for six months, sophomore year—but James still feels a little weird around Clare since she started dating that college guy.

Eventually all the fathers storm into the TV room with their drinks and do their usual grilling about school and life and this and that.

"So, James," Mr. Ashford says, "your dad tells me you applied early to Duke."

"Yeah, but I haven't heard yet." Great, now everyone knows. And now, if he doesn't get in, everyone will know that, too. Perfect. He almost envies Alex, because everyone besides Michelle seems to be steering clear of him.

"Well, if Duke won't have you, you can always go to Shelton State," Mr. Ashford says, laughing heartily to himself. Shelton State is the community college. It's not a bad school, as far as that goes, but the implication is that it is for dummies, people not good enough for a regular college. James manages a light chuckle.

"Alex is running now," his dad says, maybe sensing James's annoyance at the topic at hand. "He just made the cross-country team."

"That's great!" a few people exclaim, as if it was the greatest achievement in the world, especially for a complete head case.

He sees Alex, sitting there, offering sheepish smiles, and realizes that he also doesn't want any attention.

They're both saved when Mrs. Ashford peeps in the room, holding a glass of white wine, and says that dinner is served.

James, Alex, Michelle, Steven, and Clare—as expected—are seated at the kids' table that has been set up in the living room, within earshot of the dining room. James fills himself with turkey and ham, sweet potatoes and regular mashed potatoes, corn bread stuffing, cranberries, salad, green beans, and cheese biscuits. It's almost too much. The girls nibble mostly on salad and vegetables, with bird-size portions of the meat, afraid the boys might think they're pigs or something. Steven's a pig like James, and Alex eats heartily as well, though he doesn't really seem to be digging the turkey.

"So, Clare," Michelle says. "You haven't said anything about your college boyfriend. Who is he?"

James sees Clare stop midchew, then keep going. She looks up and puts down her fork. "Well, we broke up last week, actually."

"Oh, God. Don't I feel stupid," Michelle says.

"It's okay. I'm over it."

"You were probably too good for him anyway."

James doesn't know much about this college guy, but he feels oddly happy about the news. Not that he wants Clare back. But it's like this has brought her back down to earth. He is careful not to break into a grin.

"What about you two?" Michelle asks, meaning James and Alex.

"I'm not dating anyone," James says, careful not to look at Clare.

"What about Alice?" Alex asks, like a thud.

James says, "Uh, I . . . we broke up." He'd wanted to say, *I dumped her.* Saying they broke up makes it sound civil and mutual, which it sure as hell wasn't. Meanwhile, he's fuming at Alex for not keeping his trap shut. Like he or anyone else needs reminding of Alice. James can see Alex redden, already feeling chastised.

"God, it's like breakup time in Tuscaloosa! What about you?" Michelle says to Alex.

This girl is relentless! James thinks. Isn't it obvious that Alex does not, will not, have a girlfriend right now? In fact, as far as James can recall, he never has had one. Well, there was that girl in eighth grade, Carla, but does that count? Sure, maybe they kissed and stuff, but he just knows Alex is still a virgin. No, Alex has never *really* dated a girl, though he could have—plenty of girls liked him. But who would want him now?

"No," Alex says. "No girlfriend for me. Not yet."

"High school dating is meaningless anyway," Michelle says, and without thinking about it, James looks at Clare. Thankfully, she's focused on scooping a small pile of mashed potatoes onto her fork.

Later, after dinner and dessert—pumpkin pie and cherry pie and a caramel cake and vanilla ice cream—the adults continue sitting around the dining room table, drinking and chatting and gossiping. The rest of them resume their spots in the TV room, feeling drunk on rich food. Eventually, the girls sneak off upstairs to Michelle's room, where they're probably talking about the college guy and what went wrong.

"You really should think about Vanderbilt," Steven says. He's drinking a beer now because his parents said it was okay. As if

Steven doesn't guzzle beers at college. "I think you'd like it there. You should come visit the campus," Steven continues.

"Cool. Well, maybe I'll come visit in the spring." He wants to say, *That is, if Duke doesn't work out.* But he doesn't want to bring *that* up again.

Clare strolls in without Michelle and sits next to James.

Steven flips the channel to some Christmas movie. No matter what's on the screen, Alex's eyes are glued to it. And he seems to be smiling to himself, like he's holding in some great secret. He *has* been in a better mood since making the cross-country team, but he's still mostly quiet, at least when he's around James.

"So," Clare says, "what are you doing the rest of the weekend?"

"Uh, mostly working on a paper for English class."

"Oh yeah, you're in AP. I'm in advanced, so mine's not due for another week or so."

"Lucky you."

"But I might as well get started. I hate procrastinating."

"Man," Steven says. "You think writing papers in high school is tough? At Vandy, it's like all we fucking ever do is write papers." He goes on and on about his papers—for Spanish class, for political science—and he and Clare just nod and wait till he's finished throwing in his two cents. He finally shuts up and decides he needs another beer and heads to the kitchen.

"Well, if you want a study break, maybe we could see a movie on Saturday or something," Clare says.

Without thinking about it, he says, "Sure."

"Okay. Well, call me."

James nods and, like Alex, begins to focus intently on the TV.

A movie with Clare? He's pretty sure he won't call her. Or maybe he will, to say he's too busy. If she's trying to rebound with him, she can forget it. Besides, Saturday night is supposed to be Tyler's party, and he'll probably go to that.

Feeling like he needs an escape, James heads for the bathroom. At the door, which is just down the hall from the dining room, he can hear all the parents gossiping.

"Well, I heard that she's Jack Pembroke's girlfriend," Mrs. Ashford says. "Or she was. They've been spotted together."

"Get out of here," his mother says.

Jack Pembroke is the richest man in town, the owner of the country club that James's family belongs to, who made his fortune in the lumber industry or something like that. Maybe it was a paper mill, James can't remember. He lives in a big mansion on the country club grounds, with his prissy wife. He's got to be about seventy years old, maybe older. Notoriously grumpy, he recently banned kids under sixteen from the hot tub because he said they peed in it. James has heard all this from his parents. He's never had much interaction with the man himself.

"Old Jack can get a piece of tail that young?" Mr. Ashford says.

"Don't be crude, hon!" Mrs. Ashford says.

"That can't be true," his mother says. "I've seen her go on dates with other men. I mean, men around her age."

"Well, she has no husband to speak of," Mrs. Watson says.

James has no idea who or what they're really talking about, and he doesn't really care—it's about boring old people and has nothing to do with his life. So he shuts himself into the bathroom, turns on the sink, and wonders when they can just go home.

* * *

Around five o'clock the next day, James's phone rings, startling him out of a catnap. James got his own private phone line last summer. Not because he's a big phone talker, like a girl, but because his dad got sick of all the shouting up and down the stairs to tell him the phone was for him. Now, as the phone rings, he decides to let the machine get it. He's too groggy to talk. The machine clicks on after the fourth ring, but no one speaks—it's a hang-up. He *hates* when people can't bother to leave a message.

It's getting dark out now, so he hops off his bed and flicks on his overhead light. Maybe he should shower to wake himself up? Or maybe grab a soda in the fridge? He's actually hungry again, too, even after the pigfest from yesterday.

But the phone rings again. This time he answers it.

"Hello?"

"James?"

"Oh, hey, Tyler," he says, recognizing his voice. "Did you call a few minutes ago and not leave a message?"

"No, man. Not me."

He wonders if he's lying. "So, you still having a party tomorrow?"

"Yeah. Not a huge one, but it should be bad-ass. You gonna come? Maybe bring Nathen and those guys?"

James wants to ask, *And Alex? Can I bring Alex?* Even though he doesn't want to, not really. "Yeah, I should be able to come. What time?"

"Oh, like eight or so? Once the game is over?"

"Cool. See you then." He's still not sure if he'll go or not.

Maybe he will call one of his boys. Or there's always Clare, who supposedly wants to go to a movie. Sheesh. He's glad no obligations pull at him tonight. He can be lazy and continue to sit on his ass.

Later, after his shower, and after his mother gets home from a day of shopping and announces they'll have leftovers for dinner at seven, James's phone rings again.

"Yo," he says.

There's a pause, then Alice's voice: "I have a new boyfriend, so you can go fuck yourself."

And before he can respond, she hangs up.

Should he call Clare or not? Or should he go to Tyler's party? These are the questions that occupy James on Saturday. Not life-or-death decisions or anything, but still, they distract him, even with the Alabama and Auburn game raging on TV. It's a tug-of-war. Part of him just wants to stay home.

He sits in the den, watching the game with Dad and Mom. Mom isn't really that interested—she reads magazines and looks up only when James or his father make exclamations about good and bad plays. Alabama is winning at the half, but barely. Anything can happen. The crowd is boisterous, loud, a sea of blue and orange—Auburn's colors—with a chunk of Bama crimson in one pocket of the stadium. James imagines people all over Tuscaloosa—all over the whole state—glued to their TVs, armed with beers and soda and snacks, shouting and cursing, depending on what's happening.

Alex pops in on occasion, but he's not glued to the TV like the rest of them. He doesn't give a shit about football. Mom and

Dad entice him to stay—"It's a great game, Alex, come watch"—but he begs off, claiming he has homework to do. At some point during the third quarter, Alex pops his head in and announces he is going for a run. As far as James knows, Alex has no idea about Tyler's party later. He came in James's room last night, when he was about to fall asleep. He gave a tentative knock, like he was almost hoping James wouldn't hear it.

"Come in," James had shouted from the bed. His TV was on, a repeat of the *Late Show*, but he wasn't paying it much attention.

Alex edged his way in, pausing in the doorway. "Hey. Uh, sorry about you and Alice. I didn't know. I mean, I figured you guys were—"

"It's fine," he said, cutting him off. "She's a nutcase anyway."

"Oh."

"So don't worry about it."

"Okay. Well, I just wanted to say sorry."

And before James could say anything else, Alex had pulled the door shut and left. James hadn't meant to sound so short. But the phone call from Alice had pissed him off. He didn't even want to think about her.

After a tense last quarter, Alabama wins the game, so James can finally peel his ass off the couch. He decides to call Nathen to see if he wants to go to Tyler's party. He knows Greer has relatives in town and he has to hang out with his cousins, who are good little religious girls from Memphis. And Preston went to his mother's house in Huntsville.

"Is Nathen there?" he asks when Mr. Rao answers, sounding proper and elegant with his British accent.

"Oh, hello, James. No, he's out running. With your brother,

in fact. I expect him home in a little while. Shall I have him call you?"

"Sure," he says, then hangs up. Those two are always fucking running, he thinks. Can't they ever take a break? It's not like he's playing tennis every minute of the day.

He decides he might as well go to Tyler's later, with or without Nathen.

After dinner—chicken parmesan, a nice break from warmed-over turkey from the Watsons—and after Alex has headed to his room, James tells his mother he's going to a party.

"A party?" she says, rinsing dishes in the sink. "Who's having a party?"

"Well, it's more like hanging out, I guess. Not like a big party, just a small group."

"Okay. Just be home by twelve-thirty. Or midnight." She hands him a rinsed plate to put in the dishwasher. "Whose party is it?"

"Um, one of the guys on the team," he says.

"Who?"

"Tyler."

"Oh," she says, sounding pleasantly surprised. She has always liked Tyler, maybe because he's such a good ass-kisser. Parents love a good ass-kisser, even if that person is obvious about it. "Is your brother going with you?"

"Uh, no."

"Why not?"

"I dunno. Guess he's not really invited."

"Why not?"

"Mom, I don't know!"

She shuts off the sink and wipes her hands. "I don't get it." She shakes her head and gets this irritated look on her face. Doesn't she know that all of Alex's friends have dumped him? Is she that clueless? James wonders.

"Anyway, I doubt Alex would want to go," he says.

She nods and turns away from him, walking to the pantry, peering inside for something. "Well, like I said, be home by twelve-thirty. And drive safely."

She sounds the way she does when she's mad—her tone all snide and whiney. But what can James do? Nothing! So he heads back upstairs to get dressed.

Once he is dressed and has fixed his hair, James grabs his keys to go. He clutches his keys firmly, so they don't jingle, and walks quietly past Alex's door, afraid he'll open the door and ask where he is going. Not that James really has anything to hide.

Downstairs, Mom again reminds him to be home by twelve-thirty, and then he's safely outside. He backs his Jeep out of the driveway. Before he drives off, he looks up to the second floor and sees Alex's window. The lights are on in Alex's room, and the closed blinds are parted a little bit. And then the parted blinds drop back in place, and James drives off.

Tyler lives in a newer neighborhood not too far from where James lives. It's full of big redbrick homes with white trim that all look the same, all with decent-size yards with a few skinny trees here and there that still have a lot of growing to do. By the time

James arrives, he sees a number of cars lined up and down the street. *Small party my ass,* he thinks. Nathen had said he was too tired to go—he and Alex had run ten miles and he was beat. So James is flying solo.

Inside, the party's in full swing but not too crazy. To his left, in the main TV room, a group is gathered, listening to the stereo and watching TV and drinking and talking loudly. He sees some other juniors and seniors, a few girls, and some other guys— about thirty or forty people. Ron and George are on the couch sipping from red Dixie cups, and both seem to be working this one girl James doesn't recognize. They give him slight, distracted waves.

"Hey, you made it!" Tyler exclaims, walking down the hall from the kitchen, holding two Heinekens, one of which he hands to James. He's wearing a crimson button-down shirt. Lots of people, James notices, are in crimson—Bama colors.

"Thanks," James says.

Then Kirk walks toward them from the kitchen, also holding a Heineken. "Hey, man, what's shaking?" Kirk, Tyler's sidekick, another one of Alex's former friends. His eyes look lazy, like he's stoned. He probably is. Kirk is also wearing crimson—a Polo. They're both so hyped-up, and for a moment James wonders how Alex was even friends with them. He can't picture quiet Alex with these two guys, so brash and loud.

"How about that game?" Kirk says, holding up his hand for a high five.

James high-fives him—how can he not? "It was awesome."

"Fucking Auburn losers," Tyler says.

"You got a cigarette?" James asks Tyler. He doesn't smoke, really, but he wants an excuse to go outside, in the backyard.

"I got one," Kirk says, pulling a pack from his back pocket.

"Thanks. I'll be back in a sec."

"We'll be here, buddy," Kirk says, laughing like he's just told some funny joke.

James walks down the hallway, to the kitchen, and then out a sliding glass door onto their back patio, which is lit by two over-bright floodlights. There's a pool, but it's covered now for the winter by a big forest-green tarp. He doesn't even light his cigarette, just stares off in the distance, past the pool, over the back fence at the other houses, lined up like ducks.

He hears the door slide open behind him and turns to see Clare.

"Fancy meeting you here," she says, sliding the door shut. "Weren't we supposed to see a movie?"

"Yeah, sorry about that." Shit—what is *she* doing here?

"I'll live," she says, smiling in a way that lets him know she's a little miffed but that she'll forgive him anyway. He knows that smile well, from when they dated. Seems like he was always doing something that miffed her.

"I didn't see you when I came in," he says.

"I was in the bathroom. I came with Suzy Parker." She smiles.

James nods, then realizes he has no lighter for the cigarette. Oh well.

"Is Alex here?" Clare asks. She's in jeans and a black shirt under a little black jacket.

"Huh? Oh, no, he's not."

"Really? He's good friends with Tyler, right?" She hugs her arms to her chest, like she is cold. Her blond hair hangs loose tonight, framing her smooth face.

"Yeah, well, he *was*. You know, before all the . . . the stuff happened." James pulls the cigarette to his mouth and then realizes it's not lit.

"I see. Well, he seemed like he was doing okay the other night."

"Yeah, I guess."

"Why'd you come outside?"

"Well, I was gonna smoke. But I don't have a lighter. And, uh, I just . . . I dunno. I shouldn't have even come to the party. It feels weird."

"Yeah. I only came because Suzy dragged me. She has a crush on someone here. And, well, here I am."

"Yeah, here we are." He cracks a smile. He realizes that he feels comfortable with her now, alone, like a weight has been lifted or something. "We should have gone to a movie."

"Well, we can go some other time."

"That would be cool."

"But just as friends," she says.

He looks at her, sort of annoyed that she said that first, before he could make it clear that he only wanted to go as friends anyway. "Yeah. That would be cool. I'm over girls anyway."

"And I'm over guys, so it's perfect." She smiles to herself and stares off to the back of the yard.

"Well, I guess we should go back in."

"I guess so," she says.

Inside, in the TV room, James sits on the couch next to Tyler, who's regaling everyone with a story about how he got out of a speeding ticket yesterday.

"So, like, this cop takes my license, and I guess he recognizes my last name, and he realizes who my dad is."

Tyler's dad is the local district attorney. James's father is a

94

lawyer, too, but he mostly deals with bankruptcies and wills and shit like that. Tyler's dad, meanwhile, is always in the papers and on TV, talking about how he's tough on crime.

"So he asks me if Earl Shaughnessy is my dad," Tyler continues. "And I tell him he is, and he just smirks and gives me a warning!" He's drunk and seems almost ecstatic. James watches as Kirk hangs on Tyler's every word, laughing like this story is the funniest thing ever. Two slobbering, stinky puppy dogs is what they look like to James.

He sips his beer in big gulps and tries not to think of Alex at home in his room. *He* should be here, not James. Not with these guys he doesn't even like, not really. And then he realizes that Alex shouldn't be here, either.

Across the room he sees Clare, who seems to sense his stare. She looks at him and smiles sympathetically, like she knows exactly what he's thinking.

The Monday after Thanksgiving isn't as bad as James thought it might be when he woke up with that typical, post-holiday dread of school. It's sunny again, which always helps lift his mood. But all day he hopes to avoid seeing Alice. She's like a living ghost, haunting his days. In this avoidance he is successful, and by sixth period, he knows he is in the clear. He won't have any close encounters with Crazy Girl. And that holds true for the entire week, miraculously.

On Friday afternoon, while he is changing for tennis practice, George tells him about Valerie Towson. She's this supersmart—and superquiet—black girl in their class. James has AP English with her, in fact, and French, too.

"She got into Duke, man. Didn't you hear?" George says.

"Are you serious?" he says, his heart pounding.

"Yeah. I heard in my calculus class. Mr. Runyon was making a big deal out of it. Valerie was embarrassed about it and didn't really say anything."

"Huh," James says.

"You didn't hear yet?"

"No. Not yet." He feels like he has just missed a flight, or a bus.

"Well," George says, "I'm sure you'll hear from them soon."

All through practice, James can't focus. He hits balls into the net or into the back fence, misses his serves left and right.

"Donaldson, you're a mess today," Coach Whitley says.

After practice, James drives home quickly. He just *knows* that damn letter from Duke is waiting for him at home. He just knows it. He feels sick to his stomach, his belly full of both dread and anticipation. Good news or bad—what will it be?

When he pulls into the driveway, he gets out of his car without taking out his bags. He heads straight for the mailbox. That kid Henry is outside, but James ignores him even though Henry shouts hello.

He yanks open the mailbox and sifts through the mail—a few magazines, some bills, the usual crap. And then he finds it. The letter from Duke. Off-gray envelope, with Duke's logo in the corner. A thin envelope. Is that good or bad?

He hesitates.

"Hi, James!" Henry shouts again.

James tears open the envelope and pulls out the letter. It's only early admission, he tells himself. If they say no, it's okay.

But, now, seconds away from seeing the words on the page, he senses the news will be good. Everything, so far, has gone his way. Plus, he's in the top ten of his class; sure, Valerie is smart, too, but James plays sports, is in extracurricular clubs. How could she get in and not him? He's ready to celebrate.

"Dear Mr. Donaldson," he reads. "After careful review of your application, we are unable to grant early admission."

James stops reading. He can't go on. He just stands there, frozen, in a daze, until Henry shouts his name one more time.

"Hi, Henry," James finally says, softly, almost as if he's talking to the ground.

5

Alex

This second weekend in December, on a Saturday morning, the weather is freezing. There's hardly ever a chance of snow this far south, and there is no precipitation expected, but still, the air is so cold it makes Alex's breath feel pinched. It is not good running weather.

"Should we cancel our run?" Alex asks when Nathen calls him on the phone that morning.

"Well, it *is* cold as balls out. But I was thinking we could go to the university rec center. My folks are members, and I can bring guests if I want, for just a few bucks. They have this indoor running track. That way we could run and not freeze our asses off."

"Oh, wow. Sounds cool."

"Yeah, each lap around is about an eighth of a mile. It can get repetitive, but it sure beats the treadmill."

"Sounds like a plan, then," Alex says.

"I'll pick you up in an hour?"

"Sounds good." Alex hangs up and puts on his gym clothes—shorts and a T-shirt, and, over that, his sweats. He also packs his gym bag, putting in a change of clothes. Downstairs he grabs a strawberry-filled breakfast bar, a banana, and a glass of orange juice. Dad is reading a section of the paper at the breakfast table. Alex takes a seat across from him.

"Hey there," he says, looking up from the paper and smiling. "How's the marathon man?"

"Doing good," he says. "Where's Mom?"

"At the supermarket. You're up and at 'em, huh?" he asks, eyeing his attire.

James, Alex figures, is still asleep. "I'm going to go running with Nathen in a little bit."

"In this weather?" he asks, looking back down at the paper.

"We're going to the rec. His parents belong."

"Oh," he says. "That's smart."

"Yeah. Sure beats running outside."

He folds the paper to the side. "I'm really proud of you."

Oh, here we go again, Alex thinks. "Thanks," he says. It's like, ever since the incident, Alex is a baby, and every step he takes—from doing well on a test to eating everything on his plate—is celebrated like it's some big achievement. Mom does it, too.

Dad stares at him, like he is pondering something. "We're *all* proud. Not just because of the cross-country. Your mom and I can tell you've really turned a corner."

"I guess," Alex says.

"It's true. I know life is tough sometimes. Some days it seems pretty awful. I remember when I was your age. I'd get in bad moods. Depressed, even. Felt like the whole world was against me."

Alex nods, trying not to roll his eyes. He knows his dad was popular as a kid. Alex has even seen one of his high school yearbooks, where he was named Most Handsome and Most Likely to Succeed. But Alex listens, nods, because he knows that his dad is trying to make him feel better.

"You just have to take it one day at a time," Dad says, sounding just like Dr. Richardson during their therapy sessions.

"I know."

"Good." Dad nods and looks at Alex with a solemn but warm expression. "James says that Nathen says you're a very good runner."

"He does?"

"Yep, he sure does," he says before picking up another section of the paper.

Alex gulps down his food and drains his juice and heads back up to his room to grab his stuff. He wonders what else Nathen has said to James. Do they talk about him much to each other? Lately, James has made weird comments about him and Nathen. Like, the other day, he'd said, "Going running *again*? You guys sure run a lot together." He sounded like he was jealous or something, which is ridiculous. Alex and Nathen are friends now, for sure. But it's a different type of friendship. Or it feels like it is. It's not like he and Nathen are hanging out drinking beers, or talking about girls, or even going to parties together. Nathen still does that stuff with James and his other friends. So what's the problem? Besides, Alex knows that James went to a party at Tyler's house over Thanksgiving—he overheard him telling Mom; Alex may be quiet, but he can still hear things. He didn't really care that James went, but it bothered him that he thought he needed to keep it a secret from him.

He hears a car horn, so Alex dashes downstairs and out to Nathen's waiting Jeep, wearing a big navy blue down jacket over his sweats, carrying his duffel.

"Brrrr," he says after shutting the door. "It's freezing out there." Inside the Jeep, the air from the heater washes over him.

"Thank God for the rec, right?" Nathen playfully pats Alex's thigh, then moves his hand to the gearshift and drives ahead. "You'll like the rec. It's pretty cool. Plus, it's a little too early for most of the college kids to be there. They're all sleeping off their hangovers."

"You do anything last night?" Alex asks.

"I studied mostly. Watched some TV. Preston wanted us to come over, but I didn't feel like it. Pretty lame Friday night."

"I guess that's where James went. To Preston's." Alex had heard him leave around eight, and he heard him come back at midnight.

"Yeah, he tried to get me to go. I just wasn't feeling social."

Alex is glad to hear that Nathen's Friday was pretty much like his own—quiet and solitary, save for his parents being at home. But Alex mostly stayed in his room—doing homework, listening to the corny radio dedications on 98.3 FM, and watching sappy Christmas movies they were already running on cable. He remembers when every Friday and Saturday was spent with his friends, hanging out, going to movies, whatever. Staying at home was never really an option. Now it's the only option. But he doesn't mind. He's grown to enjoy it, to be honest. No putting on an act, no worrying about saying the right or wrong things. Tyler, in particular, used to bombard him with stinging comments, punctuated always by an empty "Just kidding, Alex." But, deep down, Alex knew he wasn't kidding. At home, alone, he is safe from all that.

The rec center is a huge brown brick building set on the edge of the campus, next to a big empty field and an outdoor running track, away from most of the dorms and frat houses and academic halls. The parking lot is mostly empty.

Inside, a male student (who, oddly, doesn't look that in shape) sitting behind a large counter checks Nathen's ID badge and charges Alex two dollars for the guest fee. He hands them each two white towels, though Alex has brought his own.

"So, here we are," Nathen says. "Our new home away from home." They walk down a long, high-ceilinged hallway, carpeted in crimson, Bama color. To the left is a basketball court, which is encircled above by the indoor track on the second floor. To the right, they pass the main weight room, which is gigantic and full of dumbbells and weight machines, treadmills and stationary bikes, and whose big glass windows overlook the empty field. At the end of the hall, past a few racquetball courts, are the locker rooms.

"Let's put our shit in here," Nathen says, opening the heavy door labeled MEN. Inside, it smells of sweat and soap and perfumey deodorant spray. The air is moist and warm, stuffy. The room is large, segmented into three dressing chambers, and all the walls are lined with gray plywood lockers, with small benches in front of them. Nathen walks to the farthest chamber and yanks open a locker and shoves his bag inside, then sits and peels off his shoes and sweats. Alex chooses a locker next to his and unpeels his sweats as well. A few older men—thirties, forties, fifties—are lingering about, naked or wearing towels, dressing or undressing. Alex tries not to look, but their nakedness is persistent, a bright naked pink in a field of gray. He finds that the sight of their bodies is not as embarrassing as it is unappealing and ridiculous, with their overly hairy torsos and flabby butts announcing themselves without shame.

Around a corner of the room, out of his view, Alex can hear sinks running and the hiss of the showers.

"So I thought we'd run about five miles? Maybe take it easy a bit?" Nathen says, relacing his shoes.

"Sounds good," Alex says, though he'd hardly consider five miles taking it easy, especially at the speed Nathen runs.

Upstairs they stretch outside the track entrance. Alex's legs feel stiff, maybe from the cold, and they almost seem to crack and snap when he bends over. Nathen stretches as well, effortlessly, his brown legs tightly muscled, dusted with black hairs.

"You ready, bud?" Nathen asks. "Let's do it."

The track is cushiony and surprisingly roomy, with six lanes. Below, on the basketball court, a few students play a game of two-on-two basketball, and their rubber-soled sneakers squeak insistently. A few female students walk around the track, but he and Nathen are the only runners.

It's weird running the track, because there's no new scenery to look at—they just run around and around, like they're on some skating rink. Alex sweats a lot—he almost misses the cool outside air. After about the tenth lap, he starts to lose count, so he just follows Nathen, an endless loop. Finally, after who knows how many laps, Nathen slows down and starts a cool-down walk around the track.

"How far was that?" Alex asks, catching his breath.

"Five miles, exactly," he says, smiling. "Next time we'll go further and faster."

"Can we come back this week?"

"Maybe. But it might be next weekend before we can come again. This is an insane week at school, with midterms and all."

"Yeah, don't remind me."

"Fucking sucks."

"But you're smart. You'll ace them." Alex knows that Nathen has applied to schools up east, like NYU and Princeton and Columbia, plus some other smaller liberal arts colleges. His grades are good, almost as good as James's are, maybe better.

"Are yours gonna be tough?" Nathen asks.

"Yeah. Well, trig will be, and chemistry. I hate math and science."

"See, that's what I love. It all makes sense to me."

"Must be nice."

"If you need any help with that stuff, let me know."

"I will," he says. James is good at math and science, too, but he hasn't helped since Alex was a freshman and sophomore. Back then he always seemed annoyed to have to do it, and impatient when Alex didn't always get what he was telling him. Now Alex flounders along by himself, though he's doing okay—solid Bs in both classes.

"Let's shower," Nathen says.

The two of them make their way to the locker room. Alex's heart should be slowing down after the run, but it doesn't—it quickens at the thought of being naked in public, and in front of Nathen.

Luckily no one else seems to be in the locker room when they enter. Still, Alex says, "We could just shower at home."

"Well, we're here. We might as well do it now. I'm all sweaty and gross," Nathen says, before yanking his shirt off. Alex tries not to look, but he can't help taking in quick glances. Nathen's stomach and chest are smooth and dark, though a shade lighter than his legs and arms. He is muscular, lean and fit from all of the running—his shoulders broad and rounded, his arm muscles long and ropey, the ridges of his stomach muscles barely poking out from under the skin. Nathen grabs a white towel and dries his face and chest. Then he looks over at Alex, who is just fiddling with his bag, stalling. "Don't be shy," he says, smiling, like it's all a big joke.

Alex forces a laugh and says he isn't shy. It's not that Alex hates his body, it's just that it's not very toned. It's boring, he thinks. He's like the underdeveloped version of James, who has big calves and strong forearms and taut biceps and broad shoulders. Plus, Alex has light clumps of brown hair around his nipples, which he thinks look goofy. And his hips are too wide. His butt a little too plump—and so damn white. Ghostly white.

He finally peels off his shirt and tosses it in the locker. By now, out of the corner of his eye, he sees Nathen drop his shorts to the ground, step out of them, then wrap a towel around his waist. Alex can't—he won't—look, even though he realizes he wants to.

"You coming?" Nathen asks, standing there, the towel barely holding on to his narrow hips.

Quickly, like he's late for something, Alex drops his damp

shorts and underwear and instantly grabs the towel to cover himself. But instead of feeling freaked out, he finds himself smiling, like he knows he is being silly.

The white tile floor is cold and damp. The showers are lined along two walls that face each other, six on each side. Each shower is covered by a crimson curtain that hangs from a rod. Thank God—Alex had almost feared one big open space of shower heads, with no privacy, like the way you always see in movies about football teams and stuff.

Alex chooses his shower and steps in, closing the curtain before removing his towel, which he then hangs on a hook just outside. When he parts the curtain to do this, he sees Nathen choose a shower across from him, then yank his towel off and hang it before even stepping inside. His butt—also paler than the rest of him, a brownish yellow—is small but round.

Alex jerks his head back and pulls the curtain tighter and starts the shower, trying to find the right water temperature. At first it's freezing, and then too hot, but finally he gets it just right. It feels good, much more forceful than his shower at home.

He lets the water pound him for a while before he realizes he needs to wash his hair and soap his body, using the dispensers on a small shelf inside the shower. The shampoo is purple, the soap green, the conditioner pink. He takes his time. Eventually, he hears Nathen's shower stop, the musical sound of the curtain being pulled open. He's tempted to look, but he doesn't dare. Why does he even want to?

"Hey, Lex," Nathen says loudly over the din of the shower. It's the first time he's called him that—Lex.

Without thinking, with the water still running, Alex parts

the curtain a bit. Nathen is out there, dripping wet, his towel draped around his shoulders but not covering his front. Alex can't help but see all of him now.

"I'm gonna get dressed. See you out in the lobby?" he says matter-of-factly. He's just standing there, with no shame, totally naked, like he's daring Alex to notice him. And Alex does, of course. How can he not look now?

"Okay, see you," Alex says, then shuts his curtain.

In the shower, the warm water still raining down on him, he looks down at his own dick. And though he should be surprised about it, he isn't surprised when he sees that it is getting hard. Not full force, but enough so that he knows he has to think about ugly things and ugly people and anything else but Nathen so that it will return to normal. He has to wash his hair two more times before he is ready to leave the shower.

Luckily Nathen is dressed and gone when Alex returns to his locker, but some students have shown up, as well as a few more older men. Alex dresses quickly and leaves.

He sees Nathen down in the lobby, waiting, wearing jeans now and a long-sleeve T-shirt under his jacket. As he gets closer, he fights off a smile. They've seen each other naked, he thinks, and it was weird, yes, but not bad weird.

On the drive home, they're both quiet but it's not awkward. It's more like the quiet of contentment, like they can relax and not have to fill the air with bullshit. Alex feels both refreshed and exhausted. He can smell the scent of the gym shampoo and soap filling the car. When Nathen pulls up to this house, Alex isn't ready to leave the car. He feels like he could sit there in its fragrant warmth and be happy forever.

*   *   *

Monday arrives too soon, opening what promises to be a rough week at school. Midterm exams start on Wednesday and end Friday, and the only good thing is that those days are half days, ending at lunch time. Two exams each day. Monday and Tuesday are full days of last-minute review sessions in every class. The air is filled with panic about trying to remember four months' worth of crap: cosines and sines; elements, compounds, and chemical reactions; the amendments and the articles of the Constitution; the words in Spanish, with their feminine or masculine forms, not to mention the verb conjugations; and all the nineteenth-century American poems, sermons, short stories, and novels and what their themes say about our great nation and its history. These facts and documents and thoughts even creep into Alex's dreams at night, creating goofy collages of people and numbers and papers.

Alex sees Nathen a few times on Monday and Tuesday, briefly, in the halls, but nothing more than that. Still, it's enough to make him feel a boost in his mood amid all this academic hell.

Tuesday, after Spanish and before study hall, he heads to his locker as usual. As he gets closer, people pass him with big grins—people he knows well, and some kids he doesn't really know at all. One of those people is Lang, who used to be one of his best friends, even if she is a girl, even if she could be snooty and self-centered and obsessed with the way she looked. She had liked him, not romantically, but as her one male confidant, she claimed. "It's so easy telling you stuff, Alex," she'd once said, before she stopped speaking to him at all. Walking toward his locker, he thinks for an odd, tiny moment that maybe Lang and other people are going to start being nice to him again, that people are going to start viewing him, once again, as just another student. But then he sees his locker.

Someone has written LOSER up and down the locker door—six times, actually. Six rows of LOSER, messy but legible renderings in white. It looks, at first, like paint, but once Alex gets close, he knows it is Wite-Out because he can scratch flakes of it off.

Alex stands there, frozen. This wasn't here earlier, between first and second period, the last time he came by. His locker is in the southwest corner of the school. He always liked it because it was near the end of a dead-end hallway, away from a lot of foot traffic.

He can hear people walking by, laughing or whispering. Finally, he unfreezes and opens his locker. It takes him a few twists on the combination because his hands are unsteady. He takes out a few books and shoves them in his backpack, which is pretty full already since he needs every damn book because of the exams this week.

His backpack feels heavy, like he's carrying a cinder block in there. The bell rings—he's late for study hall. He should hurry. But, instead, he turns into the bathroom and goes to one of the stalls. He sets his bag down and sits on the toilet without taking his pants down. He doesn't need to go to the bathroom. He just wants to sit there. He breathes, in and out, evenly. Because he *can't* start crying. He can't let himself get too upset.

He might have expected this kind of thing to occur in October, right after he came back to school. That's when people made comments under their breath; some golf team jerk named Ben

Mutert asked Alex if he wanted him to get him a glass of Drano from the janitor to drink; and he found the occasional notes stuffed into his locker. This stuff lasted, sporadically, for a month. But it's December now, school is winding down. He thought he had made himself mostly invisible.

He breathes in again and then releases a big chunk of air. So what, he thinks? It's no surprise almost everyone still thinks he is a loser. This was just a mean, childish, stupid prank. Who cares?

But he still can't move, because he feels like he might shatter into a thousand pieces if he does. He hates feeling this way, and he hasn't in a while. He has felt tougher, stronger lately, ever since he started running. He hasn't felt like the old Alex, but like a newer, better Alex. Maybe it was all an illusion. Maybe he is just a fragile little freak after all.

He sits there until he starts to feel normal again. Like the sting of a slap has receded. Like he has finally come up for air. Then he makes his way to study hall, a good fifteen minutes late. When he pulls open the classroom door, everyone turns to stare at him, and he fights like hell not to turn around and run away.

"Nice of you to join us," the teacher says to him, and he steps inside.

Somehow, he survives the week. After the locker incident, Alex is almost happy for exams, because they keep his mind occupied. He doesn't even bother to contemplate who did it. And he didn't report it to the principal. Luckily, a kind janitor washed it all off that night, so it was gone by the morning. He, of course, didn't tell his parents about it, didn't tell James, didn't tell Dr. Richardson the day after during their session. He didn't even tell Nathen.

He didn't see what good telling any of them would do. His parents might freak out and complain to the principal and cause a big scene, and Alex didn't want that. Dr. Richardson, well, what could he do except nod sympathetically and ask him how it had felt? And as for James and Nathen—he was too embarrassed to let them know. He wanted the incident to just go away.

By the time he finishes his Spanish exam on Friday morning, his brain feels dead. But then it's all over, for two weeks, at least, until school starts back up again in January.

But now what? Sure, he has Christmas to look forward to, though he hasn't asked for much: a new wallet, a watch, a few books, some money. And then how will he fill his days? He's not sure if he and Nathen will continue their jogging regimen, but he hopes so. He wants to be ready for the new year. On this Friday afternoon, he thinks about calling Nathen, but he doesn't. If Nathen wants to run together, he'll call. If not, well, Alex will just put on his heavy clothes and try to run in the cold outdoors.

His mother rouses him from a nap later, when it's just getting dark outside. "Alex, remember we have the Mackeys' Christmas party tonight."

He rubs his eyes. "Oh yeah."

"It starts in an hour, so you better start getting ready. You should wear that tailored shirt we got you, and maybe a festive tie."

"Do I have to go?"

"Of course you do. Besides, it's just down the street," she says, before walking away, leaving his door slightly ajar so that the hall light pierces the darkness of his room.

Each year, the Mackeys, from around the corner, host a big holiday party. Mrs. Mackey used to be his principal in elementary school, but she is retired now, and so is Mr. Mackey, who used to be a lawyer. Their kids are grown and living far away, with families of their own, so they have a big empty house. The party is catered, kind of fancy, full of people from the neighborhoods north of the river, the same seemingly tiny circle of doctors and lawyers and bankers and professors that his parents usually spend time with.

Alex wants to stay home. It will be crowded with drunk adults, and he's bound to run into plenty of kids from school, like Tyler and Kirk. He showers slowly and suits up in his gray wool trousers, the white shirt his mom told him to wear, and a forest-green tie that is speckled with tiny red dots. Down the hall, he can hear James getting ready, grumbling about having to wear a tie. He hears James's phone ring a few times and imagines he's making plans for after the party—with Preston or Greer or maybe even Nathen?

"Hey, there," his father says when Alex walks downstairs. He's flipping through the mail on the table in the foyer.

James comes storming down the stairs, looking almost identical to Alex in his pants and white shirt, his shiny black dress shoes. But James is wearing a light blue tie, like he's protesting against Christmas colors. He fills out his clothes better than Alex, too, and his hair is longer and messier.

"Don't you two make a handsome pair," Mom says to them, walking downstairs. She is wearing more makeup than usual and smells of her special perfume. She wears a velvety-type black dress, under a red shawl.

"What about me?" his dad says, before kissing her on the cheek. He's still in his work suit.

"You look as handsome as always," she says, laughing slightly.

"And you look like a knockout," Dad says, kissing her on the lips this time.

For a minute it feels like they're this perfect little family without a care in the world. Maybe they were, Alex thinks, before he went and screwed things up.

James gives a loud sigh and says, "Let's just go, okay?" Then they make their way outside, toward the party that Alex dreads.

"Alex!" Henry shouts. Henry is standing in one of the rooms at the back of the house, by a table covered with plates of sweets— all kinds of cookies (sugar, oatmeal, chocolate chip, snickerdoodles), a few creamy-looking pies, and a chocolate cake that no one has had the courage to cut into. Alex walks over to him, feeling relieved to have someone to talk to, even if it is just Henry. His parents got sidetracked already by some of their friends, and James vanished right away, so Alex is on his own.

Henry's mother is standing by him, holding a glass of red wine and talking to some man Alex doesn't recognize. She looks pretty, even stylish, in a red dress, her skin remarkably tan for winter.

"Hi, Henry. I didn't expect to see you here," Alex says.

"These cookies are good," he says, nudging toward the table.

As if Alex has interrupted something, the man walks away, leaving the three of them alone. "Hi there," Henry's mother says, smiling. "You excited about Christmas, Alex?"

He has never really chatted with her before, besides an occasional hello. What does he even call her? He thinks of her only as Henry's mom. "I guess so," he says. "I'm just glad school is out."

Henry continues munching on another cookie.

"Don't eat too many of those, sweetie," she says, before sipping more wine.

Alex hasn't had a drop of booze since he made the team. He doesn't really miss it, either, though in situations like this—a crowded party full of people he'd rather not talk to—he thinks a little booze might take the edge off. He's sure some of the other kids here, including James, are sneaking sips from flasks.

Suddenly, Mrs. Mackey walks up to them. "Laura, I'm so glad you could make it! Hi, Henry," she says. "And look at you, Alex. Isn't he handsome?" she says.

Alex can feel himself blush. Mrs. Mackey used to scare the shit out of him. She was a stern, no-nonsense principal, and she's always been tall for a woman. When he was a kid, she towered over them, with her perfectly coiffed gray hair and her tweedy suits. But now that he is older, she just seems like a nice old lady, not someone armed with a yardstick and a clipboard, clip-clopping down the hallways like she was the police on patrol.

"Oh, well, thanks for inviting us, Shirley," Henry's mom says. "It's nice to be included."

"Of course, dear," she says. "You're part of the neighborhood."

"Well, I'm sure some people wish I wasn't here," she says, sort of laughing uncomfortably.

"Alex, let's go get some punch," Henry says, grabbing his hand and pulling him away. Mrs. Mackey and Laura continue chatting as the two of them make their way to the room with the punch. Almost instantly, Alex withdraws his hand from Henry's, but he still follows him.

The party is plenty crowded now. All around Alex are people he knows. He doesn't want to look at them, because then he might have to stop and talk or deal with their concerned or scornful gazes. So he walks behind Henry and stares down at the back of his head. Henry's hair is a more normal, copperish red now, messy and brittle-looking, and only the tips show any trace of the bright, cartoonish red from weeks earlier. When Alex chances to look up, he sees James, slouching by a couch, where Clare Ashford is sitting with Suzy Parker. Kirk is sitting there, too, by Suzy. God. That means Tyler is probably here, too.

"There's your brother," Henry says.

"Yeah," Alex says, but he keeps moving, out of that room to the dining room, where a buffet is set up. He doesn't want anyone in that crowd to see him, period, much less see him hanging out with a kid.

"Where're you going? I thought we were gonna get punch," Henry says, now at his heels.

"I'm not thirsty anymore." He weaves through the crowd, careful not to bump anyone, though at this point it's almost unavoidable. Then, right before he enters the kitchen, he hears someone shout his name. Well, sort of his name: Lex, not Alex. He turns and sees that it's Nathen. Nathen, wearing not just a bright red tie, but a full suit, dark gray. His short dark hair is slightly gelled to make it spiky in front.

"Hey, buddy," Nathen says, slapping his hand.

"I didn't realize you'd be here," Alex says, trying not to sound too excited.

"My folks dragged me. But whatever—I'm just so fucking

psyched school is over," he says, then seems to notice Henry standing at Alex's side. "Oh, hey."

"This is Henry," Alex says, but just then Henry smiles and wanders off. Alex shrugs. "Yeah, I'm glad school's over, too."

"I thought you might call me this past week, you know, to help with your chemistry."

"Yeah, well, I guess I managed." Though he would have called, if he'd known Nathen expected him to.

"You want to jog tomorrow?"

"Definitely," Alex says, relief washing over him.

"And maybe we can run a few times next week, before Christmas."

James appears, as if from thin air. He says, "There you are," to Nathen, not Alex. "We're hanging out in there," he says, pointing with his head to the other room. "We may head to Preston's later."

"Oh, cool. I'm up for that. You going to come, Lex?"

"Uh," he says, then looks at James. He can tell James is freaking out—thinking how could Nathen invite *him*? "No," he says, "not me."

"Oh, okay," Nathen says, sounding confused. "Well, I'll pick you up tomorrow, then, okay? At ten." He smiles and walks away with James. Alex keeps staring at them as they walk down the hall, and Nathen gives one quick glance back and smiles again.

Alex decides to find Henry. It can't be easy for him being here, either. But as he goes room to room—seeing his parents chatting away in the front living room, drinking, his dad munching on a crab cake—he can't find him. He does see Henry's mother, still in the back room and armed with the wineglass,

116

chatting with another man, Dr. Horn, the chiropractor with the bushy blond mustache. Alex recognizes him from his TV commercials, where he puts his seemingly magical hands on people who are grinning like ninnies.

Alex stands by the door of the semi-crowded room, thinking maybe Henry will find his way back here. He stands next to two women he recognizes but doesn't know the names of—casual friends of his mother's probably, rich ladies wearing lots of jewelry and too much perfume, holding wineglasses. One has dyed dark hair—dyed because she's surely as old as Mrs. Mackey, who let her hair color takes its natural course—and the other is a younger lady, a blonde with a pointy nose. They don't seem to notice him, but he can't help overhearing them.

"Yes, that's her. Thank God Jack and Martha aren't here. Who knows, there might be a scene," the dark-haired one says.

"She seems nice enough," the blond one says.

Alex realizes they are chatting about Henry's mother, though there are other women in the room.

"Sure she's nice. The slut with the heart of gold. Or should I say gold digger with the heart of gold?"

"Oh, Gail, you're awful," the blonde says, giggling, clearly thinking that awful really means hilarious in this case.

"Well, it's true," she says. "She's renting that house around the corner, you know. But I heard she doesn't pay a dime. Like she's a kept woman. And she's half Jack's age. What a cliché. I swear. And now look, she's chasing Jerry Horn. She has no shame." The two of them leave the room, perhaps to look for other people to gossip about.

Just then Henry walks up. "There you are," he says. He has a cup of punch, which looks just like watered-down cherry Kool-Aid. "Oh, there's Mom." As he says this, she seems to sense his words, because she turns and waves at them. Then she turns back to Dr. Horn, turning on her charm.

Henry scrutinizes them and frowns. "Let's go to the buffet. You wanna?"

"I guess." Alex would rather hide out back here, though. He doesn't want everyone to see him following Henry around. But it's not like anyone else will talk to him, really, so he bites the bullet and follows him again through the crowd. As they walk from room to room, he catches a glimpse of Nathen, still at the party, talking with Clare and Greer, smiling and laughing and looking like he's having a blast. He wishes he could go over there, to talk more with him. But, at the same time, he doesn't want to share Nathen. He wants him all to himself.

At the buffet, Alex sees the two gossipy women again, filling little plates with hors d'oeuvres. He wonders if they know who Henry is. *The slut's son,* they would say. He feels a sudden urge to go up to them, to say something rude. Like, *What do you two know about anything?* But this burning flash of anger—or whatever it is—subsides when he watches the two of them walk away, balancing their plates with their drinks, looking like pathetic and foolish women in ill-fitting costumes.

Henry, at his side, says, "This buffet is boring. I think I want another cookie instead."

"And they have cake," Alex says.

"Cake!" Henry says, as if Alex just came out with the best suggestion in the world.

On the way back to the dessert table, they nearly collide with James, who has a plate full of cookies.

"Hey, James!" Henry says.

"Oh, hey." James smiles sheepishly. "I'm just loading up for the . . . uh, for the group."

"What group?" Henry asks.

"His friends," Alex says. And then he can't stand it anymore—this party, this crowd, all this dumb and phony holiday cheer. He turns abruptly and walks to the front of the house, bumping into people but not giving a shit. He reaches the front door and steps out into the cold night. He walks down the sidewalk and heads toward home.

"Alex, wait up!" he hears Henry shout, clopping behind him.

Alex slows down a little so Henry can catch up.

"You mad at me?" Henry asks.

Alex stops. "Mad at you?"

"Yeah. You just left without saying anything."

"I'm not mad at *you,* Henry."

Alex looks down at him, and Henry's look of worry revises itself into a grin. "I thought I might be bugging you."

Alex feels a stab of regret. "No, Henry. You never bug me."

"Oh, good," he says.

The two of them walk in silence to Alex's house. Instead of going inside, they walk around to the backyard. They both sit on the swings in the darkness. A gentle but cool wind blows through the yard, causing the pine trees to sway behind them.

"Can I ask you something, Alex?"

"Yep," he says.

"You're my friend, aren't you?"

"Of course I am," Alex says.

"Good," he says. He pauses and then says, "You're mine, too."

Alex smiles. "Thanks, Henry."

*　*　*

"Today we'll do a mile, and then run sprints, and then a mile, then sprints, and so on. Till we can't walk," Nathen says. He's talking so earnestly, like he always does when he's teaching Alex about cross-country stuff.

They are at the rec center again, on a Saturday two days before Christmas. By now, the university has let out for winter break, so the rec center is empty, save for a few professors. Nathen and Alex have come four times this past week, and Nathen says this will be their last "session" until after Christmas.

The workouts have been tough, but Alex has enjoyed them. Each morning, they run a different distance or routine, Nathen pushing Alex like a coach would. Like he supposes Coach Runyon will do next term. After their runs, they head to the showers, where Nathen undresses without shame and, day by day, Alex does as well. He tries not to obsess over it, but he feels like there is a vibe between them in those moments, though he doesn't know what it means. It's natural to be curious about other boys' bodies, right? So what if he sneaks a peek at Nathen's dick (which basically looks just like his, just darker) and balls and his butt? It doesn't mean anything, really. He knows Nathen takes a peek at his, after all.

Today's routine is particularly grueling. His legs start to feel rubbery and sore, and each time they sprint Alex feels slower and slower, his energy draining away like water from a bathtub. By the end, he just wants to collapse. And he does, lying down on the carpet outside the track.

"You okay, buddy?" Nathen says, breathing heavily himself, walking in little circles.

"I think so."

"Get up. It's better for you to walk around so you don't cramp."

Nathen towers above him and holds out his hand, pulling Alex up. And once he is standing, he feels the urge to just fold into Nathen.

"Let's shower, then we'll go grab some lunch at the mall or something. Cool?"

Alex nods, thinking about how good the water in the shower will feel.

In the locker room, he's almost too exhausted to take his clothes off. When he finally does—just dropping his sweaty stuff on the floor—he lazily drapes a towel around his waist and follows Nathen. He picks a shower and turns on the water, letting it warm up, and lets out a little groan.

"You gonna be okay?" Nathen asks.

Without turning around, Alex nods, starts chuckling. "You must think I'm a wimp."

"Not at all." He steps close to Alex and puts his hand on the small of his back. "Here, get in."

Before Alex really realizes what is happening, Nathen has nudged him into the cascading water of the shower. And Nathen has stepped in as well, yanking the curtain closed behind them, trapping them together in the tight space.

Alex can't help but grin—it's so surprising, unexpected. "Audacious" might be a good word for it. Nathen is at his side, and the water hits them both with its soft force, washing away the grime of their exercise. Nathen's not grinning, but he is looking at Alex, giving him the same look he gives when he so earnestly talks about jogging.

He continues just looking at Alex, then reaches over and squeezes the shower gel container. "Here," he says, but not too loudly, rubbing the gel onto Alex's chest. Alex lets him. He closes his eyes, as Nathen keeps squirting soap on his hands and rubs it over Alex, washing him. It's nothing more than that until he feels Nathen's lips on his face. On his cheek, nose, then his lips. Then Nathen's tongue in his mouth, which Alex accepts and then returns with sloppy eagerness.

Alex has kissed a few girls. That girl Carla, in eighth grade. He liked it, though it felt mechanical and fast. Powerful but not passionate. He kissed Lang once, too, but more as a joke. He liked the process, the act—but not really the people he was doing it with.

This is different. It's not mechanical. It's not a joke. It feels right. He'd do it forever, if he could. He realizes it is how a kiss is *supposed* to feel.

He can't help but move his hands to Nathen's hips, pulling them toward his. They're pressed up against each other, kissing hard now, and finally, when Nathen pulls back, he's smiling that confident grin of his. Above the hiss of the water, he says, "That's all for now," and then gently shuts off the water. But it's not all, not yet, because he kisses Alex again—a few quick pecks on the lips—and then whispers, "Guess we better go get dressed."

They're both hard down there, of course, but that's not going to change if they keep standing here behind the curtain together, so Alex reaches out for his towel and the two of them head to their lockers.

* * *

Nathen drives them to the mall, only a few minutes away. On the drive, they don't really say much, and that's cool with Alex. He's sort of feeling light-headed anyway. If talking about what they just did would ruin the moment, then he's fine with total silence.

The mall is swarming with crowds, the parking lot jammed with last-minute shoppers. Inside, the two of them lumber to the food court, a long stretch of fast-food joints with common-area tables in the middle. Nathen decides on a sandwich and waffle fries from Chic-fil-A, and Alex gets the same.

Alex usually hates the mall, because invariably he sees people he knows. But now he doesn't care if he sees people, or if they see him. Let them see him. Here, having lunch with Nathen.

"So," Nathen says once they sit down at one of the few empty tables. "How you feeling?"

"Worn out. But good." He wonders if Nathen is asking about the jog or the shower.

"Good," he says. He sips from his soda and chews on some ice. He stares at Alex and smiles again. "I feel good, too."

"I guess we should take a break from running till after Christmas?"

"Yeah. But we can still hang out."

"Okay." Alex is starving, and he's been wolfing down his food. But his stomach starts to hurt a little. "You think that James will think it's weird, you know, if we hang out?"

"Why would he? Can't we be friends?"

Alex nods. "Yep."

"Besides, he doesn't have to know all the time."

"True."

"Good."

Alex sips his soda till it slurps.

"Alex?" Nathen asks.

Alex almost wishes they'd stop talking. Like, the more they say, the weirder it will all get.

"You know, about earlier?" Nathen says. "I mean, I liked it. And I hope you did, too. Because it's not a joke or anything to me. I mean, I wanted to do it. I just wanted you to know, okay? So you're not freaked out or anything. I don't know. It's weird, I guess. But I liked it. I like you. And you should know that. So, if you don't wanna hang out anymore, if you're freaked, then just—"

"I like you, too," Alex says, interrupting Nathen's onslaught of words. And there goes his heart racing, like he's running fast, like he's chasing Nathen around the track, with no end in sight.

James

On a cold Saturday in early January, James and the gang gather at Preston's garage apartment. It is a few days after New Year's and just two days before school starts again on Monday. Christmas came and went without much fanfare—besides parties and presents and a lot of eating, James mostly sat around and watched TV or read a few Michael Crichton novels. He wasn't the beacon of productivity that Alex was—running every other day, or else doing push-ups and crunches, even getting a jump on reading for next semester. No, James was a lazy bum. He's almost looking forward to school starting in a few days, because then his days will have some structure and order.

Tonight James has come by himself. Greer is here—his college-age girlfriend broke up with him over the holiday, so he's finally joining in (until he finds a new girlfriend). It was supposed to be a low-key deal, a guys-only night of card playing, movie watching, drinking, smoking. Nothing special. A way to ease into the new year, before the last five months of school leading to graduation. But somehow Tyler Shaughnessy got invited, and he brought Kirk and Beth Hayes with him. If James had known *they* were going to be here, he probably wouldn't have come. They're juniors, for one thing. And Beth, as the one girl in the room, throws everything off balance. She's like an interloper from another world, and they have to watch what they say. They can't really talk about the girls in their class, for instance, or she'll rat them out.

"Where's Nathen?" Tyler asks, then cracks open a can of Bud Light that he brought. At least he and Kirk had the courtesy to BYOB.

"He said he was tired and wanted to stay in," James says, repeating what Nathen told him earlier on the phone. "He did a lot of running today."

"God, he takes that shit so seriously," Greer says. He is on a beanbag thumbing through a *Sports Illustrated*. He's acting all aloof, like he has better things to do. *He may be on to something,* James thinks.

"Hey, isn't your brother going to be on the cross-country team with him?" Kirk asks.

"Yeah. He and Nathen are best friends now," Tyler says, like it's some crazy joke.

"Not really," James says, feeling tinges of alarm. "They just run together."

"Well, I saw them at the mall together last week. Having lunch or something," Tyler says.

"So? They'd probably just worked out together," he says, trying to sound calm and unperturbed. "Was it Thursday? I think they did run together that day."

"Hmm," Tyler mutters, as if he's thinking something else but not saying it.

"I didn't know your little bro could run," Preston says, rolling a joint, taking his damn sweet time, like it's an art form.

James sighs and nods. "Well, he can." He wishes they'd move to another topic.

"Yeah, he runs like the wind," Tyler says, giggling with Kirk. Even Greer laughs at this.

James has no idea if that's supposed to be some kind of joke between them. Until recently, he liked Tyler fine. But now Tyler is starting to seem like a menace. First of all, why is he inserting himself into their social circle? Doesn't he have his own junior-class friends? Sure, they're on the tennis team together, but so what? It's like, from out of nowhere, Tyler is breathing down his neck. Their necks. And second of all, why does he have to mock Alex right in front of him?

"Let's call Nate and see if we can get him off his sorry ass to come over here," Preston says.

"Okay. Hand me the phone," Greer says without much enthusiasm, finally putting down the magazine.

Preston takes a break from rolling the joint and hands him the cordless.

Kirk and Beth, meanwhile, are holding hands and stealing kisses. If they wanted to make out, why did they come *here*?

James heads to the kitchenette to get a beer from the fridge, but he can hear Greer talking on the phone.

"He's not there? . . . Yes, ma'am, it's Greer. . . . Doing great, thanks." Greer circles his hand in the air to let everyone know that Mrs. Rao is talking his ear off. "Okay. . . . No, no need to tell him I called. I'll call him tomorrow. Okay. Bye." Then Greer hangs up. "What the fuck? 'He went to the movies,' " Greer says, imitating Mrs. Rao's English accent.

"The movies?" Tyler frowns.

"Who with?" But the minute James asks, he knows the answer and wishes he'd kept his mouth shut.

"Well," Greer says. "She said he went with your brother."

"Weird," Tyler says, softly, before laughing to himself. "See, I told you—they *are* best buddies now!"

"What an asshole," Greer says. "Why would he go to the movies with Alex?"

James knows he should respond. He wants to ask them all, *What's so bad about my brother?* Why wouldn't Nathen want to go to the movies with him? They run together, they're about to be teammates, it makes sense they've become friends. And sure, Alex is—well, he's got his issues. But so what? Everyone has issues if they really think about it. James knows he's not exactly the best brother in the world—knows that he could be nicer, could make an effort to get back the closeness they had, or at least stick up for Alex now.

But he doesn't have the energy tonight. Instead, he just shrugs and says, "Don't ask me."

James calls Nathen the next morning. "So how was the movie?" he asks, knowing that he has failed to mask the edge to his voice.

"Oh, hey. Uh, it was good." Nathen's voice sounds strained, maybe nervous. "Listen, I'm sorry I didn't go to Preston's."

128

"Why'd you lie to me, Nate?"

"I didn't lie. I mean, shit, I just didn't feel like going over there. I was gonna stay home, but I'd mentioned a movie to Alex earlier, after our run. And he called me, so I went. We went."

Alex called *him*? "Well, everyone at Preston's thought it was weird that you ditched us and went off with him. They thought you were an asshole."

"Well," he says, "that's their problem."

Something about this comment should bug James—how Nathen just dismisses a whole group of their friends. But it *doesn't* bother him. He sort of agrees with it. Individually, Preston and Greer can be great. But sometimes, the way they act together in a group—like last night—makes James wonder, *Why am I friends with these guys?* Greer is focused mainly on his constant string of girls, and Preston on pot and drinking and his BMW. They don't sit around worrying about college and grades like James; they know where they are headed—to Alabama and the frat life, more or less a continuation of their lives right now. Lately, around them, James feels like they are becoming strangers. Or that *he* is becoming the stranger.

He doesn't really feel that way about Nathen. Nathen has purpose, goals, smarts. And kindness—something that James feels he himself sometimes lacks, especially when he's with Greer and Preston and so many of his other classmates. So he can't stay mad at Nathen.

"Well," James says. "No worries. You didn't miss much. Just the usual."

"So we're cool?" Nathen asks, now sounding relaxed.

"We're cool."

After he hangs up, James heads downstairs to make himself

something to eat. He finds Alex in the kitchen. "Are Mom and Dad here?" James asks.

"No, they went grocery shopping. But Mom made blueberry muffins," he says. That's what Alex is eating at the table in the breakfast nook.

James grabs a muffin from the plate on the counter and also pours himself a glass of milk. The muffin isn't hot anymore, but it doesn't matter—he devours it, standing up.

"Nathen and I saw a movie last night," Alex says.

"Yeah, that's what he told me."

Alex looks over at him. "You don't mind, do you?"

James takes another gulp of milk. When he's done he says, playing it off, "Why would I mind?"

"I don't know."

James grabs another muffin. "I mean, Preston was a little pissed that he wasn't hanging with us. But I didn't care. It was boring over there anyway." He thinks about mentioning Tyler, Kirk, and Beth, but he decides against it. What would be the point? "Was the movie good?" James asks.

"It was okay," Alex says. "Nathen liked it a lot."

"Cool," James says. He finishes his muffin and takes one last sip of the milk and dumps it into the sink. "Well, I'm going up to my room."

Alex just nods, staring out the window, but James can see that he is smiling, like he is lost in some pleasant daydream.

Monday brings a new semester, and the temperatures drop below freezing. James has to let the defroster run in his Jeep before he can drive to school. On the way, he thinks about his classes this semester. The counselors and teachers and even the admissions offices claim that his grades this term *still* matter, but James doubts that's true. His college applications are already in. He'll still work hard and probably get all As anyway. It just comes naturally to him.

During lunch Preston ribs Nathen about Saturday. "So why'd you ditch us, man?" he asks. He's moving soggy fries around on his tray, dousing them in ketchup before putting them in his mouth.

Nathen tells Preston just what he told James the day before. He sounds self-sure and unguilty about it.

"Well, next time you better show up," Preston jokes, accepting Nathen's excuse, or brushing it off. "This is our last semester, man. We gotta hang out as much as possible."

James exchanges a private glance with Nathen, who winks.

On the way to French class James sees Alice at her locker. Luckily there haven't been anymore phone calls since that one around Thanksgiving. She doesn't notice him at first, but as he gets closer to passing her, she slams her locker and glances his way and gives him an icy stare.

If looks could kill, he thinks. James just hopes he can survive another five months of this crap. Now that she has a new boyfriend—whoever the unlucky guy is—can't she just get over it? It's not like Clare harbors any bad feelings toward him over their breakup during their sophomore year. They saw a movie together over the holiday, and there was no temptation to hold hands during, no real awkwardness. Like him, she just seems to be coasting along, ready for graduation and a life after Central High.

French class ends, AP English begins. The reading list for this semester is heavy—novel after novel after novel, poem after poem, story after story. The class groans, and Mr. Harris reminds them, "Well, this *is* advanced placement, after all." At the end of the term they have the option to take a test to see if they can get college credit. But James isn't even sure he'll do that; he just wanted to be in the smarter class. Plus, it looked good on his application.

It's too cold out for tennis today, Coach Whitley decides at the start of sixth period, so they all hang out in the hallway outside the gymnasium, which is a big waste of time. Once the weather gets a little more bearable, they will start practicing harder, even staying after school, to get ready for the new season, which starts in April, right after spring break.

When the bell rings, James dashes out to the parking lot. On the way, he sees Alice again, wearing her down jacket and standing by her blue Ford Taurus, smoking in quick puffs that are indistinguishable from her normal breaths in the freezing air. Alice sees him and flips him the bird. He thinks about flipping her back, but he doesn't. He almost wants to go and tell her to grow up, to get a life. But he just sighs and gets in his car and gets the hell out of there.

A few nights later, his mother announces that they are having Henry and his mother over for dinner on Sunday.

"Really?" James asks. "Why?"

"They're our neighbors," she says, like that explains it all. They've been neighbors for months, so why now? he wonders.

"I thought you didn't like her," he says.

"James, why would you say that? That's not true. I never said anything like that."

"Okay, *sorry*," he says.

"I mean, she's a bit odd, yes. But Shirley Mackey told me she's had quite a hard time of it. You know, raising a child on her own, making ends meet. So I thought having them over would be a nice thing to do. And you're friends with the little boy, right, Alex?"

"Yep," Alex says, not looking up from his plate.

This is no big secret. If Alex isn't off jogging with Nathen or shut up in his room, he's outside chatting with that kid. It's weird, James thinks, someone Alex's age being friends with a ten-year-old. Kind of pathetic, too. But in the end he doesn't see the harm in it. Neither do his parents, he guesses. A kid friend is better than nothing.

"What does she do?" James asks.

"What?"

"Mrs. Burns. What does she do?"

"Oh, well, I think she does secretarial work at Pembroke Paper. She may work part-time only. I'm not sure."

His father chortles to himself, and James sees Alex give him a quizzical look.

"So how does she afford that house?" James asks.

His mother seems irritated by the questions. "Well, I don't know, honey. I suspect she has family money. Who knows?"

James could go on with his questions: Like, what family money? He remembers that Henry doesn't even have a father in the picture. And, even if she had family money, why rent *that* house? It's way too big for two people. But he lets it drop. What does he care anyway?

For the Sunday dinner Mom makes pork chops, roasted new potatoes, asparagus, and a salad, plus corn bread. For dessert, she has made a chocolaty Coca-Cola cake. Henry and his mother show up right on time. Under her winter coat she is wearing slacks and a royal blue blouse; she smells of a flowery perfume, and her face is made up to give her a healthy glow. She looks nice up close— a small woman the same age as some of his younger teachers, probably in her thirties, with dirty blond hair cut in a stylish fashion. Henry, meanwhile, has blond hair now. Not that peroxide, almost whitish blond, but more like yellow. He wears black pants and a blue cardigan over a white polo and green sneakers.

"I'm so glad y'all could make it," his mother says, noticing Henry's wild hair but masking her surprise with a smile.

"Here," Henry says, handing Mom a bottle of white wine that he has been holding.

"Oh, well, thank you," she says.

"Mom bought it, but I picked it out. I liked the bottle."

"Well, I'm sure it's a wonderful wine," she says, smiling at Mrs. Burns, who giggles nervously. The two of them then head to the kitchen, because Mrs. Burns—who says they should call her Laura—insists on helping get the food ready.

James, Alex, and Henry, meanwhile, park themselves in the living room. Dad has been watching *60 Minutes,* but now that Henry is here, he focuses on him.

"And you're at Verner Elementary, Henry?"

"Yes, sir. I'm a fourth grader. Next year I'll be a fifth grader."

"Wonderful," Dad says. "Do you like it at Verner?"

"Not really," he says, very matter-of-fact.

Dad thinks this is so funny and laughs, but James can tell that Henry isn't trying to be funny. After Dad ends his laughing fit, he says, "A man I work with, his daughter is at Verner. Jennifer Goodwin, do you know her?"

Henry nods. "Yes, I do. She's okay."

Again Dad laughs. Maybe he's just nervous or not used to kids anymore? "So, do you like your teachers, at least?"

"Dad," Alex says, "stop grilling Henry about school."

James is a little surprised at Alex's assertiveness, and so is Dad, because he looks at Alex with a confused smile on his face, like he can't believe his ears.

"My teachers are okay," Henry replies. "Yes, I like them."

James can look at Henry and see he has a hard time at school. The goofy hair, always a new color, plus the mismatched clothes. He's also, well, weird, the way he speaks in clipped sentences, the way he stares at you so pointedly. Surely he has it rough. After all, kids are mean, and they don't get much better as they get older. Hell, maybe it will get *worse* for him. All of a sudden James feels oppressed by Henry's sad existence, almost suffocated by it. And with Alex right here, too, it's like the whole room is flooded with rejection.

But then Henry looks at him and smiles, revealing his set of slightly crooked teeth. James can't really say why, but the feeling of oppression vanishes as quickly as it appeared.

Mom does most of the talking during dinner. Or, rather, she does all of the *asking*. She asks Mrs. Burns question after question, like she is interrogating her on a witness stand, though with much more cheer and friendliness than a prosecutor.

Where did she grow up? (Virginia.) Did she go to college? (Yes, briefly, at a small college in Virginia.) Where were they before they moved to Tuscaloosa? (Georgia, then Florida. Before that, Virginia, then Tennessee.)

"I'm afraid we've had a nomadic life," she says, laughing, then looking at Henry.

"Mom says a change of scenery is a good thing," Henry says, then nibbles on an asparagus stem.

"Well," she says, looking at Mom and Dad in turn, "I grew up in Virginia and lived there my whole life, even for college, and I, well—I just didn't like being stuck in one place."

James can certainly understand *that*.

"And then Henry came along," she says, giggling again. "So that's why I dropped out of school. It seemed like a good time to get away, make a new start. Nothing has really tied us to one place ever since."

James can sense that there's more to this story. Something is missing. Or many things are missing. Crucial details. Like how she said "and then Henry came along." Like he was dropped at her doorstep or something, like a newspaper.

"And what kind of work do you do, Laura?" Dad asks.

"Oh, secretarial work. I used to do transcription, too. When Henry was little. I could do that from home. And in college towns, I would type students' papers for them."

Dad nods, and Mom says, "Oh, how interesting."

"Yeah, it was. I sort of got my own college education just by reading those papers. Read about all kinds of things. The Cold War, Vietnam, ancient Rome. It was fun work, I must say. I may put an ad in the paper, since the university is here."

"Why'd you move to Tuscaloosa?" James asks. It seems like a reasonable question, but he notices Mrs. Burns sort of struggle with the answer: her eyes squinch and she looks up, as if she is thinking up a good reason.

"Oh, well, it seems like a nice place. And I've always liked college towns. And, well"—she giggles—"I don't know, really."

"Mom says we'll probably stay here," Henry says.

"Oh, good," Dad says. "It's a wonderful place to raise your children."

Yeah right, James thinks. *A real great place.* As if his own child, Alex, didn't try to off himself. Is his father just saying that, or does he believe it? He looks at his mother, but she doesn't seem to have registered the comment.

"Alex and James, do you boys like it here?" Henry's mom asks.

Alex has been quiet for most of the meal, more so than usual, just eating his food and sipping his water, like a machine. But before James can answer, Alex speaks. "Yeah, I do. I mean, it's not the greatest place in the world. But I like it. It's home, you know? No matter what, it will always be home."

James is stunned into silence. His parents are both staring at Alex, pleasantly surprised by his statement. Hell, James is surprised. How could *Alex* like it here?

"Well, I hope we can stay," Mrs. Burns says, breaking the silence before taking a sip of her wine. James eyes her, and she smiles at him with clenched lips.

If you guys want to stay here, fine, he thinks, *but I'm so out of here.*

* * *

137

"So, how's Alex doing on the team?" James asks Nathen. It's a Friday night a few weeks later, and they are at a University of Alabama basketball game at Coleman Coliseum. Nathen's parents get discounted tickets, so here they are during halftime, in the large auditorium, midcourt, in seats halfway up, just above the rowdy student section. Big crimson banners hang from the high ceiling, announcing all the championship victories for both the men's and women's teams.

"He's doing really well," Nathen says. "Coach R isn't being too rough on him, and the other guys seem to like him. It's intense, but he's learning." Nathen nods. "Yeah, he's doing great."

"Cool. That's great."

Alex has been on the team for two weeks. Most days he comes home just as it gets dark out, exhausted but also, James notices, strangely buoyant. Not that he is chattier with James—they rarely talk other than at the dinner table. But James hears him talking with his parents, going on and on about the team and training and this and that, sounding eager and excited. And their parents, in turn, sound excited, too.

"You guys don't talk much, huh?" Nathen says, as if reading his mind.

"Not really. I mean, we do. But not like we used to."

"Why's that?"

"I don't know. I mean, ever since he did that crazy shit, I just feel weird around him. Like if I say the wrong thing or something, he might, like, I don't know. . . ." He stares off at the action on the court. Some middle-aged guy has missed his big chance to win some prize on the court, and a cheerleader is patting him on the back. When James looks back at Nathen, he asks, "Does he talk to you?"

"A little. Mostly about running and stuff."

James feels little tinglings of jealousy, but he knows that is silly.

"I like him a lot," Nathen says.

James just nods. Why shouldn't he be cool with the two of them being friends? It's girly to get possessive of a friend anyway.

After the game's over, when they're stuck in the postgame traffic jam, James remembers that there's a party tonight at George Thirkell's house. Every weekend, it seems, someone's parents are out of town. "You wanna go to George's party?" he asks.

Nathen turns the radio to the local college station, and the lead singer of a band called Wing Ding sings acoustically about how some girl broke his heart. "Man, you tennis boys are always throwing parties," he says, smiling. "I don't know. You want to go?"

"I don't know."

Nathen is quiet for a minute, then asks, "You think Tyler will be there?"

"Probably. Why?"

"Honestly? I'm not too fond of that kid."

"Yeah. I mean, he's my teammate, but he gets on my nerves."

"Uh, yeah, no shit. Plus, he's been a real jerk to Alex, it seems like."

"Yeah," James says, and a surge of guilt rises up in him. Here's Nathen, a guy who barely knows Alex, taking a stand for him. Which is much more than James has done. But he wipes the guilt away like a smudge. Alex brought it on himself, after all.

Besides, James has got five more months of school to go, and he needs to focus on college and graduation and tennis. He has enough on his plate without having to worry about all the kids who are being mean to his brother.

"I guess we can just skip it, then," James says.

"There'll be other parties."

Yep, James thinks. More parties. More of the same old shit.

Nathen finally clears the campus traffic and heads across the river on McFarland, up the hill toward their neighborhoods. A lot of the trees are bare and skeletal, now that winter has made up its mind to be winter. Homes are lit up with the glow of lamps and televisions.

"Just think," Nathen says, "next year we'll both be somewhere else on a night like this. You'll be scoring the ladies at Duke, and I'll be living the Ivy League life." He starts laughing, and James joins in, because though it's all quite possible, and though he thinks about it all the time—this future life in college and beyond—he still feels bound to this city, to this life, like things will never change.

The next night, James goes to see another movie with Clare. It's *not* a date, he tells his parents before he heads out. Everyone thinks they're dating again, and it's annoying always having to explain the situation.

He picks her up at her house, which is near the hospital in a nice neighborhood tucked away behind a busy part of town. He rings the door and she answers right away, not even giving him a chance to say hello to her parents, which is fine with him. Her hair is in a ponytail and she is wearing a white knee-length wool coat over jeans and a sweater. She clearly didn't get dolled up for the occasion, but neither did James.

"I can't believe you're dragging me to this movie," she says.

"Dragging? Whatever," he says, smiling. They're going to see a movie about an undercover cop infiltrating the Mafia. It'll be bloody and tense. "You picked last time, remember? I had to see that Julia Roberts crap."

"It wasn't crap! It was good."

"It was crap. Thank God she's good-looking, because her movies stink."

"You're a jerk," she says, laughing. "Just because it was about love and all that, and not about blood and guts. Boys are all the same."

"Boys?" he says. He mocks a tough-sounding accent: "I ain't no boy."

"Oh, I forgot, you're a *man*." She laughs.

He feels himself blush, suddenly remembering her old college-age boyfriend. Of course he seems like a boy to *her*.

"Anyway, this one will be good. I'll pay."

"Okay. But it's—"

"Not a date. I *know*!" He meant to sound like he was laughing it off, but when Clare is quiet for a minute he realizes he sounded testy, like he is mad it *isn't* a date.

The theater is across town, at the older mall, the one with no good stores in it anymore. The parking lot is crowded, and James has to circle around a few times before settling on a spot far away from the entrance, near where the lot edges up to the highway. If he looks to his left, he knows he could see the glowing sign of the

La Quinta, which is just across the street. He can almost feel the light of the sign burning into his face, a shameful reminder. He slams his Jeep shut and turns toward the mall, careful not to look the other way. What would Clare think if she knew? She'd think he was a scumbag, probably.

"It's packed," Clare says, seeing the inside of the theater lobby as they approach. "All of Tuscaloosa out for a night on the town."

And it's true, all kinds of people are out for a night at the movies—young and old, black and white, couples and groups of friends, even parents with kids. Right away James sees a few people from school, not great friends but acquaintances. He and Clare wave to a few of them, but nothing more. There are also a lot of kids from the county schools here. A lot of the guys are in tight jeans and snakeskin boots, like they're going to a rodeo or something. Their girlfriends are wearing tight jeans, too, or else miniskirts, even in this weather. He sees one guy, tall and beefy in jeans with a blue plaid shirt tucked in, his longish black hair tucked under a trucker cap. A football player, probably. And the girl holding hands with him is Alice.

"Shit," he mutters under his breath, but Clare hears and says, "What?" Then she sees them.

"It's no big deal," he says.

Clare narrows her eyes at him. "Whatever you say."

"It isn't," he says. "I just hate running into her. She's such a psycho."

Clare sighs. After Alice and her oaf boyfriend—or whoever he is—buy their tickets, they walk over to the concession area, thankfully not noticing him and Clare.

James buys the tickets from a girl who seems way too happy for such a busy and annoyingly crowded night. Clare insists on buying the popcorn and Cokes and Sno-Caps.

The inside of the theater is warm, smells of popcorn, and is swarming with people, dotted throughout in every row under the milky orange lights. They manage to find two seats midway down, not too close to the screen, but not too far away. The floor of their row is sticky with spilled soda and melted candy and who knows what.

James is careful to stare straight ahead at the screen, afraid of turning and seeing Alice. If she's in here, she's probably seen them already. Maybe she's kissing her boyfriend, maybe hoping James will turn around and see her, all in love and shit. He keeps his hands on his thighs, careful not to use the armrest because he doesn't want to bump arms with Clare. He especially doesn't want her to think he might be putting the moves on her.

When the lights of the theater fade and the movie screen bursts with activity, James breathes easy, feeling safely hidden away in the dark embrace of the movie.

After the movie lets out—it was pretty good but reminded James of too many other movies he's already seen—he feigns interest in the credits so they can avoid the mad dash out the door (and, of course, Alice). Then, when the crowd has thinned, they both hit the bathrooms. The girls' has a line that eases out the door, and by the time James finishes peeing, Clare is still nowhere to be seen.

He stands off to the side in the lobby, waiting for her. Soon he sees Alice exit the bathroom, and he thinks about ducking behind one of the big potted plants. She sees him before he can make any attempt to hide.

He looks away, hoping she'll just sneer from afar. But before he knows it, she's in front of him. He can smell her perfume. "So, you and Clare Ashford are back together, huh?" she says, arms folded over her chest.

"No, we're not. We're just friends."

She smiles and rolls her eyes. "It doesn't matter if you are, James. I don't care."

Yeah, sure you don't, he thinks. He sees her turn away, maybe searching the theater lobby for her meathead boyfriend.

"I'm going out with Shane Rollins," she says, turning back to him. "He's the quarterback at Hillcrest. A football player."

"Oh, really? Gee, I thought he was quarterback on the basketball team."

Just then, Clare walks up and stands next to him, like she is unsure of how close she should get, maybe afraid that Alice will try to scratch her eyes out. Clare says, "Hi, Alice."

But Alice just gives James a shit-eating grin and turns and walks away.

"Let's get out of here," James says.

In the Jeep, Clare says, "Sorry about that."

"About what?"

"Alice. Sorry that you had to talk to her. I know it must be weird."

"*She* came up to me. She told me about her new redneck football-playing boyfriend."

"God, I'm lucky I don't have to run into Mason at school."

144

"Who?"

"Mason, my ex. You know, the college guy."

"Oh yeah." Mason. Shane. All the guys who came after him. Well, he can see why Shane wants Alice—he clearly just wants an easy lay. That's the only reason any guy wants Alice. And she just likes him because of the football thing. Whatever.

"I feel sorry for her," Clare says.

"Why?" he asks, incredulous, almost laughing, thinking immediately of his slashed tire.

"I don't know. I mean, she seems nice. She just . . . she has a chip on her shoulder, I guess. I've always tried to be nice to her, unlike some of the other girls. But she hates us, so I guess we all hate her back. Except me, really. It just doesn't seem like she has any friends."

"Well, she's a psycho bitch, if you ask me."

Clare sighs. "Oh, James."

"What?" he says.

But all Clare says is "Never mind."

After he drops off Clare—she gives a cursory good-bye and then dashes to her house—James drives around the city. It is late, but not past his curfew, and he doesn't want to go home yet. He drives away from home first, through the mostly empty city streets, past strip malls with Laundromats, hair salons, copy centers, past a McDonald's and a Subway and a Chinese buffet place. There's the Krispy Kreme where their dad used to pick up doughnuts on Saturday mornings. Alex always wanted the powdered ones, but James liked the glazed and the chocolate iced, washed down with a glass of milk. They haven't gotten dough-nuts in a while.

He drives by Central High, which looks eerie in the darkness, devoid of lights and activity. Will he ever miss this place one day? Grown-ups are always saying these are the best years of their lives. But is this as good as it gets? He hopes with all his heart that it's not. For his sake. And for Alex's.

When he finally gets home, the house is dark, though his mother probably has one ear open in her light slumber, waiting for the sound of James's return. He enters through the kitchen door and goes directly to the fridge for some water. After he takes a big gulp from a bottle, he hears a voice.

James follows the sound, walking softly through the foyer to the living room, where he sees the moonlight framing Alex in the front window. His back is to James, and he is holding the cord-less to his ear. "Yeah, tomorrow is good," he hears Alex say softly. Then Alex chuckles. "We'll see about that."

Who is Alex talking to? James knows he shouldn't be snoop-ing in the dark, but Alex has to have heard his Jeep pull up, right?

"Okay, I'll see you tomorrow. You'll pick me up, right? . . . Okay. . . . Yeah, you sleep well, too." He chuckles again. "Night." Then James hears the beep of the off button. He quickly backpedals across the foyer, then into the kitchen. He coughs so Alex knows he is there.

Alex walks in right after that. "Oh, hey. You scared me there for a second."

"Sorry. Just got home."

Before James can ask him who he was on the phone with, they are both bathed in the headlights of a car that has turned onto their street. James expects the car to zoom on by, but it doesn't. It slows and stops across the street, at Henry's house.

"Who's that?" Alex asks. They both go to the window and peer out.

The car looks like a sedan or something, a dark color. Maybe a BMW, maybe a Mercedes, it's hard to tell. Then its lights flick off, though James can still hear the engine running.

"It's right in front of the mailbox," James says. Soon, James can make out a hand reaching from the driver's window and placing something in the metal mailbox.

"Weird," Alex says.

The car's lights suddenly flick back on, and both he and Alex pull back from the window. The car drives off, and as it passes James can see now that it is a Mercedes, can hear the distinctive gurgley sound of its diesel engine.

"I wonder what that was all about," James says.

"Did they leave something in the mailbox?"

"Looks like it."

"Weird," Alex says again.

It's like they are in some creepy movie, like the one he saw previews for at the theater tonight. Feeling caught in the moment, James makes for the front door, which he unlocks and eases open.

"What are you doing?" Alex whispers.

James steps out into the cold night and creeps down the steps, across the lawn. Alex, he realizes, is following him now, even though he's barefoot in sweatpants and a T-shirt. They both pause at the curb, as if waiting for cars to come by. Then James walks to the mailbox.

"James," Alex whispers loudly, before approaching.

He pulls down the mailbox lid. Inside he sees an envelope. He pulls it out. Alex is now at his side, peering at the envelope as well. The nearest streetlight provides a little light, enough for James to see that no name is written on the envelope.

"It's thick," James says.

He hands it to Alex, who hesitates before grabbing it and squeezing it. "What is it?"

"Money. It feels like money."

Alex looks up at him in the darkness and nods before shoving it back inside the mailbox. James reshuts the lid. They both dash back across the street, inside the house, where James relocks the door. They both stand there for a minute, as if they've escaped some close call, before Alex says, "This is so strange."

"Yeah. Who'd be dropping off money?"

Just then the upstairs hall light flashes on. "Boys? Is that you?" Mom shouts.

They look at each other, and to James the moment is almost electric, like in just a few short minutes they've bridged a divide.

"Yeah, Mom," Alex says.

She appears at the top of the stairs. "What are you two doing?"

"Nothing," James says.

"Well, go to bed. It's late." She flicks off the light and they hear her go back to her room.

They climb the stairs, then pause at James's door.

"You want to look out my window?" Alex whispers. Alex's window faces Henry's house, but James's looks out at the back-yard.

"Nah, I better get some sleep," James says.

"Okay," Alex says, sounding a little disappointed.

"Good night," James whispers.

"Good night," Alex whispers back.

Later, in bed, James wonders who the hell would have dropped off an envelope full of money in the middle of the night. Now that he can't sleep, he wants to cross the hall to Alex's room, to see if he is looking out the window, thinking the same thoughts he is. It's only then that James remembers he forgot to ask Alex who he was chatting with on the phone. But he knows it was Nathen. No doubt about it.

Alex

Alex had touched the envelope himself, and it *felt* like a wad of money—soft and papery and just the right size. But who would leave money in a mailbox in the middle of the night? And why?

Instead of trying to get some sleep—he is, after all, running with Nathen the next morning, so he needs his rest—he stations himself in front of his window, opening the blinds just so. Henry's white house is lit by the moon and the spillover from the streetlight. Maybe Mrs. Burns will creep out of the house and grab the envelope and run back inside. Or maybe Mrs. Burns's mailbox is some weird drug drop spot, and whoever left the envelope is using it unbeknownst to her, and soon another car will swing by for a pickup. Whatever it is, Alex feels a charge of excitement, like something dangerous is going on right under their noses.

He thinks about waking up James, having him stand here with him to keep watch. He wants to talk with him about it.

Maybe he has an idea of what's going on. It's like this sense of mystery has bound them together again. Even if it turns out to be nothing, can't they laugh about it?

But he just stands there, frozen, like he's afraid of even crossing the hall and knocking on James's door. That's the thing with James lately. Sometimes—like tonight—he seems like the brother of old, like he's slowly but surely coming to see Alex as his younger brother again and not some oddball. But then there are the days—more common—when he shoots Alex those dismissive looks, when he is silent and aloof. Alex also feels a little guilty about the situation with Nathen—like he's somehow betraying James, or wronging him in some way. How could James ever understand? So Alex keeps quiet, too, keeping this secret deep inside.

He takes one last look out the blinds, hoping for more intrigue. But nothing happens. It's just a quiet and cold January night, so he crawls into bed and closes his eyes and waits for sleep to take over.

In the morning Alex puts the envelope incident out of his mind. Nathen is picking him up for their Sunday jog at the rec in a little while. Each morning when he wakes now, Alex still can't believe he is a full-fledged member of the cross-country team—it's all real, not some hazy fantasy he has dreamed up. For the first time in his life, he's on an *actual team*. And he earned his place through his own skill and hard work. (Not like T-ball, when they basically had to take any kid who wanted to play.) James has always been the one to excel at sports. It's not that Alex was never interested in them, it was just that James always got there first.

James conquered soccer, and then baseball. Even basketball for a while. Then he found tennis. By the time it was Alex's turn, he naturally shied away, because he knew he wouldn't be the star that James was. What was the point?

But now, with running, he feels like he has found *his* spot in the athletic realm, one that stands apart from James. In the practice runs so far, Alex keeps up with most of the other guys, except for the best runners like Joseph Ewusi-Mensah or Donald McClendon. It's tough, of course, because there are technical things to consider now—he can't just go out and run mindlessly like he used to. This is a sport, and there are tactics and methods. He has to focus on his stride and how his feet land on the ground. "Get up on your toes," Coach Runyon will shout at him when he lands on his heels too much. Then there's the pacing. "You're going out too fast," Coach says. Some days he feels like he has a limp, his legs are so sore. Still, he is adapting to the schedule and to the rigor of it all, slowly but surely. Coach says it just takes time for a body to get used to the distances and speeds and routines and all the hard work. Plus, Coach reminds him, his body is still growing, which further complicates things.

He likes his teammates—a serious, hardworking bunch, both tall and short, lean-bodied, all business during practice. But after practice, they're nice to him, talking to him, giving him encouragement and pointers. He thinks some of them might even be his friends.

During their most recent session, Dr. Richardson said he can tell Alex is doing better. "You seem more upbeat, positive. I think this cross-country thing is great. It's good for you both physically and mentally." Alex nodded in agreement.

What Alex didn't mention to Dr. Richardson was Nathen. He really doesn't know what's going on between them, but something *is* going on, that's for sure. Something good. Ever since that day at the rec, they've been more than just teammates. More than just friends, even. Though they are both of those things, too. It's like they are explorers in some new, uncharted land, explorers who don't really know how or why they got there. And for now, they haven't stopped to ponder it—they just keep exploring, discovering, never looking back. Mainly it has been kissing and touching here and there, when they can find safe moments. They haven't even really talked about the situation. When they're together, stuff usually just happens.

But there had been one night, when Nathen whispered, "Let's take this slow." Whatever "this" was. They had been in his Jeep, making out while parked in the deserted Foodmax parking lot. Between each kiss they had nervously looked around, making sure no one was watching, that no other cars were coming.

"Okay," Alex had said back, feeling relieved but also excited and anxious.

Because what they are doing is wrong—right? Wrong and unnatural. Sinful. Boys should only kiss girls. (Kiss and all that other stuff.) *Not boys.* Yes, it is wrong, wrong, wrong. Well, at least that's what they always say—the Bible, the preachers, the politicians, the other boys in his school who use the word "faggot" like it's the only putdown they can ever come up with. Everyone, it seems, says it's wrong.

But maybe it's not. Maybe *they're* wrong.

He wants to chat with Nathen about it, but he's afraid to disrupt what they have. Like if he makes one false move, everything will collapse and he'll go back to his old life, a life without purpose. A life of things that are simply meant to be good for him but really aren't.

After their run and shower, Nathen and Alex stop off at Subway to get a sandwich. The rec had been crowded today, full of students still caught up in the New Year's resolution workout frenzy, even though it is the end of January. The locker room, too, had been packed with guys, which made Alex a little nervous. He and Nathen barely looked at each other while they undressed, made toward the showers, and then dressed again.

Now, in Subway, seated at a table by the door, they wolf down their sandwiches.

"Maybe we'll just start running outside again," Nathen says.

"Yeah, okay."

"I mean, it was almost too crowded at the rec to get a good rhythm going, you know? All those sorority bitches and their fat asses." He burps and Alex gets a whiff of roast beef.

"Disgusting."

Nathen laughs and balls up his napkin and tosses it at him. Under the table, their legs touch, like by accident. But Alex knows it's on purpose.

Alex turns to look out the window, and he nearly spits out his Coke when he sees Tyler drive up and get out of his car. He doesn't say anything, but Nathen turns to look out the window and says, "Oh, great."

At least Tyler's alone. No Kirk in sight. He's wearing khakis and a pale blue oxford with a dark green tie under a navy blazer. Just getting out of church, Alex guesses.

The bell on the door jingles as he enters. Tyler notices the two of them right away. "Oh, hey, guys." He comes over, his hands in his pockets.

"Hey, man," Nathen says, but Alex says nothing, just looks down at his half-eaten chicken marinara sub.

"Let me guess," Tyler says. "You guys just came from a run?" He smiles, like what he said is really amusing.

"Yep."

"You two are, like, always together. You dating or something?" he says, laughing.

"Ah, fuck off, Tyler," Nathen says, smiling like he knows it was just a joke. "Why are you all decked out?"

"Some of us go to church on Sundays."

Alex wants to say, *Wow, aren't you a saint,* but he just turns away and looks out the window at the cars whizzing by. He wishes Tyler would just whiz on by, too. Tyler's only acknowledging him—barely—because Nathen is around.

"Not me, dude," Nathen says.

"What, no Hindu church on Sunday?" Tyler says, laughing again. He's a real comedian, this guy.

"Dude, I'm not Hindu," Nathen says, sounding more exhausted than angry.

"I'm just kidding, man," he says, smiling big, all self-satisfied. "Well, listen, I'm gonna grab a sub and head out. But let's hang out soon, okay?"

Nathen just nods. Alex continues to stare outside.

"Later."

He's gone, but not completely. Alex can still feel his eyes on the two of them while he's in line getting his sandwich. Alex feels raw, exposed. He even shivers, like he's standing naked in the cold outside air. He has half a sandwich left, but all of a sudden he feels full. He wraps it up for later.

"You okay?" Nathen says.

"Yep." He slurps the rest of his Coke.

It seems like Tyler will never leave, but he finally does. They both watch as he struts to his car, his sandwich bag swinging along beside him. "That guy's a real asshole," Nathen says. Under the table, Alex feels Nathen's knee against his own, a gentle rub.

Nathen drives him home, the songs on the radio the only noise filling the air. It's a sunny day, a washed-out blue sky dotted with a few cottony clouds. Soon it will be February, the last stretch of cold before March ushers in the beginnings of spring.

"So, my folks are gonna be away this weekend," Nathen says. He pulls the Jeep up to Alex's house. "At some conference."

Alex's heart swells and races.

"You maybe want to come over one night? Maybe sleep over?"

"Like, spend the night?" Alex says.

"Yeah, like, spend the night." Nathen drums the steering wheel and stares ahead, all casual about it.

Alex pauses so he doesn't sound too eager. "Sure."

"You think your folks will let you?"

He'd forgotten about them. And about James. For a moment, the outside world had slipped away. But now it's back, demanding explanations. "Oh. I don't know. What would I tell them?"

"Well, you can tell them that we have a six a.m. run the next morning and that it'll be easier if you're here so we can wake up together. I mean, sometimes Coach makes us do that on weekends, usually when it's warmer. Tell them it's his idea."

"Okay. I'll tell them that." Though Alex is not sure if he will. He doesn't want to lie to his parents, but what can he tell them? No matter what he comes up with, James might smell a rat.

"Cool," Nathen says.

"Well, I'll see you tomorrow."

"Okay, bud." Nathen pats his hand, briefly.

More than anything he wants to lean over and kiss Nathen. But who knows who's watching from the house. It's too risky. So he just smiles and steps out. "Bye," he says as Nathen drives off. Before he goes inside, he stares across the street at Henry's mailbox. He's almost tempted to go check it for the envelope, but he doesn't have the nerve, here in the daylight.

Upstairs, he sees that James's door is open. James is lying on his bed with a book. He pauses at the doorway. "What are you reading?"

James puts the book down, then flips it back to show him the cover. "*Pride and Prejudice* for AP."

"How is it?"

"It's not bad for a chick book."

Alex steps inside. "Um, so, what do you think about last night?"

James sits up, becoming animated and interested. "That was weird, huh?"

"Yeah, totally weird. I mean, who do you think did it?"

"No idea. But something's fishy, for sure."

"Yeah. It is. You think we should maybe tell Mom and Dad?"

"Why?"

"I dunno."

"Let's leave them out of it for now."

"Yeah, you're probably right."

"Maybe you can find out something through Henry," James says.

"Yeah, maybe." But, really, what could Henry know? Clearly, by dropping the envelope off in the middle of the night, this person—whoever he or she is—is trying to keep everything a secret.

"It's something to do with his mother, I bet," James says.

"You think?"

"Yeah. There's something off about her."

"I guess so," Alex says. It's not like he hasn't thought the same thing.

James lies back down and picks up his book but still looks at Alex, as if waiting for more. But Alex has nothing to offer. Alex can't really imagine grilling Henry, nor can he imagine snooping around in Henry's house like he's a Hardy boy or something like that. He feels at a loss.

"Well, I'll let you get back to your reading now," Alex finally says.

James just nods, like all of a sudden, he doesn't really care about the previous night's intrigue.

Thursday night after dinner, Alex sits downstairs in the den with his parents, who are watching a TV show about lawyers. James is upstairs, studying or on the phone, who knows. Alex is trying to study vocabulary from an SAT prep guide, but he's having trouble concentrating on the words—or the TV.

"Mom? Dad?" he asks during a commercial. "We have an

early run on Saturday, with Coach Runyon. And, uh, Nathen wants me to . . . He wants me to sleep over so we can wake up early and just go together."

"Don't you run enough all week at school?" his mother asks.

"Well, it did rain a few days this week," he says. "So this is a make-up run."

"I don't see why not," his father says. He then turns back to the TV, as if it's all settled.

"Well, are Mr. and Mrs. Rao okay with you staying over?" she asks.

"Uh, I think so."

"Maybe I should call them," she says.

"Well, I think they may be, like, going out of town." There, he has said it, the truth. He feels relief at not having to construct a lie on top of another lie.

"So it would be just you boys?" she asks.

Alex is unable to read her tone. Is she suspicious, or just being matter-of-fact, or a worrywart? "Yeah. But, I mean, you guys left me and James alone all weekend, remember? Back in November?"

She seems to ponder this for a minute, nodding. "Well, I suppose it's okay, if it's okay with Mr. and Mrs. Rao. Hon?"

"It's fine with me," his father says. This time he looks at Alex and nods.

"Okay, then," she says.

Alex sits with them while the rest of the show plays, forcing himself not to smile or jump up and down. He thinks about how tomorrow night, at this time, he'll be at Nathen's. Just the two of them. The whole night together.

Friday afternoon is dreary but dry, and after cross-country practice, Alex and Nathen say their good-byes, knowing they will see each other in just a few hours. Alex is sweaty and winded but not exhausted—he has a nervous buzz about him that prevents that. But he has forgotten his trig notebook, and he will need that this weekend, so he heads back inside the school to his locker.

Inside, it is mostly quiet, with just a few teachers lingering in their classrooms. Alex pads down the hall in his jogging shoes. As he gets closer to his locker, he worries about what might be scrawled there in Wite-Out. There have been no incidents since the last one, and today, thankfully, his locker door is bare, unviolated.

He retrieves his notebook and walks back down the hall, turns a corner, and that is when a girl dashes out of the bathroom and nearly slams into him.

"Jesus!" he says, bobbing out of the way. When he sees that it is Alice, the girl his brother used to date, he feels himself redden. "Oh, hi. Sorry." Like he's apologizing for James or something, and not for the near collision.

Her face is puffy and pink, and her eyes show the strain and wetness of a good fit of sobbing. She wipes a few tears away with her hand and says, "It's okay. I'm the one who almost knocked into you." She isn't carrying any books, but her hands are bunched into little fists.

"Are you okay?" he says.

She sniffles and looks at him. He thinks she may start sobbing again. But she doesn't, she just nods and holds in her tears.

"You sure?"

She forces out a breath and looks toward the ceiling, as if gathering herself. "Yeah," she says. "I'll be all right."

He knows that she is just saying that. But what can *he* do? He barely knows her. "Okay, well, I hope you, uh, have a nice weekend."

She forces a smile and nods. He still gets the sense that she is moments away from another crying jag. When he cries—and he hasn't cried since the incident—he does not want anyone to see him. It's an ugly, pitiful sight, meant for privacy. So he just walks away, leaving her there in the empty hallway. But with each step he takes, he feels the urge to go back and try to comfort her or something. He doesn't know what he would do, what he would say, and when he drives off he feels a flicker of regret before he remembers the night ahead of him.

Later that afternoon, when he's in the kitchen getting a soda, Alex hears James come in the front door (probably after checking the mailbox). Alex had hoped to avoid him before going over to Nathen's—what was he going to tell him about tonight, after all? Will he believe the Saturday jogging story? Even if he believes that, will he still think it's odd? Guys don't really have slumber parties.

James walks into the kitchen and looks into the pantry. Without missing a beat, he says, "So, Nate says you're sleeping over at his place tonight."

Alex cracks open the can of Pepsi. "Uh, yeah."

"Because of a crack-of-dawn run with your coach?"

"Yep. It sucks."

"Why wouldn't he come over here instead?"

"I don't know."

"Yes, you do."

Alex's heart starts pounding.

"I'm not an idiot," James says. "I know his folks are out of town. Nate told me. Y'all are going to have some of the guys from the team over for a little party."

Alex's heart steadies, and he says, "Oh yeah. We are." He stands there with his soda, trying to appear calm.

James leaves the pantry and opens the fridge and takes out a half-drunk bottle of Gatorade. He drinks it right from the bottle. When he finishes guzzling, he exhales. "Don't do anything stupid," he says. He narrows his eyes at Alex, like he's holding something back, and then leaves to go upstairs.

Nathen greets him at the door with a mischievous smile. He's wearing jeans and a gray T-shirt, no shoes. "Welcome to the Rao home," Nathen says. Inside, the house is warm and smells of books and furniture polish and a spice of some sort. Alex drops his overnight bag in the foyer. He has packed his running clothes, just in case, but also pajamas—cotton shorts and a thin white undershirt—and his toothbrush.

The Rao home is more modern than his—more large glass windows, more angles and pitched ceilings, sleeker furniture. Nathen gives him a "tour," first through the living room, where the walls are lined with bookshelves and dotted here and there with watercolors and small exotic-looking paintings. Then to the kitchen, which is gleaming and sparklingly white, even the appliances. Then down a long hallway that is covered with family photos.

"This is the wall of shame," Nathen says.

On the wall are framed photos of the Rao family through the years—Nathen as a Little Leaguer, kneeling on a grassy field with a baseball bat pitched over his shoulder; the Rao family dressed to the nines in front of some important-looking building at the university; then the family again, with Sarita in her cap and gown at graduation, a slightly younger-looking Nathen with his arm around her, smiling his big smile. Then there is one of the family in front of what Alex recognizes as the Taj Mahal. They are all smiling and squinting in the sunlight, looking hot and ragged, not equal to the majestic building behind them.

"Wow," Alex says.

"Yeah, that's when we went to India a few years back. I was twelve."

"Looks awesome. I've never even been out of the country."

"It was okay. I remember it being hot as hell. And crowded. Mom insisted we go to see my grandparents. She acts more Indian than Dad does. That's what Sarita says anyway. Sarita's always riding Dad these days, saying he's lost touch with his heritage." He tells Alex how his sister has rediscovered her roots while at college, getting into yoga and spirituality and all things Indian, even though Nathen reminds her that she is half English, too. Not to mention American. "But she gets it from Mom. Mom probably wishes *she* were Indian and not Dad. She collects all these Indian paintings of dancing women with eight arms and stuff."

"That sounds kind of interesting."

"I guess," Nathen says. "I must say, she's a good cook. The Indian food she makes is really delicious."

"I went to Star of India once," Alex says, referring to the Indian restaurant near the campus. "It was good." But he feels foolish after saying it, like he is trying to score points.

"Ah, that place is okay." Nathen turns from the wall and smiles at him. "Maybe we'll have you over to dinner sometime."

"Yeah," Alex says, giddy and terrified at the thought.

"Well, want to see my room?"

"Sure." He follows Nathen down the hall, past a few other rooms and a bathroom. Nathen's large room is at the back of the house, and it has its own bathroom and walk-in closet, as well as a big window that overlooks the backyard. He has a double bed and a messy desk that is covered with schoolbooks and papers and a lamp, a long dresser on which is perched a mirror, where Nathen has inserted photographs into the edges of the frame—snapshots of him running or with friends (Alex spies a few with James) and with family. The walls are decorated with framed certificates for all of his awards, both academic and athletic. Third Place, Tuscaloosa Fall 5K, 16-and-Under Division. National Honor Society. First Place, Citywide Mile Run. National French Honor Society. Young Chemists' Honor Society. James's room is like this, too, a wall of accomplishments. Alex's is paltry in comparison— his only real prize was second place in a third-grade art fair and third prize in the science fair in sixth grade.

"So this is it," Nathen says, walking around the room.

"It's nice," Alex says.

Nathen just shrugs and smiles. Alex can feel an odd charge in the air, like they are delaying something. He wishes he had the courage to walk over and kiss Nathen, to get something started, but he feels frozen.

"Well, you wanna order a pizza and watch a movie?" Nathen asks.

"Sure," he says, both disappointed and relieved.

Nathen walks up to him and grabs his hands, though he doesn't look at him. Instead, he stares down at his feet and says, "I'm glad you're here tonight."

"Me too."

Then Nathen reaches in for a kiss, and it sends sparks of joy down Alex's body. Because, finally, they are able to kiss without fear of being seen. It doesn't feel dangerous or risky anymore. It feels safe and good.

Later, they are under the covers of Nathen's bed, lying on their backs, Alex's head resting on Nathen's outstretched arm.

"How did you know that I liked you?" Alex asks.

"I dunno. Guess I could see it in your eyes."

Alex smiles, says, "Really?"

"Sure. Couldn't you see it my eyes?"

"Not really. I mean, I don't know. I guess I didn't know what to look for."

"Hungry eyes," Nathen says. "You had hungry eyes."

It is late, and they have spent the entire night either fooling around or drinking beers or talking. Nathen has already told him about how he always knew he liked guys from a very young age, when he'd sport woodies looking at the men in underwear in the

Sears catalog. But how he never acted on it until math camp one summer, with a kid from Birmingham. Hearing about his past makes Alex feel a little queasy—queasy and jealous that there were a few guys, and just a few, Nathen is careful to point out, before Alex, none of whom live in Tuscaloosa. But also queasy because Nathen is so sure of himself, so confident in who he is.

"So," Nathen says. "What are you thinking about?"

Alex sighs. "I don't know." After a bit, he says, "Are we, like . . . I mean—"

"Fags?" Nathen says.

"Shut up," Alex says, laughing it off, but still jarred by the sound of that word. Besides, he was about to ask if they were boyfriends.

"Well, we *are* fags. And that's fine by me." Nathen's leg pushes into his, and Alex finds himself getting hard again. His head is swimming with so much feeling and so many thoughts and fears, but lurking underneath it all, there are steady waves of relief and happiness. He wishes he could bottle it up and save it.

"You okay?" Nathen asks.

"Yeah," Alex says, rubbing Nathen's hip with his right hand.

"You know, we can't tell anyone about this."

Alex says, "I know."

"I mean, it kind of sucks." Nathen rolls toward him and hovers above him, looking down. He rubs Alex's chest with his free hand. "It has to be our secret. I mean, if anyone found out—"

"We'd be dead."

"Well, I don't know about *dead*," he says. "But it's definitely *not cool* down here."

Alex wants to ask if that is why Nathen is applying to schools in New York and up north, but he doesn't even want to think about that—the fact that, in August, Nathen will be gone. Instead, they start kissing again and that leads to more of the usual. Before, with girls, Alex got nervous about the idea of sex and messing around, so he never pursued it. It didn't really light his fire anyway, so he figured he'd be bad at it. But this, with Nathen, doesn't feel weird—it feels so natural, like he's picked up a skill he didn't know he had.

Afterward, they both linger in a state of restlessness. Alex has never slept in a bed with someone else in it, except on vacations when he and James had to share a room or a hotel bed. But this is, obviously, different. He feels too wound up to fall asleep.

"What are you thinking about?" Nathen asks. Once again, he cradles Alex against him.

"Just thinking about how good this feels."

Nathen squeezes him. "It sure does."

A few minutes of silence go by. Then Nathen says, "Can I ask you about something?"

"Yes." He takes a deep breath.

"I mean, I understand if you don't want to talk about it."

"What?" he asks, a slight twinge of dread rising in his belly.

"About, you know, Marty Miller's party and what you did."

Normally, it is a subject Alex wants to avoid. But now, he feels a sense of relief that Nathen has brought it up. "What do you want to know?"

"You sure you're okay with it?"

"I'm sure."

"Well, I guess . . . Well, mainly I want to know why you did it."

Of course, Alex thinks. Everyone wants to know why. So in the dark, Alex tries to explain it. It is the same story he has told Dr. Richardson countless times.

"I guess it was March or April of last year?" Alex says. "I don't know. Tyler and Kirk started acting weird. Or maybe it was me acting weird. But they looked at me like I was some freak or something. Something changed between us."

At home, he explains, he'd look in the mirror, trying to figure out what it was that his friends and all the other people at school saw when they looked at him—he looked the same, didn't he? It was like they sensed something in Alex that he himself couldn't recognize. Something they should avoid. Like he had some contagious disease.

He tells Nathen that he hadn't seen much of his friends that entire summer—Tyler went away to tennis camp for a month, Lang had traveled through Europe with her older sister, and Beth and Kirk both took summer jobs. "I'm too tired, man," Kirk would say whenever Alex called. Alex also left messages for Beth, but she never even called back. When Tyler got home from camp, he always seemed to have some excuse to avoid hanging out with Alex, too.

"So what happened when school started?" Nathen asks.

"I guess I thought maybe things would go back to the way they had been. But it didn't work out that way. From the very first day of school, things were off. Just like they were in the spring."

The night of the party, Alex remembers that all his friends ignored whatever he said, how Kirk had told him that his taste in music sucked, how Tyler kept giving him sidelong annoyed glances. Alex drank a rum and Coke that he'd mixed himself. He drank it fast and felt light-headed but in control, the alcohol suppressing the unease he felt.

"So, Alex," Tyler had said that night. "You lose your virginity this summer?" Then everyone started laughing.

Alex had smiled and laughed, too. "Very funny."

"What the fuck *did* you do all summer?" Tyler asked.

"Mowed yards and stuff," he said. Which was true. He also read books, but more often than not, he never finished any, his interest lagging midway through. He raised his cup and realized it was empty. Kirk had the flask. "Can I have some more?" Alex asked.

Kirk rolled his eyes and dumped a little more into his cup. Alex drank it down in one gulp.

"You're so weird," Lang said, laughing.

Then they went back to acting like he wasn't there. At times, Beth hooked her finger into Kirk's belt loop and took puffs from his cigarette, like they were a couple. Lang talked about the French or German boys who had hit on her. Tyler mentioned some girl at his camp, how she was such a slut.

"Tell me you fucked her," Kirk said.

"Kirk, that's gross," Beth said, but she smiled like she didn't really mind.

"I never fuck and tell," Tyler said.

Listening, holding his empty cup, Alex felt confused, out of place. It was as if he were with a group of strangers. Or, if not strangers, people whose lives now had little to do with his. "Only a few months had gone by, but in a way it felt like years had passed," Alex explains.

"And then you went to the party?" Nathen asks.

"Yeah. Then we went to the party." He remembers being in that bathroom, feeling a tremendous ache. It was an ache that had spread through his body that summer, growing and growing. It was an ache of emptiness. Something was missing. Something that other people seemed to have without even realizing they had it. Alex couldn't bear the future if it meant living with this feeling, day in and day out. He didn't think the ache would ever go away. But it did, of course. Alex breathes out, like he has just run a sprint. "It was a mistake," Alex says. And he believes this. "A stupid mistake."

A long silence takes over, as if Nathen is just processing what Alex has said. Finally he says, "Thanks for telling me."

"Do you think I'm crazy?"

"Of course not."

Alex pulls himself more tightly against Nathen. He could say so much right now, but instead he closes his eyes and tries to relish this bizarre contentment. This relief.

"You know you can talk to me, if you need to," Nathen says. "Always."

Alex nods in the dark and says, "I know."

Soon, he can hear Nathen's breathing, slight little snores. But Alex refuses to let sleep take him. He wants to stay awake, he wants to drink in every last moment of their first night together.

8

James

Greer and Preston get their acceptance letters to the University of Alabama in the middle of February, and they waste no time announcing it to the world.

"This is the best fucking Valentine I could have gotten!" Preston exclaims at lunch, because it's the Friday after Valentine's Day and all four of them—James, Nathen, Greer, and Preston—are dateless wonders. But that's okay, because there is a big party tonight, for couples and noncouples alike. A sort of anti–Valentine's Day party.

"You're looking at two Bama freshmen," Greer says, giving Preston a high five.

Big deal, James thinks. So what if he and Preston got into Alabama? It's not like there was any doubt that they would. Anyone can get in there, especially anyone whose parents are rich alumni. All the Alabama-bound kids—and there are a lot of them at Central—are getting the acceptance news. Over half the senior class seems to be in a state of euphoric relaxation, and the other half is sitting on pins and needles.

"Must feel great," Nathen says. "Knowing where you'll be going this fall." Like James, Nathen has yet to hear from the schools he applied to, like NYU and Columbia.

"It sure does," Greer says, smiling and then flashing a mouthful of half-eaten hamburger.

"Sick," James says. He picks at a half-eaten roll, which is doughy and sweet. The cafeteria is crowded and noisy and smells like burned meat.

"So no news from Duke yet, man?" Preston asks.

He shakes his head and drains the rest of his orange juice. "Not yet. They don't let you know till early April."

"Well, my man," Preston says, patting him on the back, "there's always Bama."

"Yeah, what more do you want? Beautiful campus, great football team, hot sorority girls!" Greer says. He and Preston laugh.

Nathen smirks and looks over at James, as if in commiseration.

"You two boys can go get your fancy-pants degrees at some private school," Greer says. "I'll think of you when I'm banging a Tri Delt after a football game at the KA house."

James laughs, and both Preston and Greer laugh, too, thinking that James is laughing with them. But really, he's laughing at them. Is that really all college means to them? Football, frats, and sorority girls?

Nathen shakes his head and rolls his eyes. "You guys are pathetic," he says, though he, too, manages to laugh.

"So, Nathen, are you coming to the party tonight or are you gonna pussy out on us again?" Preston asks, switching gears.

"I'll be there. But I can't drink much. Our first meet will be here before I know it, so I have to be good."

"Sucks for you," Greer says.

Tennis season starts soon, too, but that won't stop James from drinking a little. Still, James isn't really looking forward to tonight. Parties, parties, parties—they are all starting to seem the same. All the same old faces, the same old antics, the same old conversations, the same old cliques. Sometimes it feels like everyone is gathered on a dock, surrounded by glassy dark water, while James is tethered to the side in a little rowboat, and the rope holding him there is slipping away. Soon the boat is loose and the dock and the people on it become minuscule dots in the distance, and James is floating in the vast body of water, all alone.

"Earth to James," Preston says.

"Huh?"

"I asked if you need a ride tonight?" he says.

"Oh. No, not tonight. Nate and I are going in his car, since he's not drinking." He looks over at Nathen, who is smiling to himself. It's a look James has seen on Nathen's face a lot lately. The smile of someone at ease with himself, the smile of someone who looks unreasonably happy. Lately he's asked him, "What are you smiling for?" But all Nathen says is, "Can't someone smile?"

The Valentine's party is in a huge subdivision on the other side of town, at Jay Atkinson's house. Jay's a football player, a big guy with curly honey-brown hair, someone all the girls have swooned over at one time. Despite that, James thinks he's a good guy, and surprisingly smart for a football player. He's also the type of person that most everyone at school likes, so the party will probably draw a big crowd from all social circles.

Nathen drives, weaving his Jeep through the wide streets and up and down gently sloping hills.

"Are we lost?" James asks.

"No. Jay's house is all the way at the back of the neighborhood."

"God, it's like a small city here."

The houses are diverse but unremarkable—some two-story, some split-level, some modern, some colonial, with well-tended yards and two-car garages. As they get closer, they see a horde of cars lining the street. Groups of people amble toward the brightly lit house, a beacon in all this suburban darkness. Behind this stretch of houses, James can see a thick forest of pine trees that looms over the houses like a forbidding curtain. Nathen parks behind a Honda, and the two of them make their way inside.

A lot of people are gathered on the back patio, where the kegs are, and the rest are jammed into the hallways and the living room. Jay, the host, is crowded in the kitchen with a lot of other football players, black and white guys who look older than everyone else because they're so oversized. They're all smiling big and laughing, basking in the glow of their athletic celebrity. Out back, Nathen and James see Preston and Greer and a few others standing around smoking cigarettes as if that will keep them warm. A bitter wind weaves through the forest behind the house, shooting spurts of coldness onto them.

"I'm gonna get a beer. You want one?" James asks.

"None for me, remember?" Nathen says. He heads over to the guys, leaving James waiting in line with an empty red Dixie cup. James scans the crowd as he waits, and he recognizes most of the people. Even though he is tired of such parties, there is a slight comfort in all this familiarity. He feels a tap on his shoulder and turns.

"Happy Valentine's Day," Clare says, smiling. She's bundled up in her coat and a maroon scarf. Suzy is with her, as well as a few of her other girlfriends—Meg and Stephanie and Melody, all with sour expressions on their faces.

"You too," he says. He glances around. "I guess no one really has dates."

"Yeah, well, dates are overrated," she says.

George, his teammate, is manning the tap on the keg when they get up to it. "Hey, man! Good to see you here," he says, sounding drunk and exuberant.

"Fill 'er up," James says, holding out his cup. He takes Clare's cup for her and has George fill it first.

"What a gentleman," she says.

He shrugs and smiles. They move away from the keg and sip the cheap beer. Nathen and the boys are standing off the patio in the brittle grass, talking among themselves.

"You heard from any schools yet?" Clare asks.

"Not yet. Have you?"

"Well, I got into Alabama. But I just applied there for safety's sake."

"I didn't even bother."

"I should hear from Davidson next month, and Vandy. And Tulane. It's kind of stressful, all the waiting."

"Tell me about it." He suddenly remembers sophomore year,

when he and Clare dated. That Valentine's Day they had watched a movie at her house, had pizza, made out, traded stupid gifts. It seems so long ago, especially as they stand here now, a few months from graduating.

James hears someone shouting his name. He glances over and sees Greer motioning for him, seeming impatient. "Well, I better go join the boys."

"Okay. See you later," Clare says.

He joins the guys, who are egging Nathen on to go talk to some girl. "See that chick? That junior? See her?" Preston says, pointing with his cup to a girl with short reddish blond hair and wearing a pink sweater and jean jacket. "She's been making eyes at Nate ever since you guys got here. But he won't go talk to her."

James recognizes her as a soccer player. Brittany? Brenda? Short and cute, but maybe too goody-goody and fresh-faced to be all that hot.

"Dude, I told you I'm not interested," Nathen says.

Lots of girls have had crushes on Nathen, but as far as James can remember, Nathen hasn't had crushes on any of them. He talked about this one girl he had a summer fling with a few years back, at a math camp, of all places. And sure, he's made out with girls at parties and gone on a few dates, taken girls to homecoming dances and prom and stuff like that. But he's never had a serious girlfriend. And so what? James thinks. They're nothing but pains in the ass anyway. Nathen is smart, smarter than the rest of them.

"Just go talk to her, man. She clearly wants your jock," Greer says.

"Leave him alone," James says.

"I gotta go pee anyway," Nathen says, then beelines for the backdoor of the house, disappearing inside.

"What's up *his* butt?" Greer says.

"Maybe he isn't interested in that girl. Just leave it alone."

"Yeah, well, it's weird," Greer says.

"What is?"

"All these chicks are hot for him and he just, like, brushes them off. All the time. I mean, he could have more pussy than even me." Greer laughs.

"Maybe he does and he just doesn't brag about it all the time like you do," James says.

"Whatever." Greer chugs the rest of his beer, and even in the dim light of the back porch area James can see that his eyes are ragged and red and glassy. He is drunk, and sometimes he can be one of those mean drunks.

"Hey," Greer says, starting to smile, as if some bright idea just occurred to him. He sort of snorts and then he sucks on his cigarette and blows it in their faces. "What if Nathen is a fag?"

"Shut up, Greer," James says, fighting back a cough.

"Hey, he may be a pussy about chicks, but no *way* he's a fag," Preston says, looking directly at Greer.

Right then, Clare, Suzy, and George walk over with their cups of beer. "Hey, guys," George says. "So, who's not a fag?" he asks, smiling.

"What?" Clare says.

"No one's a fag," James says.

"Except maybe Nathen," Greer says, letting out another snorty laugh.

"Nathen?" Clare asks. "Our Nathen?" she says, like they all lay claim to him.

James looks toward the house, nervous that Nathen will come back and find himself in the middle of this awkward conversation. But luckily there's still no sign of him. "You guys are ridiculous."

Preston says, "Hey, Greer said it, not me. I don't think he's a homo."

James glances at Clare, who looks back at him with annoyance in her eyes.

Greer is smiling big, like he's the funniest guy in the world. "Well, it would sure explain a few things."

"Shut up, Greer. Before he comes back," Clare says.

"Yeah," Suzy says.

"Explain what things?" James asks.

Greer smiles and runs a hand through his hair. "Well, for one thing it might explain why he and your little brother are such good buddies."

Everyone's quiet a second, as if they've all been slapped in the face and don't know how to react.

James feels his heart pounding, his face burning with rage. He feels a hand on his elbow, a gentle touch anticipating restraint, but it's too late, because before he knows it his fist has flung out and hit Greer smack on the cheek. And then again. Two quick punches.

"*Fuck,* man!" Greer says, stumbling back and shielding his face before James's next assault.

"Stop, James!" he hears Clare shout, but mostly everyone has grown quiet. He's about to punch again when two sets of arms pull him back.

"Easy, buddy," Preston says. He resists their arms at first, but when he sees that Greer is on his knees in the grass, touching his face pathetically, he eases up and shrugs himself away.

"I'm cool," James says, walking off to the side, away from everyone.

He breathes heavily. As shafts of wind hit his face, he almost feels like he is frozen. He's certain that he has drawn the attention of the entire backyard crowd. It is Clare who eventually pats him on the shoulder. "Come with me," she says, leading him away, back inside. That's where he sees Nathen, on the couch talking with a few of his cross-country teammates, drinking a Coke and smiling obliviously.

Clare leads him to the front of the house. "You okay?" she asks when they reach the front foyer, which is empty and quieter.

"I can't believe that fucker."

"Let it go," she says. "He's just a drunk idiot."

"Don't tell Nathen," he says. "Okay? Promise?"

"Okay, James. *Okay*," she says, so calmly. "I have my car. I can drive you home, if you want?"

"I came with Nathen."

"I'll tell him you feel sick. Just stay here. Hold on, okay?"

The funny thing is, he does feel sick. Or not sick as much as nervous, on edge, his head buzzing. He closes his eyes for a bit, and when he opens them he sees Clare coming back. Nathen is following her, looking worried, that calm smile gone from his face.

"You okay, buddy?" he says.

"Yeah. Yeah. I just don't feel well."

"You already had too much to drink?" he says, sounding baffled and amused.

"I don't know."

"Listen, Nathen, I'm gonna drive him home," Clare says.

"You sure?" he asks both of them, his eyes darting from face to face, unaware of what Greer said outside. Ugly lies, stupid insults.

"Yeah, I'm sure. I'll call you tomorrow."

"Okay, but I'm ready to leave, too," Nathen says.

That's a wise idea, James thinks.

"I don't mind dropping James off," Clare says, smiling. "Really. Stay a little longer and have some fun."

"Okay," Nathen says, eyeing them suspiciously.

Clare drives him home in her Acura. She's a careful, slow driver. This used to drive James nuts, but now he is glad she is cautious. It allows him to calm down and collect his thoughts. In fact, just sitting next to her calms him.

"You okay?" she says.

He nods. "I can't believe I hit him."

"I know," she says, at first sounding all serious, but then she fails to suppress a giggle.

"Shit, it's not funny," James says.

"I know. But Greer deserved it. He's deserved a good punching for a long time."

"I guess he was just being drunk and stupid, like you said." Though even *he* knows that those are not good excuses. Greer is always drunk and always says stupid stuff. James would expect such bullshit from someone else, but not from a friend. A supposed friend—to both him and Nathen.

When they reach James's house, Clare stops the car and they sit there in the silence.

"Thanks," James says.

"Thanks for what?"

"For taking me home. And for, I don't know, just being there. I feel like such an ass."

"Don't be silly," Clare says.

"I'm so ready to fucking graduate," he says, as if that will solve everything.

"I know."

He feels, all of a sudden, the urge to kiss her. Maybe because it's so soon after Valentine's Day. Maybe because he knows what it's like, kissing her, and because it always felt good. Maybe because he just needs to. But he knows that would be a bad move. Friends. They have to remain friends.

"Well, I better go in," he says.

"James? Don't let what Greer said bother you, okay?"

"I won't," he says, though he knows it *will* bother him, if he thinks about it. He'll just have to try to erase it from his memory. And he'll have to call Greer tomorrow and apologize, which kind of stinks because, if anything, Greer should apologize to *him*. Still, he hopes he didn't give him a black eye or anything. Maybe everyone will have been too drunk to remember the fight and what was said. Maybe by Monday all will be forgotten and forgiven. Maybe.

He smiles at Clare and gets out of the car, and then walks to the front door without turning back. He's home well before curfew, but his parents are already in bed, either asleep or watching TV with the lights off. Upstairs, he sees the light of Alex's room under the crack of the door. He goes to his own room and undresses and crawls into bed, turning the lights out. Soon he hears a knock. "Yeah," he says.

The door creaks open. The hallway light allows him to see that it is Alex. "Why're you home so early?" Alex asks.

"Because I was tired," he says, hoping that will settle the matter.

"Did Nathen drop you off?"

"No," James says. "He stayed." He knows he should leave it at that. But something—that voice in the back of his head, that buzzing sound—makes him add, "He was hitting on some girl or something."

"Oh," Alex says. "Well, I'll let you sleep."

In the darkness James tries to look at Alex's face, as if searching for a clue, some secret sign that his interest in Nathen goes beyond friendship. But Alex, after a brief pause, shuts the door, leaving James alone in the dark. James shuts his eyes and wills sleep to come to him, but for a while he tosses and turns, the sound of Greer's shrill voice echoing in his head like a warning.

That Monday at school things are understandably weird between James and his friends. He apologizes to Greer during lunch, before Nathen gets there. Greer doesn't look scarred or beaten up at all, just some slight reddishness on his cheek, and he brushes James's apologies off.

"No big deal," Greer says. "Besides, I was a jerk. I'm sorry, too." But James can tell some damage has been done. It's like all of the unspoken, underlying division between them keeps growing and growing.

Nathen finally joins them with his tray of food. He's mostly clueless, though he asks, a few times, if something happened at the party. "You sure you guys didn't fight? You guys cool?"

"We're cool," Greer says.

"If you say so," Nathen says.

James considers telling Nathen the truth, but what good will that do? It will just upset and embarrass him. But, at the same time, shouldn't he get a chance to defend himself? Because what Greer said is clearly bullshit.

The bell rings and they all scatter to their classes. Nathen sits across from him, as usual, during AP English. Valerie Towson sits in the front row, taking notes like a robot. If she weren't so quiet and so harmless, James would feel a lot of rage directed at her for getting into Duke already. Preston said she only got in because she's black, but James knows she's smart, deserving. Maybe, just maybe, they'll continue being classmates next year.

Mr. Harris is lecturing about Jane Austen and satire and comedies of manners and social expectations of women in eighteenth-century England. Whenever he asks a question he almost always answers it himself, so it is easy for James to zone out. He glances at Nathen, and though he tries not to think about it, he can't help pondering what Greer said at the party. Is any of it even possible?

Last year, in his American government class, Mr. Wiley would frequently break the class into groups and assign them debate topics about current political events and issues of the day, one group taking a pro viewpoint and the other taking the con. Once, the class had debated gays in the military. No one had wanted to take on the pro view, even though Mr. Wiley had told them, again and again, that their individual viewpoints didn't matter. They just had to research and argue and convince Mr. Wiley of their assigned position. Still, no one had wanted to even *pretend* to be on the pro side of gays—except for Mary Beth Hastings, who was always going on about animal abuse and how the president sucked and how eating meat was inhumane and how recycling was a moral imperative. So it became Mary Beth against the rest of them, saying how gays were no different than you and me, and that they could serve just as well as any other man and woman, all the while putting up with hoots and under-the-breath comments from the guys (and some girls) in the class. James had felt bad for her, but after class he didn't give the topic much thought. He didn't know any gays, so what did this have to do with him?

Even now, most of the gay people he knows about are on TV shows, funny and witty and sophisticated characters who live in big cities. Or else they are like the guy who cuts his mother's hair, or that male nurse from their church—what's his name?—men who seem more like women to James, with their girly way of talking, their constant hand gestures, their wide-eyed expressiveness and glued-on smiles. They're like friendly extraterrestrials, harmless but totally foreign.

Nathen is nothing like any of those guys. Nor is Alex, now that he thinks about it. They aren't girly at all. So what could make Greer think they're homos? Is there something James can't see? Sure, neither of them has girlfriends or seems interested in acquiring one anytime soon, but so what? That doesn't mean a thing. Hell, James doesn't want a girlfriend either, and he knows *he's* not a homo.

Near the end of class Nathen glances over and stifles a

yawn and rolls his eyes, then smiles. It's that smile again, that look in his eyes of total happiness. No homo would smile like that, never.

When James gets home from school, he notices a strange car parked near Henry's house. It's not exactly in front, but sort of between Henry's yard and the house next door, as if it is undecided about which house it is visiting. The car's not a Mercedes but a navy blue BMW with darkly tinted windows all the way around. James walks to the mailbox and steals glances at the car. He can't tell if anyone's in it or not, and he can't see the license plate in the back.

Again, there are no letters from colleges today, but James is almost relieved. No news is good news, as they say. Besides, he knows it's still too early.

Inside, he drops his books in the kitchen, grabs a bottle of Gatorade from the fridge, and sits in front of the kitchen window, spying on the car. A few minutes pass, and then Mrs. Burns pulls up in her Volkswagen. James sees Henry dash out from the passenger side and run up the walkway to the front porch. He bounces on his heels, like he has to pee. Mrs. Burns makes her way there, and James notices that she stares at the BMW. But instead of letting her gaze linger, she unlocks the front door and the two of them head inside.

Soon, he sees Alex pull up in his Honda. Alex is in his track clothes, carrying a gym bag and his book bag as he comes through the kitchen door.

"Oh, hey."

"There's another weird car in front of Henry's house," James says.

Alex sets his stuff down and joins him at the table. "You mean that BMW?"

"Yeah. I can't tell if anyone's in it."

Just then, someone opens the driver's-side door. It's a man in shades, with wavy brownish red hair with too much gel in it, wearing a suit without a tie.

"Who is that?" Alex asks.

"How should I know?"

They watch the man hesitate and then ease the car door shut. He looks around, west and east, as if watching for traffic. Just then, James sees Mrs. Burns come outside and stand on her front steps. The man sees her and they stare at each other, saying nothing.

"She's shaking her head," Alex says.

James sees that. He can also see her saying something—not shouting exactly, but with force, as if she's issuing a warning.

The man moves forward a bit, but Mrs. Burns says something that stops him in his tracks. As if suddenly embarrassed, the man moves back to the car, gets inside, and starts the engine.

Mrs. Burns crosses her arms and continues to stand protectively on the steps, until finally the car drives off. James thinks about trying to get a glimpse of the license plate number, but the car is gone too quickly. Finally, satisfied that the car is gone, Mrs. Burns goes back inside.

"That was weird," Alex says.

"Totally weird," James says.

"Who do you think that was?"

"I have no idea. Maybe an ex-boyfriend?"

"Yeah, maybe." Alex peers out the window, and James studies him, like if he looks at him long enough Alex will reveal something about himself, will open up. But then he thinks some things are better left unexplored, unsaid. And maybe this applies to Henry and his mother, too—maybe they should stop being nosy, suspicious.

Just then Alex turns and notices him staring. "What?"

"Nothing," James says.

February gives way to March, and the weather gets a little warmer and springlike, though a nip in the air lingers. The month passes slowly, but nothing really happens besides the usual—school, practice, waiting for that letter from Duke. Tennis practice intensifies as the days go by, so James stays at the courts until four-thirty, sometimes later. During practice some days, he glimpses the cross-country team across the soccer practice field in the smaller stadium. He can make out Alex, his lanky frame and clipped haircut, going through the drills with his teammates. He looks, amazingly, like he belongs there—he looks like an athlete. But besides that, he and Alex only really see each other at dinner, and by then they are exhausted by full days.

Finally, the first day of April arrives. April Fool's Day. That day, some members of the senior class—including Preston, of course, but not James—sneak out to the parking lots during lunch and soap the windshields of a bunch of the junior class's cars with lame stuff like SENIORS RULE! and JUNIORS SUCK! When James gets home, he sees that Alex's car, thankfully, is clean of any soap smearing. Maybe they avoided Alex's car on James's behalf, or maybe he just got lucky.

After dinner that night James sequesters himself in his room. Spring break is just a week away, and James is looking forward to a reprieve from the toil of tennis practice and the boredom of school. When his phone rings, he lets the machine get it. He's on his bed reading *Great Expectations,* too lazy to get up and answer it. Besides, it's probably someone he doesn't want to talk to, which includes most everyone these days.

At first there is dead air. But then a familiar voice says, "James?" There is a pause, then the voice continues: "It's me, Alice. I . . . I don't know why I'm calling." For a moment James thinks it's Preston or Greer pranking him, because the voice sounds odd, too high-pitched for Alice. Then the voice, after a pause, begins again: "I guess . . . I just wanted to talk." The voice cracks then, and then he knows it is Alice, not a joke at all. She starts crying, right there on the phone. *Oh, great,* he thinks. But there *is* something different in her voice. She doesn't sound hostile and bitter and ready for a fight. She sounds sad, scared, vulnerable. Alice quits crying, sniffles, and gathers her faltering voice. "I know I'm the last person you would want to talk to," she says. "But, I really . . . I really wish you'd pick up. I swear I'm not calling to . . . to, uh . . . Well, I'm calling as a friend."

James picks up. "I'm here."

"Oh," she says, sounding surprised but relieved.

"What is it?" he asks, not trying to sound short but knowing he does.

"Listen, I'm sorry to call like this. But, you were always so easy to talk to. And . . . I don't know." She starts crying again.

What can he do but wait and listen?

Finally, she gathers herself and says, "Sorry. I'd rather talk in person. Can you, like, maybe meet me after school tomorrow?"

He wishes they could chat now, not later. "I don't know. Tomorrow's real busy. I have tennis practice and then I have some shit to do."

"Please, James? I won't take up much time."

She sounds so sad and needy, he can't deny her. "Okay, fine," he says, feeling totally put out and annoyed.

"Thanks," she says softly.

They make a plan to meet at four o'clock at Monnish Park, the little park that is adjacent to school, though it is blocked from view by rows of hedges and old, fat oak trees.

After he hangs up he tries to read, but there's too much crowding his head. Nathen. Alex. The weird shit going on next door. Clare. Greer. Preston. Colleges. And now Alice.

After tennis practice the next day he drives his car over to the park, even though it's a short walk away. He wants to be able to get away quickly, if he has to. He wonders what Alice wants to talk to him about. It has to be something bad—why else meet in person, shielded from their classmates' eyes?

From his car James sees her sitting on a bench close to some monkey bars, where no kids are playing. He walks to her, feeling apprehensive each step of the way. As he gets close he can tell that she looks tired, worn out. She is wearing her royal blue down jacket over some jeans and brown flats. She is not wearing much—if any—makeup, so her eyes look funny, naked and unkempt. Still, she almost seems prettier this way.

"You came," she says, smiling faintly.

"I said I would." He sits down next to her and looks around the park, which is strewn with dead leaves and pinecones and downed brittle tree branches. Behind him, he can hear the traffic of Fifteenth Street.

"Thanks," she says. "I didn't mean to cry last night. I'm sorry if that freaked you out."

"Nah," he says, though it did freak him, a little bit.

"Shane dumped me, so I guess that was part of it. But that was, like, a while ago, and I'm over it."

"That sucks," James says, though he feels a surge of satisfaction. He's no longer the only bad guy.

"Yeah, but I feel better today. Actually, I kind of feel silly now."

"Why?"

"Well, I don't know. I guess we could have just chatted over the phone instead of meeting like this. But I just wanted to see you. And apologize."

"Okay."

"You know, for being so . . . well, for acting so emotional back in November. And for being a real bitch since then."

"Okay," he says again, not really knowing what he should say. Part of him feels like he is owed this apology, that it is overdue. But he knows he was a jerk, too.

"You were always real nice to me. I mean . . . when we were together. We had some good times, didn't we?"

He only nods.

"You're not like a lot of the other guys."

"Yeah, I am," he says.

"Not really."

They pass a few moments in silence. Then he can't bear it anymore. "You know where you're going to school in the fall?" he asks. This time he looks at her, but quickly. It's like she has this weird aura of calm about her. Like she's a different person.

"Not yet. I mean, maybe Bama. But I may have to go to Shelton State at first. My mom says I have to pay my own way, and I don't know if I can afford Bama. So, we'll see. . . . What about you? Did you get into Duke?"

He almost feels guilty answering, because his choices are limitless. He can go anywhere he wants, if he gets in. But not Alice. "No, I haven't heard yet. They actually rejected me for early admission. But I should hear soon. Hopefully before spring break. It's driving me nuts. I just want to know."

"Oh, you'll get in. You always get what you want. Things always go your way," Alice says, though she says it without bitterness, like it's just a fact.

He wants to dispute this, but he doesn't. He rubs his hands, which are callused from tennis. They sit there for a while, not saying anything more. He wants to leave, but he knows he should stay put until Alice dismisses him.

"Well, I better go," Alice says. "Lots of homework." She stands, her hands tucked into her jacket.

"Yeah, me too."

They walk together toward the little parking lot, which is empty except for their cars. It's a funny park. No one ever seems to come here, and he wonders why. Sure, Fifteenth Street is noisy and busy, but the park is like a little sanctuary.

"Thanks for coming," Alice says. "It means a lot that you showed up. I hope we can be friends now." She reaches in for a hug, and James is powerless to stop her. It feels nice, actually, like all the anger they both carried around is melting away into a puddle beneath them. And he thinks maybe Alice senses this, too, because it seems like forever before she lets go.

When James gets home, Henry is outside sitting on the curb, elbows on his knees, looking rejected. He isn't wearing a coat, just some brown pants and a yellow sweater, with white sneakers. Since he has to go to the mailbox anyway, James knows he has to talk to him.

"Hey, Henry," James says. That's when he notices the extra car in their driveway. A shiny black Mercedes, like the one they saw that night weeks ago, dropping off the envelope.

Henry looks up. "Oh, hey."

"What are you doing outside? Aren't you cold?"

"Yeah. But some old man is inside arguing with Mom," he says.

"Who?"

Henry shrugs. "Mom told me to go outside. She says they need to talk privately."

James pauses at the mailbox and eyes Henry's house. "You can come in our house if you want."

Henry shakes his head. "I want to wait."

"Okay," he says, about to open the mailbox, that nervous twitch rising in his chest. But before he does, an old man comes out of Henry's house and slams the door shut. The man heads straight for the Mercedes, not giving Henry or James the time of day, like he is purposely ignoring them.

"Oh," James says, but softly. He knows this man, of course. It's Jack Pembroke, the rich guy who probably owns half the city. The grumpy owner of the country club. Mrs. Burns's boss, right? *And* her landlord. He's seen the man countless times—in person and in the paper.

When Jack Pembroke gets in the Mercedes and zooms away, Henry dashes to the front door and disappears inside, leaving James standing there.

There's nothing else to do but open the mailbox. There are two magazines inside—Dad's *Newsweek* and Mom's *Vanity Fair*— and one thin envelope. Another thin envelope from Duke, the blue letters of the return address blaring at him. He feels sick. His hands feel fat and heavy, too. But he wants to get it over with, so he tears along the edge and yanks out the letter. It is on creamy white paper, folded tightly. He unfolds it, steeling himself, all but ready to rip it in shreds when he reads the bad news.

But it isn't bad news. "Holy shit," he whispers, "I got in."

9

Alex

Spring break arrives in early April. And although the cold weather seems to be slowly fading away, Alex doesn't think it feels like spring yet—flowers are not blooming, the bees aren't littering pollen everywhere, the grass is still yellowed and dry, and he still needs a jacket outside.

At school the run-up to spring break had been intense. All of Alex's teachers piled on the homework and stepped up their lesson plans, packing in as much stuff as possible before everyone went off for a week and forgot everything.

And Coach Runyon had intensified their practices. "Our first meet is right after spring break," he'd said on the Friday before the break began. "So I don't want you slacking off over the holiday. You've got to sneak in some workouts next week. And don't screw up your eating habits."

He and his mom are going to spend the break at the beach

house in Gulf Shores. His father and James were supposed to come, too, but now that James has gotten into Duke, they are headed up to North Carolina to tour the campus and stuff like that, to make sure this is where James really wants to spend his next four years. Nathen is doing the same sort of thing—he got into NYU and Columbia, so he is going to the Big Apple with his parents, to check out both schools. So, while Nathen and James are off preparing for their future lives, Alex and his mom are heading south, just the two of them. Alex is glad to get away—from school, therapy, Tuscaloosa—even if the trip will be a little boring.

They leave on Saturday and take turns driving the five-hour trip. Alex drives first, cruising down Highway 69, but then his mother takes over after lunch at McDonald's. Just past Thomas-ville, she hits Highway 43, a four-lane highway that courses through southern Alabama, past one sleepy town after another. The landscape shifts from rolling hills and pine trees to flat fields and streets lined with cypress trees and stately oaks.

Perched at the side of one vast cotton field there is a white billboard with fading red lettering that says: GO TO CHURCH OR THE DEVIL WILL GET YOU! It has been there as long as Alex can re-member, and he finds it amusing, ridiculous even—anything but sinister.

"Your father and brother are probably still driving through Georgia," Mom says.

"I guess so," Alex replies.

"We'll still have fun, just the two of us," she says, slapping him playfully on the thigh.

"Yep," Alex says. He's actually kind of glad that James won't be here. James had been moody and grumpy for many weeks, until he got the Duke news. And he still mostly avoids Alex. Or, when not avoiding him, looking at him oddly, Alex can't help feeling, as if trying to read his mind.

As they get closer to the Gulf, Alex notices how the horizon seems bluer, like the sky is announcing the ocean. When they hit Mobile, his mother drives through the Mobile Bay tunnel. When they were kids and came down to the Gulf, he and James would hold their breath when their father drove through this very tunnel. They pretended that they were truly underwater, instead of protected by tons of concrete and beams, and the first one to exhale was the loser. James always won.

When they clear Mobile, all the stores and shops along the highway start to look familiar—the shops that sell seaside bric-a-brac; the stores fronted with colorful displays of inner tubes and rafts and folding beach chairs; fruit stands stacked with watermelons, cantaloupes, and strawberries.

"We're almost there," his mother says.

Even now, when it's just the two of them, he gets the same excited feeling that he always did when they first catch sight of the Gulf and its green-blue choppy waters and pale sand dunes. When they come here, it always feels like they have driven to the edge of the world.

The house they own is at the western side of Gulf Shores, far from a lot of the development in the center of town—the high-rise condos, the arcades and tacky gift shops, the bait shops and boat rental places, the seafood restaurants with white gravel parking lots. But some smaller condos are popping up on the western end, here and there amid the private residences, a fact that his parents lament every time they come down here.

All the homes are on stilts and made of wood, but they are all painted different colors—dusty pale blue, canary yellow, plain old white, a wintery gray—and are different sizes, some large, others no bigger than the garages beneath them. Their house is yellow with white trim, with three bedrooms and a large deck that looks out over the Gulf. It's the perfect size for a family—nothing huge or showy. Years ago his mother named the house "Happy Returns," and over the garage there is a little blue-and-yellow-painted sign that acts as the house's name tag.

When he steps out of the car, Alex smells the salty sea air that blows at him. He can hear the afternoon waves crashing peacefully.

"This is wonderful, isn't it?" his mother says, standing next to him, gazing out at the beach. The temperature is mild, warmer than at home, though the ocean wind provides a little bite.

"Yeah, it's nice," he says. But even as he drinks in the air and the beauty of it all, he thinks it would be that much better if Nathen were here.

They spend their first few days lying on the deck, sunning and reading, occasionally taking mostly quiet walks along the beach. The ocean is still way too cold for swimming. In the afternoons, Alex goes for runs down the beach road—not on the beach, since the shifting sand is bad for his feet. It's not very crowded on this end of the beach, but when they go into town for dinner each night—Mom refuses to cook on her vacation—the restaurants are bursting with families and rowdy spring breakers. Their favorite place to eat is called Sea and Suds, and it is perched on a pier that juts out into the Gulf, where fishers cast their lines and

kids lean over the railings and try to spot jellyfish and other crea-
tures. Tonight, as always, Sea and Suds is busy and noisy. Waiters
and waitresses zip by, taking orders on little notepads, dropping
off baskets of food or taking them away, refilling glasses of water.

"What a lovely night. Don't you just love it down here?" she
says while gazing out the window. She has had a few glasses of
Chardonnay, and Alex can tell that it is loosening her tongue,
feeling contemplative.

Alex nods and takes a sip of his Coke. He sees two other boys
that look his age at a booth nearby, and they are with two girls.
He wonders where they are from, and if they are on dates with
these girls, or if they are brothers, and did they meet here or
travel together. It's sometimes hard to believe that there are other
kids his age all over the country, other kids living their own lives
at different schools. After he got out of the hospital, Alex had
fantasized about moving to a new city and changing his name.
No more Alex, no more Alexander—just Xander. He imagined
an entirely different life for himself with a name like that—he
would be the cool kid, the rebel, the wild child. Happy-go-lucky
Xander. No one would know the old Alex, and he could start
over, with new friends, where no one knew anything about his
past. He wonders if that's how Henry feels each time he lands in
a new city. Like he's been given a fresh start. In the end, it doesn't
seem to have mattered much—Alex figures Henry will be an
oddball no matter where he goes. And maybe Alex will, too.

"What a difference a few months makes," his mother says,
gazing out the window. She then turns to him and smiles. "You're
happy now, aren't you, honey? Happier, I mean."

"Yeah," he says.

She nods. "I can tell. I'm glad."

Alex can see tears welling in her eyes. "Aw, Mom, not here."

"I'm sorry," she says. She grabs her napkin and wipes her eyes, then smiles. "I won't be sappy. But your father and I . . . we're so proud of how far you've come." She gazes at him warmly, and for a second Alex thinks about telling her about Nathen. About what is happening between them. He wants to share that with someone, his secret happiness.

But right then the waiter comes and asks if they want dessert. "I'm full," his mother says.

"Me too," Alex says.

The waiter leaves to get the bill.

The moment has passed. But that's okay. It's too soon to tell her, to tell anyone. He has considered telling Dr. Richardson during one of their sessions, but so far he has held back. He thinks that it is better for him and Nathen to live in their secret little world. He's not sure how she or his father or Dr. Richardson would react. It's the great, scary unknown.

When they get home, they put on their pajamas and watch TV. When the phone rings, his mom says, "That's probably your father." But when she answers, she says, "Yes, he's here," looking over at Alex.

"For me?" he says.

"I think it's Nathen," she says, and hands him the cordless.

"Hey," Alex says, walking with the phone to his bedroom, speaking softly.

"Hey there," Nathen says. "How's the beach?"

"It's good. Relaxing. I've been jogging every day. How's the Big Apple?"

"It's awesome, Lex. It really is. But it's cold as shit up here."

"It's nice down here."

"Listen," Nathen says, "I can't talk long. I'm down in the lobby. But I wanted to call."

"Okay," Alex says, his disappointment tempered by the fact that Nathen called in the first place. He'd given Nathen the number here, but he figured he'd be too busy to use it. Too busy to even think about Alex.

"I get home Sunday, so I'll call you then, cool?"

"Cool."

"Okay, buddy. Listen," he says.

"Yeah?"

"Uh," Nathen starts, sounding unsure about what he wants to say next. "Uh, okay, yeah, I'll see you Sunday. I better go!"

"Bye," Alex says. He turns off the phone and brings it back to the front room.

"That was sweet of Nathen to call," Mom says.

Alex doesn't look at her. "Yeah, it was cool." He can feel her eyes on him, like she's reading the secret right off of his face. "Did I miss anything?" he says, staring at the TV show he doesn't care about, his mind somewhere very far away.

Later that night, Alex lies in bed, listening to the sound of the waves landing against the shore. Something gnaws at his brain. He climbs out of bed and puts on his jeans and a jacket—but no shoes—and steps out onto the deck, careful not to make too much noise. He could stay on the deck, sit in a lounge chair, and take in the night air. But he feels like moving. So he walks down the steps of the deck onto the beach. The sand is cold and gritty, but it feels good on his bare feet. He starts walking in a westward direction. It is dark, but there is faint moonlight, so he can see where he is going, can see that the beach is empty. The houses he passes are mostly dark except for an occasional floodlight.

He can't sleep, he realizes, because he misses Nathen. Their brief conversation earlier has only made him miss Nathen more. He is used to seeing him every day. Used to sneaking kisses when possible, used to trading secret glances with each other. In bed each night, he grabs his pillows, pretending that he is holding Nathen. He pretends that he smells him—the Lever 2000 soap, sour and fresh at the same time, his minty shampoo, and that unique scent of his that Alex can't even describe, really. But he knows, in the end, that he is just holding a pillow and that Nathen is really miles away.

He walks and walks and finally sits down on the beach, facing the dark ocean. The water is calmer, the waves smaller, now that no boats or Jet Skis disturb it. He doesn't know how far he has walked, but there are still houses behind him, at least, so he knows he hasn't walked past the point where the road dead-ends up to a private property. James once said that some crazy old rich lady lived in a cabin at the end of the road and that if you happened onto her beach she would shoot you with a shotgun, but he is sure that that is just one of the dumb stories that James used to tell him.

Sitting there, Alex feels an odd mixture of sadness and happiness. Sad because he misses Nathen, but happy because he has someone to miss. Maybe, he thinks, this is what love is like. All of those people in movie love stories, acting so mopey and dramatic, tormented and ecstatic. It all seemed silly to Alex, but not anymore.

It hits Alex that if he misses Nathen so badly now, then it will be even worse when Nathen goes away to college. Far worse. He pictures Nathen now, up in New York, meeting new people, excited by the life ahead of him, far from Tuscaloosa. It's a future that does not involve Alex.

He leans back in the sand and looks up at the sky, but it's too cloudy to see many stars. He thinks about what his mother asked him earlier. *Are you happy?* He said he was, and that is true. But he realizes how his happiness is built on a shaky foundation. If Nathen goes away, does his happiness collapse? Maybe, maybe not. Dr. Richardson has said that happiness is fleeting, that no rational person could be happy all the time. But he said that is okay, that is normal. So maybe Alex's life will always be that way—fleeting happiness surrounded by the ever-present reality of life, with all of its problems and difficulties and shitty occurrences.

Alex stands and dusts the sand off his jeans and his back. He walks back to the beach house, tired and cold. He has a few more nights here, and he is determined to make the best of them. He crawls back into his bed and clutches his pillow. He knows it's not Nathen, but for now it will do.

"Your dad called. He and James are having a good time," his mother says out on the back deck on their last full day. "James really loves it there, so it looks like he's Duke-bound."

"Cool," Alex says. He's wearing shades and reading a creepy

novel about a grandmother who locks her grandchildren in an attic.

"What about you? You have any idea where you want to go to college?"

"I don't know," he says, though he has given it *some* thought. But where he wants to go and where he might get in are different stories. His grades are good now, but he is not the high achiever that James is. Plus, he is terrible at those stupid standardized tests. He doubts he could get into Duke, not that he wants to anyway.

"It's probably time to start thinking about that. You have the SAT in a few weeks."

"Don't remind me."

She sits on the lounge chair next to him, with her own book, a crime novel. "You'll do fine," she says.

"Maybe."

They soak in the sun for a bit, but then his mother starts talking again. "I can't believe it's our last day. It's been nice, hasn't it? I just wish the boys had been with us." Her tone strikes Alex as thoughtful, sentimental. Must be the beach and the ocean that do this to her, he thinks.

"Will you be sad when James leaves?" he says.

"Of course," she says. "But I knew that day was coming." She chuckles to herself. "I remember when you were born. I already felt so attached to James, so when you arrived, I was so happy, relieved almost, that there was this new little person for me to take care of."

Alex smiles at the image of himself as a swaddled baby, clutched against his mother, safe and crying, innocent and dumb.

"I never had any siblings," she says.

Alex knows this already, but he lets her continue.

"When my mom and dad died, I was all alone, really." She sounds calm now, not teary. "I mean, I had your father, of course, and you two. But if not for you guys, I don't know what I would have done."

Alex closes his eyes and listens as the waves lap onto the beach. He hears a few annoying seagulls making their squawking sounds.

His mom continues: "I guess I wanted my boys to have each other."

Alex nods, not knowing what to say. He can feel her eyes on him, like she's checking to see that he is actually listening to her.

"You know your brother loves you," she says. "He may not show it much. But he does."

Alex nods again. He knows she's right. But he feels embarrassed, too. It's like one of those sappy moments in a Hallmark commercial.

As if she recognizes that, his mother stands and says, "I know you think I'm hokey, Alex, but I just hope you believe what I say." She pats him on the knee and then approaches the stairs of the deck. "Well, I think I'm gonna go for a walk. You want to come?"

He shakes his head. "Nah, I'm okay right here," he says. He closes his eyes again and dozes off. When he opens his eyes later, he stands up and looks up and down the beach. At first he sees no trace of his mother, but then, when he squints, he sees her, a tiny speck in the distance, getting larger and larger. When she gets closer, Alex waves, and even from so far away, he knows she is smiling.

The drive back to Tuscaloosa on Saturday is uneventful, though it seems longer to Alex, maybe because he is so eager to get back. The radio stations all repeat the same songs again and again, and the sights along the road—the old dilapidated houses, the small churches, the local cafés and mom-and-pop shops—are less interesting the second time around. By the time they get home and pull into the driveway, Alex is exhausted—and relieved to be home.

His father and James greet them outside and help them unload the car.

"Look how tan you are," his father says, mussing his short hair.

James doesn't say much as he lifts bags out of the trunk, but Alex can tell he's in lighter spirits, like the invisible black cloud hovering over him has moved on.

"So you liked Duke?" Alex asks.

"Yeah, it was pretty cool."

"The campus is gorgeous," his father says. "All these old buildings of limestone. You'll love it, honey."

When Alex goes back outside to retrieve the last bag, he sees Henry on his porch. Alex waves but Henry doesn't seem to notice him or even look his way. He's probably off in space, Alex thinks, as he heads back inside.

Up in his room he unpacks his bag, which is full of dirty clothes that smell of the beach, sand, and suntan lotion. What he really wants to do is call Nathen. But Nathen won't be home until Sunday, and Alex resigns himself to waiting.

Later they order pizza for dinner and sit in the TV room, but mostly Mom grills James about Duke and the trip. James is more animated than Alex has seen him in a very long time, going on and on about Duke and the classes he might take and other prospective students he met.

After dinner Alex goes up to his room. He has plenty of schoolwork to catch up on, stuff he avoided over the break, but the thought of doing any of it bums him out. He would jog, except it's now too dark out. The truth is, he doesn't feel like doing much of anything. He has carried the relaxed lethargy of the beach home with him.

He's just about to crawl into bed when James knocks on his door and comes in without waiting. "Here, I got this for you," he says, tossing a gray T-shirt his way. Alex opens it and sees that it says DUKE TRACK AND FIELD in blue letters.

"Oh, cool. Thanks," he says, surprised that James would even have given him a thought while at Duke.

James nods and walks to Alex's window. He lifts a blind and looks out. "Henry is still out there," he says.

"What?" Alex joins him at the window, and sure enough, Henry is still sitting on the porch. "That's weird. He was out there earlier."

"And I saw him out there before we ate dinner."

Without saying anything to James, Alex laces up his sneakers and grabs his jacket. As he heads downstairs, he can hear James following him. Together, outside, they cross the street and march right up to Henry. He is still sitting on the steps, elbows on knees, looking down at the ground as if watching for ants.

"Henry? You okay?" Behind Henry, the house is mostly dark, though Alex can see a trace of light burning behind the living room curtains.

Henry finally looks up, wearing a blank look, like he hasn't heard Alex but has at least registered his presence. "Oh, hi, Alex. Hi, James." Then he looks down again.

"Henry, is something the matter?"

He doesn't say anything.

"Where's your mom?" James asks.

"She's inside," Henry says. "But I'm mad at her."

"Why?" James asks.

"She says we have to move away again. Maybe."

"What? Why?" Alex says, not bothering to conceal the alarm in his voice.

"I don't know. She didn't say why."

"There has to be a reason," James says.

Alex sits down next to Henry and tries to think of what to say. But nothing comes to him. He looks over at James, who's standing in the middle of the walk with his hands in his pockets.

"Maybe she's just upset," James says.

"Yeah, that could be it," Alex says, urging Henry to agree.

But Henry is silent. Alex knows Henry has been through this before. The moves from one town to another. Why should Tuscaloosa be any different? Still, Alex wants to do something, say something.

"I don't want to leave," Henry says so quietly that Alex isn't even sure he hears him correctly.

They stay for a bit longer, in sulky silence. Alex knows there is nothing that he can tell Henry that will make him feel better. Instead, he wants to go inside the house and shake Mrs. Burns, ask her what she is doing, uprooting her kid like this again and again. And for what? But Alex can't do this. He knows that.

Kids can't do such things to adults. Manners and respect and decorum—these are the things his mother always tells him are the most important qualities a young man can have.

"It'll be okay," Alex says, knowing his words are empty and unpersuasive. Henry just nods and, all of a sudden, stands up and goes inside.

"That went well," James says.

Alex frowns and then they both walk across the street. When Alex opens the door, the heat from inside blasts him like a slap of guilt.

The next day, Sunday, Alex tries to catch up on some homework, but he is distracted. He keeps waiting for the phone to ring to announce that Nathen is finally back. He also can't help looking out his window, expecting to see Henry. But all day there is no sign of him.

Finally, after a steady diet of junk TV and halfhearted attempts at reading for English class, the phone rings, and it is Nathen.

"You're back," Alex says, as if he hasn't been sitting around waiting for this very moment.

"You wanna come over?" he says. "My folks went to their campus offices to catch up on some stuff."

"Sure," Alex says, feeling his stomach lurch.

He puts on his running gear and tells his mother that he and Nathen are meeting at the rec for a jog. It's only half a lie, and he's not even sure why he said it. Maybe in case James asks where he went. Then he drives to Nathen's, because walking would take too long.

When Nathen opens the door, Alex is almost surprised that he looks the same—same black hair, same light brown skin, same dirty green eyes, same big dimpled grin, same prominent nose. When they hug, he feels a balance restored inside his body.

"Look at you," Nathen says, pulling back and looking Alex up and down. "You're so tan. You're almost my color now!" He laughs.

"Yeah, well, the sun will do that to you."

Nathen smiles and says, "Wiseass."

Back in his bedroom, they sit on his floor, backs against the bed, as Nathen tells him all about New York. "It was nuts, man. Very cold, but still an awesome place." He describes NYU and Columbia, telling him they were both great but different. "NYU is in the middle of the city, but Columbia is further uptown and has a real campus, like Bama's but smaller." He says he met students, observed classes, took tours—pretty much what it sounds like James did at Duke. He and his parents saw a few Broadway shows and ate at nice restaurants. "We went to this swanky place on Park Avenue. I had to wear a tie, even. But I had the best steak in the world. There were *so* many places to eat there. You walk one block and there are like five different restaurants. And places to shop. And bars. And museums. There's so much going on there."

"Sounds more exciting than Gulf Shores."

Nathen looks over at him, breaking out of his New York reverie. "But you had a good time, right?"

"Yeah, we had fun. It was relaxing." He doesn't tell him that he missed him.

Nathen gently slides his hand to Alex's and starts rubbing. "You're quiet today."

"I'm just listening," he says. He smiles to reassure Nathen, though his smile is hard to pull off.

"I'm glad to be back," Nathen says. He grabs Alex's hand and squeezes it. "I missed you."

"Liar," Alex says, smiling as he says it. Because it's exactly what he wants to hear. What he has been waiting to hear—and what he has been waiting to say himself. Nathen reaches in and they start kissing. Gently at first, then ferociously, like they're making up for lost time. Nathen's light stubble tickles Alex's chin, but he doesn't mind. They keep going until they hear the front door jiggle open.

"Damn. Mom and Pops are home," Nathen says, but not in a panic or anything. He's the usual calm Nathen.

"I better go home anyway," Alex says. "Got a ton of homework to do." Though, really, he wants to stay. Part of him never wants to let Nathen out of his sight again.

"Coach is gonna kick our ass this week," Nathen says.

"No kidding."

"Our first meet is next weekend. *Your* first meet. Can you believe it?"

"No, not really. It's crazy, but I think I'll be ready."

"Of course you will."

They stand and embrace and then kiss one last time, careful to listen for his parents' footsteps, though his door is shut. "I'll see you tomorrow, okay?" Nathen says.

Alex nods. He manages to avoid Mr. and Mrs. Rao on his way out, and he's thankful for that. Not that he doesn't like them—they're both super nice—but he always feels like he's wearing a scarlet mark on his face when he is facing them.

On his way home Alex can't help remembering that, a year from now, Nathen won't be here. He grips the steering wheel tightly. He will just try not to think about it. Besides, there are many days left—weeks, months—before Nathen leaves him.

The next day at school everyone seems tanned or rested and in good spirits, despite being thrown back into the drudgery of everyday routine. Alex overhears tales of spring break—ski trips and keg parties on the beach and visits to big cities, even some woeful tales about being stuck at home—but no one asks him where he went or what he did, which is just as well.

After English class Alex makes his way past the cafeteria to the library. But this time he pauses in front of the library doors. Through the glass panes, he can see the other regulars—Jess, already surrounded by his books and papers, and Valerie, quietly absorbed in a novel. And though he can't see her, Alex is sure that the sour-faced librarian is in there, too, shelving books or re-arranging her desk.

He turns around and walks back toward the cafeteria, which he can hear and smell before he can see. Today, he decides to make a change. He won't isolate himself anymore. He won't hide. So he pushes through the door and heads to the food service area. He doesn't look around—not yet. He focuses instead on deciding what to eat. It's all disgusting—squares of greasy pizza, mystery-meat hamburgers, overcooked and overbuttered greens and other vegetables. He decides on a prepackaged salad and an apple and also some Little Debbie oatmeal cookies. Nothing that anyone had to cook. He pays at a register and then steps back out into the seating area. Now, he realizes, he has to look around, has to find a table. He almost regrets his decision—almost feels like dumping his entire tray into the trash and bee-lining it to the door, back to the safety of the library—when he sees two of his teammates at one end of a long table: Jake Blume and Pete Hong. The guys on the team call them Bloomie and Hong Kong.

He makes his way toward them and Jake seems to brighten when he sees him. "Oh, hey, Alex." Alex sits down next to him, on one of the uncomfortable, round little built-in seats. Jake has curly dark brown hair and big blue eyes and is short, the shortest guy on the team, but that doesn't seem to slow him down—he may have a shorter stride, but he is quick as a cat.

"I didn't know you had lunch this period," Pete says.

"Yeah," Jake says. "We haven't seen you in here."

"I usually do homework in the library," he says, surprising himself by admitting this. "But, I don't know, today I didn't want to do that."

"Yeah, man, you shouldn't skip out on lunch," Pete says. Pete is tall, with a head that is almost completely shaved, revealing his lean and long skull under a sprinkling of black hair. His serious face belies the fact that he is the team jokester. He's the one who gives everyone nicknames, the one who tosses off sarcastic jokes and insults. He's a junior, too, and so is Jake, but before Alex joined the team he didn't know them very well. Neither of them really belongs to a group. They are just normal guys who happen to be athletes, which seems to suit them just fine. "It's essential that you get your daily nutrition, man." Pete holds up a soggy piece of pizza and smiles before biting off a chunk.

"I bring my lunch," Jake says, holding up his sandwich. "It's healthier." Alex sees a plastic bag of carrots, too, and a carton of apple juice.

"Bloomie thinks he's better than us, man," Pete says, "because he brings his lunch."

"Of course I'm better," he says, smiling. "Not to mention faster."

"Yeah, whatever," Pete says. "Anyway, why are you always hiding out in the library?"

"I dunno. I wasn't really sure I'd have anyone to sit with in here," he says, shrugging it off.

"Well, now you do," Jake says.

"Yeah, Rookie," Pete says. "Now you're *stuck* with us."

Alex smiles. Apparently he has a nickname now.

For the rest of the lunch period, they talk about cross-country and practice and the big meet this weekend. Alex doesn't even look around to see if any of his old friends notice him. But he knows where they are—behind him, closer to the windows, a small group of strangers.

When the bell rings, Jake says, "See you at practice, Alex." He and Pete dash off together, to their pre-calc class.

Alex gathers his stuff and walks to the big garbage can by the door. Someone brushes by him, as if intentionally knocking into him, and when Alex looks to see who it is, he isn't surprised that it's Tyler, walking next to Lang, the two of them chuckling. But, oddly, this doesn't bother him. He is moving on, but Tyler, for some reason, can't let go.

All through his next class, Alex is distracted by how relieved he feels. Or maybe not relieved. More like content. He certainly doesn't feel his usual postlunch gloom after hiding out in the library. Now he feels different, more a part of things. Like just another high schooler, and not the freak roaming the halls.

This feeling carries him to cross-country practice. As he changes in the locker room with the rest of the team, he feels light and strong, like he is ready to run a marathon.

Jed Callahan, tall and freckly with dark red hair (his nickname is Red), is doing some groin stretches on the ground. "Hey, you guys hear about Alice Hudson?" he asks.

At the mention of the name Alex's belly turns a flip-flop and then tightens. He looks over at Nathen, who is busy lacing his sneakers.

"You mean the girl who smashed her car up over break?" Joseph asks.

"Yeah, her," Jed says. "She drove right into a telephone pole or something."

Alex sits down on the bench. He puts on one of his shoes, but his hands are shaking, so he leaves it untied for now. "Is she okay?" Alex asks.

"I guess so. She's out of the hospital, with a broken arm and nose or something. She got lucky."

"This just proves that girls are shitty drivers," Pete says.

Alex bends down and works on his shoes. He wonders if James knows what has happened. Alice is his ex-girlfriend, after all. Alex remembers the day he saw Alice, when she had nearly run into him in the hallway. Before, she had kind of scared him—her aggressiveness, her forthright attitude—but that day she seemed pitiful, vulnerable. He wants to know more about the accident, but now his teammates are making their way outside, leaving Alex alone with Nathen. He wonders how Alice managed to drive her car right into a telephone pole. Was she drunk? Were the roads slick?

"You ready?" Nathen says.

Alex nods, even though he *isn't* really ready to practice. Not now anyway. Not anymore. He feels heavy, like his feet have weights on them.

"That's awful about Alice, huh?" Nathen says. Alex manages to stand and they exit the locker room. Nathen drapes an arm over his shoulder.

"Coach is gonna work us to death today, isn't he?" Alex says, eager to get his mind focused on something else, hoping his legs regain their life. He hears Coach Runyon shouting for them to hurry up, which they do, pulling apart and breaking into a light jog.

It is a warm day, the first true day of spring, and the afternoon sun is bright, causing Alex to squint and shade his eyes to see. The inside part of the track field shows signs of greenery now—grass and small darker weeds, a few random yellow blossoms—and Alex can hear birds chirping in the park beyond the track. It is a beautiful day. Deceptively beautiful, like a Venus flytrap. It is a day that would suggest that nothing bad could ever happen to anyone.

After practice Nathen stays late to chat with Coach, since he is one of the cocaptains, along with Joseph. So Alex walks toward the tennis courts to find James. Not that he knows what to say to James if he does find him. But when he gets there, the team is gone, the courts empty, and James isn't at home when he gets there, either.

Alex eats an apple and sits at the kitchen table and waits. James probably just stopped to get gas or something. He'll be home soon. There is no sign of life at Henry's house, either—no car in the garage or driveway, no Henry on the porch, no odd cars parked in front, nothing. Alex waits, eating his apple down to the core.

Maybe Alice is just a bad driver. Maybe it was a mistake, an accident. Maybe she did get lucky. He barely knows Alice, but he doesn't want what he's thinking to be true—that Alice wrecked her car on purpose. Maybe he's making too much of the day he saw her, but he recognized that look in her eyes. The eyes of someone who is tired of being alone, tired of feeling like shit, tired of feeling trapped. He knows that when it piles up, you get blinded. Blinded to everything that's *not* wrong with the world. Alex wouldn't wish those feelings on anyone.

Finally he hears James drive up. He sees him get out of his Jeep, still dressed in his tennis clothes. Alex stays where he is, and when James comes in through the kitchen door, he stands.

"I heard about Alice," he says, not even giving James a second to set his stuff down.

"Yeah, well, the whole school heard," James says.

"You okay?"

"Yeah. Why wouldn't I be?" He sets his bags down and goes to the fridge, which he opens and peers into, deciding what to nab.

Alex has an incredible urge to go up to James and punch him in the shoulder. He wants to tell him that it's okay to care about someone. It's okay to be sad. It's okay to be a fucking human being sometimes. But he just says, "I don't know. You're always okay, I guess."

With that he heads upstairs. He goes into his bathroom, peels off his track clothes, and showers, appreciating the warm water as it rains down on him, washing all the filth of the day off.

When he turns off the water and gets out, he hears someone in his room—the sound of his blinds being lifted. He wraps himself in his towel and opens the bathroom door. James is standing by his window, staring out.

"What do you want?" Alex says, knowing he sounds short.

"Jack Pembroke is out there again, with Henry's mother."

"Who?" Alex joins James at the window and peers out. He recognizes the older man, who is wearing a suit and talking by his Mercedes with Mrs. Burns.

"I saw him leaving their house a few weeks ago, too," James says.

"You did?"

"Didn't I tell you that?"

"No."

"I meant to. It was really weird. Henry was outside, and Pembroke was inside talking to his mother, and then he stormed out."

"How could you forget to tell me that?" Alex says.

"Well, that was the day I found out about Duke. Guess I forgot."

Outside, Jack Pembroke pats Mrs. Burns on the shoulder and then gets in his car and leaves. She stands in the driveway and waves as he drives away.

"What do you think is going on?" James asks.

"I don't know." But then Alex remembers the Christmas party, and the two women gossiping about Mr. Pembroke and his wife. "Do you think they're having an affair?"

"Gross," James says. "He's like a million years older than she is."

"So. There are lots of older men with young wives and girlfriends. Like Mr. Kirkland? And Dr. Sheldon?"

"I guess you're right."

But Alex doubts this explanation, even if he suggested it. The way they said good-bye didn't seem, well, lovey-dovey. It almost looked paternal. "I don't know. I mean, *something* is going on between them." He clasps his arms over his chest because he feels cold. He wishes James would leave so he could get dressed.

James nods and then says in a drawn-out whisper, "Wait."

"What?"

James looks at him. "What if Mr. Pembroke is Henry's father?"

Alex glances out the window again, but Mrs. Burns is gone. "No way," he says.

"It's possible. It might explain a few things."

"Like what?"

"I don't know. Like how they afford to live in that house. And why they moved here in the first place."

"And it *would* explain why she's so secretive about telling Henry anything about his dad," Alex says.

"Yeah, I mean, he's an important man. He's married and has kids. If anyone knew about this—"

"His reputation would be in the toilet," Alex says.

Reputations. They are so damn important, Alex thinks, especially in this town, where people's secrets are like well-guarded jewels. No one wants to be known as an adulterer or a crook or a mental case. Or a homo, for that matter.

"So, why would they move away, then?" James asks. They both continue to stare out the window, like if they look long enough, the answers to all their questions will drop out of the sky.

Just then, Alex sees Henry wandering up the street, his bright blond head shimmering in the afternoon sun, a red backpack hanging from his shoulder. He's kicking the ground, and his lips are moving, so he's probably singing or talking to himself. Alex has an incredible urge to open the window and shout for Henry to come over. It's like he wants to warn him, to protect him. But from what?

Alex stands there with James, frozen, until Henry disappears inside his house.

"Poor kid," James says.

The next day at school Alex tries to pick up more information about Alice's wreck. But most of the information he gathers— from overheard snippets, mostly, but also from Jake and Pete at lunch—isn't really new: she's injured after her car accident but at home now, resting, taking pain medication. One girl in chemistry class claims some west-side gang members drove her off the road, and someone else says she fell asleep at the wheel. But no, that's not true, some other guy claims: she was drunk.

Listening to all this rumor and speculation, Alex wonders, briefly, what kinds of things were said about *him* after his incident. God only knows. Do people just pluck ideas from thin air?

Outside, the weather is gloomy—overcast and windy. It

starts pouring rain during Spanish class, the drops pelting the windows like tossed pebbles. All day, the gloominess outside has slowly seeped inside Alex, and it's still with him as he walks to his locker to grab his track clothes. He's not sure what they will do during practice, since the weather sucks. Running would be nice, to get his endorphins running, to clear his head, but with the rain this seems unlikely.

When he yanks open his locker, he sees a yellow sheet of paper, folded into fourths. Someone must have stuck it in through the grates. He looks around before he peels it open. The black-ink handwriting is familiar, but blocky and precise, like maybe someone is trying to disguise his usual messy penmanship.

The note says: "I know you're a FAG!"

Alex folds the note back into fourths and shoves it in his pocket. His heart is pounding, and he can feel his face reddening. He shuts his locker and locks it, but then realizes he has forgotten to even take out his track stuff. *Don't panic,* he tells himself. *Someone's just playing a joke.*

He glances down the hall and sees Tyler. He is just standing there by the bathroom door, holding his tennis bag and smiling at him. It's the grin of someone who thinks he knows something. The grin of someone who *used* to be your friend.

10

James

When the bell rings to end the day, it is still raining out, but not as heavily as it has been most of the afternoon. Since there was no tennis practice today, James's Jeep is still parked in the back lot. He makes his way out there, not bothering to open his umbrella, letting the cool droplets land on his face. He passes Nathen's car and notices that he is sitting inside and that someone is in there with him. James stops and taps on the window and then sees Alex in the passenger seat. Nathen lowers the window.

"Hey, buddy," he says.

James peers over at Alex, who looks all serious-faced. "What's up?" James asks both of them.

"We're just chatting," Nathen says, acting all offhand about it.

Something is off here, James thinks. He knows how Alex looks when he's upset about something—he clenches his lips and his eyes look dewy and wide, like by keeping them open he can prevent tears from welling.

"Having a serious powwow?" James says, managing a phony smile.

"Not really," Nathen says.

"I'm just a little nervous about the meet on Saturday," Alex says.

"Yeah. I'm just giving him a little pep talk."

Meanwhile, the rain picks up again and James is getting wetter and wetter. "Okay, well, call me later." Then he dashes off to his own car. Once inside, he sits and watches the shadowy shapes of Nathen and Alex through the wet glass and rain. *Pep talk, my ass,* he thinks. But what is it? What were they chatting about, looking so grave?

He feels jealous on two counts, he hates to admit to himself. On the one hand, why is his own brother clearly confiding in Nathen and not him? Sure, maybe James isn't the easiest guy to talk to. But they've been getting along fine lately, haven't they? Plus, he's family. He's the big brother, for Pete's sake.

And, then, why is one of his supposed best friends becoming better friends with his little brother? At first he didn't mind their friendship because it seemed like a good thing for Alex, something he needed. Plus, he figured Nathen was humoring Alex, maybe even taking pity on him. But now the closeness seems to be growing and growing. James feels like he's being pushed aside.

Instead of fretting about it anymore, James cranks his car and speeds off. He turns on the radio and blasts the volume and cracks the windows ever so slightly, despite the rain. He has to remind himself not to worry about Alex and Nathen and whatever the hell is going on between them. Why should these things bother him? He's graduating soon, and he will be a Duke freshman in the fall. It's enough to make him break into a smile as he cruises down Fifteenth Street, feeling lucky as he runs a string of yellow lights.

Up in his room he sits down at his desk to get some homework done. It still piles up—French paragraphs to translate, AP reading galore, and on and on. Greer and Preston are always talking about how they don't give a shit about schoolwork anymore, and it's true that they have been blowing off a lot of their assignments. Not that they were ever scholars or anything. But James can't bring himself to quit caring completely. Good study habits are in his nature. And he'll need to maintain them for college.

When his phone rings, he thinks it might be Nathen, calling to tell him what was up earlier. Instead, it is Clare.

"How you feeling?" she asks, her voice full of sweet concern.

"Fine. Why?"

"I thought you might be a little upset. You know, about Alice."

Here we go again. Ever since he found out about Alice, people act like he's still her boyfriend or something. Like he has some special claim on her. "Not really," he says. "It's not like she died."

"Well, I'm glad she's okay."

"Yep," he says.

"Have you called her?"

"No. Why would I?"

"I don't know," Clare says in a leading tone that suggests she *does* know.

"You think it's my fault?" James blurts.

"What?" she asks.

"You think it's my fault, don't you? You think Alice did this on purpose."

"Of course I don't think that! You're being ridiculous."

There is silence for a while, then Clare says, "Anyway, I didn't call to argue."

"Okay. Sorry." When he and Clare dated, they fought a lot, and it was James—always James—who did the apologizing. Clare had a way of making him feel at fault for things, even when he wasn't.

Clare says, "I called because I wanted to ask you to do something with me. But now I'm not so sure."

"What?"

"Well, I made Alice some cookies and got her a get-well card. I thought I'd get some people to sign it and then bring it to her. To her house."

Cookies and a card, like she is recovering from chicken pox. "And what? You want me to go with you?" he says.

"Well, yeah. I was hoping."

He sighs. "When?"

"Tomorrow. After school?"

"But what if she doesn't want company? What if her mother tells us to get lost?"

"Well, I don't know. I guess we'll leave, then. But I want to try."

"Okay," he says. "I'll meet you after tennis practice, by the courts. Coach may keep us late, so don't expect me to leave right at three."

"Okay," she says. "Thanks. It means a lot to me."

When he hangs up, he almost feels like screaming. Instead, he just rubs his forehead like he has a headache or something. Outside, the rain picks up again and the wind pushes against his windows.

He hears Alex now, climbing the stairs. He sits still, thinking maybe Alex will knock. Thinking maybe Alex will come in and spill his guts. But no, he hears Alex shut his door, sealing himself inside his own room.

Later, at dinner, Alex is still quiet and barely responds when their parents ask him questions. They eat baked chicken and mashed potatoes and store-bought rolls and a limp salad.

"Big weekend coming up for you two," Dad says, eating the chicken like it tastes a lot better than it does. Their dad works his ass off at the firm, but he always manages to catch James's tennis matches. Mom, too. But Saturday, James has a match in town—versus Walker High—and Alex has a cross-country meet in Anniston, which is over two hours away. So they are splitting duties this weekend. Mom will stay and watch his tennis match, and Dad will make the drive to Anniston—the team is going up the day before. "You excited?"

"I guess so," James says. "Walker usually stinks, though."

"Don't get cocky now," Mom says.

"I'm not being cocky, just being honest. They have, like, two good players."

"Alex?" his Dad says.

"Uh-huh?"

"Everything okay?"

"Yeah. I'm just feeling a little tired."

"That coach has been working you too hard," Mom says.

"Not really."

"Well, you better get a lot of rest before then. We don't want you to be sick for your big debut," Mom says. "And eat up. You need fuel."

James looks over at him, almost willing Alex to look his way, but he doesn't.

"Has Coach Whitley decided on your doubles partner yet?" Dad asks James.

"Uh, yeah. It's Tyler," he says. He's not very happy about this, even though they play well together. Tyler annoys him with his puppy-doggish chatter and stupid need to always high-five after hitting good shots.

"Tyler?" his mother says, and then makes a little noise under her breath.

James looks at Alex, to see if he's changed his expression at all. But he hasn't. He still sits there quietly, eyeing and picking at his food.

The next day is overcast but dry, so the tennis team practices with a vengeance—backhand and forehand drills and practice games and sprints up and down the court length. Coach keeps them late, and James can see Clare sitting in her car, waiting for him to finish.

"I think you guys are closer to being ready for this weekend," Coach says when he gathers them at the fence after practice ends. "We'll stay late tomorrow, too, weather permitting."

James exits the courts after saying his good-byes and walks to Clare's car. She unrolls the window. "You ready?" she says.

"I guess, but I'm all sweaty. Maybe I should shower before we go." He hates showering at school, but he thinks it might be rude to show up at Alice's in his tennis clothes.

"Okay, but hurry," Clare says, sounding annoyed.

He thinks the locker room may be free and clear—it's a small one used only by the tennis team and golf team—but he finds Tyler inside, undressing. "Oh, hey," he says.

"Oh, hey, James."

Tyler, instead of undressing quietly like a normal person, starts jabbering to James about tennis practice and the match Saturday. "I can't wait to kick Walker's ass. Bunch of dumb hill-billies."

To discourage him, James barely replies. Plus, he doesn't care to see Tyler standing there in his underwear. James has stripped down to his underwear and just an undershirt, but he refuses to get totally naked when he has an audience. Tyler, finally getting a clue, grabs his towel and saunters off to the showers before him. James isn't even sure why Tyler is here, why he isn't showering at home. He figures Tyler is wondering the same thing about him.

The showers are kind of gross, the floor cold and wet and mildewed. The shampoo dispenser is empty, so he washes his hair with the green liquid body soap, which makes his hair feel clean but gritty. He towels off inside the shower. He can still hear Tyler's shower running, so he gets out and hopes he can make an exit before Tyler finishes. But no, he hears Tyler turn off the water and yank his shower curtain open.

James pulls on his jeans and sits on the bench with his shirt off. He dries his feet and puts on his socks. Tyler comes into the main room from the showers. James glances up briefly and sees Tyler smiling at him, looking goofy. He is flat-chested and scrawny, with freckled arms and pale, slumpy shoulders. Not that James wants to look at his body—it's just there, in front of him. He averts his eyes and starts putting on his shoes.

"You wanna grab a burger or something?" Tyler says.

"Can't," James says, not looking up. "Got some stuff to do."

"Okay, no worries."

James hears Tyler fiddling with his duffel bag, and when he looks up to grab his shirt from his own bag, he sees that Tyler is buck naked. Not only that, but he is still smiling and staring at James.

"Dude, put some clothes on," James says, turning away so that he faces the other direction.

"Sorry," he says, still chuckling like he is so funny, such a clever joker.

James finishes dressing in a hurry. "See you tomorrow," he says, barging out of the locker room, not waiting to hear Tyler's response.

What was that all about? he thinks.

Clare is outside her car now, clearly ready to get going. More than anything, James wishes he could just go home. Even homework would be more fun. But he knows he's stuck doing this, so he braces himself.

"Here, sign the card," Clare says, handing it to him, along with a black ink pen. It is a simple card—nothing cutesy or humorous—that says "Get Well Soon" in florid gold lettering. Inside, James sees a number of signatures, some with personal notes like "Hurry back" or "Feel better!" A lot of these signatures are from people Alice despises, or people who never gave her the time of day before. What a bunch of phonies, he thinks. It takes a car wreck for people to stop being assholes. James signs his name to this gathering, and is glad there is no room left to write out a message.

They take separate cars, with James leading the way. He knows how to get there. Not that he spent much time at Alice's house while they dated—while they dated *briefly,* he is always careful to remind everyone. But he did pick her up a few times, and one time her mother had him in for dessert and for an informal chat. Nothing serious. Alice's mother—Mrs. Tidwell, because she had remarried—was not one of those hovering and nervous types, the kind who quizzes you or glares at you as if she is trying to read your dirty thoughts about her daughter. James remembers her as very chatty, with a raspy smoker's voice. As Alice always reminded him, James was different from other boys she'd dated. "A good guy," she said once. "A smarty pants." So he was probably a welcome change of pace for Mrs. Tidwell. But he's not so sure what she might think of him now.

Alice's parents divorced when she was little and she barely knows her father, who moved away. (At least she knows who he is, James thinks, unlike poor Henry.) Her stepfather, Mr. Tidwell, works long hours at the JVC factory, and James has never met him.

Alice's house is in a modest but not shabby neighborhood not far from the high school. The evenly plotted streets are dotted with small ranch houses that have small front yards and small fenced-in backyards, with carports that are not walled in on all sides. Alice's house is set downslope from the street, gray brick with black trim and a beige-tiled roof.

He parks on the street, and Clare pulls up right behind him. He takes a deep breath before leaving the car.

He and Clare walk down the slope to the front door, and Clare rings the doorbell. He hears the doorbell as it echoes inside, then the shrill barks of a dog. The barks get closer and closer until he can tell that the dog is right by the door, scratching, eager to see who is there, ready to jump up on them. He remembers the dog—a pug-faced, black Boston terrier who looked mean but was really sweet as pie.

He and Clare look at each other and exchange nervous smiles. Then he hears Mrs. Tidwell shouting the dog away— "Bitsy! Bitsy, hush up, now!"—before she cracks open the door, so that only her face is visible. James registers her initial look as one of mild confusion.

"Oh, hi there," she says. "Hi, James." Behind her, Bitsy is whining, wanting to get out and see who's there. Alice's mother looks the same as James remembers her—slight and thin, with short honey red hair tucked behind her ears, a tan face, a slight overbite that shows her even but large, slightly yellowed teeth.

"Hi, Mrs. Tidwell," Clare says. "We came by to see Alice, and to give her this." Clare glances down at the chocolate chip cookies, which are cellophaned to a sturdy paper plate, on top of which rests the card in its white envelope.

"Oh, well, how kind," she says, not budging.

"I mean, if she feels up to seeing anyone," Clare says. "Oh, I'm Clare Ashford."

Mrs. Tidwell nods. "Hi, Clare."

"Can we see Alice, do you think?"

"Well, she was napping earlier. And she's on some pain medication, so she may be groggy. Can you wait here a sec? Bitsy, get back!" She gently shuts the door, leaving them there with their cookies and card.

"This was a mistake," James says.

Clare says, "Shhhh."

In a few minutes Mrs. Tidwell returns without Bitsy, and this time she pulls the door all the way open. "She's in her room if you wanna go back. But she's tired, so I can't let you stay too long, okay?"

"Thanks," Clare says, stepping into the living room, which has matted blue carpet. Against a wall there is a comfy-looking gray sofa, which is covered by a white blanket and a few magazines. An ashtray is on the chipped wooden coffee table, and the TV is tuned to one of those afternoon shows with a judge scolding people about their absurd lives.

"Her room is last one on the left," Mrs. Tidwell says.

The door is shut, so James knocks gently.

"Come in."

Clare goes first, since she is carrying the cookies and the card. Alice lies on her full-size bed, under the covers, with her right arm in a white sling. She doesn't look as bad as James expected. She only has a few scrapes on her face, a bandage on her forehead, and on her nose a bruise that is the color of a prune. Her hair is tied back in a ponytail, exposing her roots, and her face looks dry and colorless where it isn't scraped. Still, she doesn't look like someone who just cheated death.

"Hi," Clare says, sounding tentative and bashful all of a sudden. "We brought you these cookies. And this card." Clare sets them on Alice's dresser. "You can read the card later if you want," Clare says, though she walks over and hands it to Alice, who takes it with her free hand.

Alice's room looks the same as James remembers it: a few posters of actors with their shirts unbuttoned, white wallpaper with small pink stripes, a pink bedspread, fluffy pillows, and a few stuffed animals on the floor. Plus the perfumes and beauty aids that cover a lot of the dresser top. He is always amazed at how much stuff girls have—bottles and tubes and cases and jars of stuff meant to make them presentable to the world.

"How are you feeling?" Clare asks, standing near Alice's side.

"I'm feeling okay. Mostly I feel out of it."

"Your mom says you're on some pain medications," Clare says. Alice nods.

And what is James supposed to say? He stands there, feeling like a bump on a log, as Clare makes more polite chitchat and Alice responds. She doesn't seem angry or bitter or surprised, nor does she seem happy to see them. She only seems zoned out.

"It must have been scary," Clare says, about the crash.

Again, Alice nods. But then she says, "Well, not really. I don't remember much about it."

That's what Alex said, James thinks. That he didn't remember much about the night he swallowed the Pine-Sol. And James believes him, just as he believes Alice right now. Because maybe—probably—they are choosing to forget. Like their minds won't let them remember, because it's too painful or embarrassing.

"They say you got lucky," James says, finally speaking.

Alice looks over at him, offering a slight smile. "Mom says God was watching out for me."

"She's probably right," Clare says.

James nods his head, but he hates when people say shit like that. Like God has all the time in the world to watch over and protect every single person on the planet. And what about the people who die in accidents or wars or whatever? Does God think less of them?

"I don't know," Alice says, as if reading his mind. "I think James may be right. Maybe I just got lucky."

"Well, we're just glad you're okay," Clare says.

"Yeah," James says.

Alice gives Clare an odd look, like she can't figure out why this person is here being nice to her. Then, as if noticing it for the first time, Alice fondles the card.

"Want me to open it for you?" Clare asks.

"No. I'll read it later." She closes her eyes. "I'm getting sleepy."

"Okay. Well, then we better get going," Clare says.

James can tell Clare wants to say more, can almost hear some sweet speech waiting to pour out of her. But she doesn't say anything, she just looks over at him and bares a smile.

"Okay," Alice says, eyes still closed.

Clare leaves before him, and James hesitates at the door. He feels relief. Not only that he can leave. But relief that he can see Alice, lying there in front of him. He doesn't want to know what really happened that night she wrecked. Nor does he want to know why Shane dumped her, or why she met with him in the park, or if she is still depressed, or any of that. The less he knows, the better, as far as he is concerned. It's over and done with. Still, she is here, hurt perhaps, maybe still sad, but here. It is then that she opens her eyes again and sees him standing there. She smiles. A real smile. "Thanks," she says.

James nods and pulls the door closed.

Mrs. Tidwell is waiting to show them out. "Well, I can't say I expected anyone to come by like this."

"We wanted to," Clare says.

"Well, I'm sure it meant a lot to her. She may not show it, but . . . well, like I said."

"Is she gonna come back to school soon?" James asks.

"I sure hope so. She doesn't feel up to it right now. I went and picked up some of her homework, but she hasn't touched it. We'll see."

Outside, they both make their way to their cars.

"See, that wasn't so bad," Clare says.

James nods. "Yeah."

"Thanks for coming with me."

"No problem," he says.

"You okay? You seem, I don't know—"

"I'm just tired. It's been a long day. But, yeah, I'm glad we came."

After they make their good-byes, James drives off. He *is* tired—that was not a lie. This day has worn him out. But he's also thinking about Alex. About how no one came to see *him* when he was recovering, when he was lying in his bed at home, away from school for a few weeks. No one brought a card, no one brought cookies. The only people who called were family friends, and Clare and Nathen. But none of James's other friends or classmates called—and none of Alex's supposed friends called, either. Like Tyler, who's been nothing but puppyish and nice to James. Why is he treating Alex like such shit?

All of a sudden James feels angry. Angry at everyone. And angry at himself for now, finally, being angry. What kind of a brother is he? He wasn't there for Alex before, and he hasn't been there since. He pulls into the neighborhood and picks up speed. Mom always says to drive slowly down these streets, to be careful for kids playing or for the walkers, but James's anger makes his foot heavy. He enters the driveway with such force that the Jeep gives a large bounce before he steps on the brakes.

Alex is at home in his room, and Mom is home, too, cooking dinner. James sets his stuff in his room and takes off his shoes and calms himself down. His flash of anger has tempered, but he still feels a sort of restlessness, an excited sort of energy.

A few minutes later he crosses the hall and knocks on Alex's door.

"Come in."

James walks in and shuts the door behind him. Alex is lying on his bed, staring up at the ceiling. The lamp on his desk is burning, and his schoolbooks are stacked on top, ready to be used. But Alex isn't studying.

As a force of habit James walks over to the window and looks out at the darkening sky. He sees no activity at Henry's house, nothing to distract him.

"Something's the matter, isn't it?" James says.

"Nothing's wrong," Alex says.

James sits at the foot of Alex's bed. "I know something's wrong. Ever since Monday."

"It's no big deal."

"Then tell me."

"I said it's not a big deal," Alex says. But James can hear the hesitancy in his voice, like he wants to tell James but is barely holding himself back.

"Is it something with Nathen?"

Alex shakes his head. "Let it go, please?"

But James can't let it go. Not this time: "I'm not leaving until you tell me."

Alex laughs at this, sounding both amused and exasperated. James laughs, too, and he feels the wall between them inching down. "I'm serious," he says.

And then Alex, too, gets serious. He sits up and gets off the bed and walks to his backpack. James watches as he rummages in one of the compartments. He finds a folded yellow sheet of paper, then another one. Alex comes back to the bed, lies down again, and then hands over the pieces of paper. "Someone has been leaving these in my locker."

James unfolds the first note, which reads "I know you're a FAG!" The second one says, "You and your boyfriend better watch out!" He looks at Alex, who now has his hands over his eyes, like he's a kid who thinks he can hide from the world that way. "Who the hell left these?" he says.

Alex doesn't say a word.

"And why would . . . why would someone leave these?"

"It's Tyler."

"What?"

Alex opens his eyes and stares up at the ceiling. "Tyler is the one leaving the notes."

"How do you know?" he asks, though he isn't surprised.

"Because I saw him the first day. Well, I saw him watching me open my locker. And then he smiled at me, but in a mean way. Plus, I remember his handwriting. He tried to disguise it, but I can tell it's his."

James is quiet for a second, taking it all in. "Why would he do this?"

"I don't know!" Alex says, raising his voice for the first time.

James studies the notes again, like he is looking for clues. But really, he knows he is just stalling for time. He doesn't know what to say. He doesn't know what to do. "I mean, why would he write this stuff?" James asks again. He feels like he is scraping away at something, getting closer and closer to a discovery.

Alex finally looks at him. "You want to know if it's true, don't you? You want to know if I'm a fag?"

James almost flinches when the word is thrown at him. "Fag." The reality of it seems to be pounding on a shut door. Pounding and pounding, like an insistent salesman. His head feels light.

"And what if it *is* true?" Alex asks, his voice cracking.

Just then they hear their mother shouting at them: "Boys! Your dad's home! Dinner's almost ready!" This is their cue to go down and set the table.

James looks at Alex, who is barely containing himself, breathing heavily, like he has an ache in his chest. Alex's face is flushed, more so than usual—hell, maybe James's is, too. James's mouth is dry and he can't speak, so he stands and leaves and walks downstairs, gripping the banister tightly as he goes.

He walks into the kitchen and grabs some paper napkins and opens the cutlery drawer, all without being told.

"Thanks, sweetie," his mother says.

As he's setting the table, Alex walks in. James had almost expected him to stay in his room, unable to face James and their parents. But here he is, sullen and still flushed. He sits at the table, his usual spot.

Dinner is risotto with chicken and asparagus, something daring for their mother. "I hope it's okay," she says.

"It's delicious," his dad says. He likes everything.

It *is* tasty, and James devours it, rarely lifting his eyes from his plate.

"Alex, honey, you've been so quiet all week," Mom says.

"You okay, big guy?" Dad says.

"I'm fine," he says. He smiles.

"He's just nervous about the meet," James says.

"Yeah," Alex says.

After dinner James helps his mother load the dishwasher. When that job is done, he has only one option left: to go upstairs and talk with Alex. To continue where they left off.

When he knocks, Alex lets him in right away, as if he expected him. They both stand there for a few seconds, and then Alex sits on the bed.

"Before you say anything, I just want to say . . . I want to say that I'm happy. For the first time in a long time," Alex says.

"You are?"

"Yes." He nods and stares off to the wall. "I mean, I'm confused, too. But happy. As happy as I've ever been." Then he looks James in the eye, quickly. They have the same eyes, big and brown, the color of tea, or weak coffee. It's funny, but standing there, James can see so clearly that Alex is just a younger version of himself. Not identical, but close. And yet in many ways, they are strangers to each other.

Still, he knows it's true that Alex has been happier these past few months. And he knows—he can't deny it anymore—that it probably has something to do with Nathen. That maybe Greer was right all along. And Tyler is threatening that happiness. He knows that Nathen is his friend, no matter what, and Alex is his brother. And he can't live in a world where Alex is unhappy again. He couldn't stand this world if Alex were to leave it, as he almost did. And so whatever it is between Alex and Nathen, whatever it is—he doesn't care.

He sits down next to Alex. He puts his arm around him. "I know you're happy. And I'm glad. I mean it." He pats Alex on the shoulder.

"But I'm scared, James. I'm . . ." And with this, Alex starts crying.

Normally, James would pull back from such a display. Tears and crying usually make him cringe. But not now. He knows it's all Alex can do right now. James lets him go on, but not for long. "Hey, hey," he whispers. "Don't be scared."

He hears Alex sniffle and wipe his eyes. "I'm such a baby."

"No, you're not." He pats Alex on the back. "I don't want you to worry. Okay?"

Alex nods, sniffles some more.

"Because I'm not gonna let anything happen to you, okay?"

"But Tyler . . ."

"You leave him to me," James says.

"Okay," Alex says softly.

James releases Alex and stands up. "It's gonna be okay," he says, before leaving abruptly. He walks to his room and locks the door. He lies facedown on his bed and does what he didn't want to do in front of Alex: he sobs. One of those gut-wrenching sobs that seems to drain his body of strength. The pillows muffle his sounds, he hopes. And when it's over, he feels lighter, almost at ease.

Because for a change, he feels like a good brother.

The weather on Saturday clears, just in time for the tennis match with Walker. The night before, James had called Tyler, offering him a ride to the match the next morning.

"That'd be awesome, dude," Tyler had said.

So James picks him up bright and early. On the drive over to the high school courts, he lets Tyler do most of the talking. James will do his talking later, after the match.

"Our first match of the season. I hope we beat the crap out of them," Tyler says.

When they arrive, Coach pairs everyone up for warm-ups. The sun is bright today. The air smells of wet grass and baking bread from the Sunbeam plant across the street. It is a perfect spring day. James hits balls back and forth with Tyler. On the other courts the Walker players, decked out in purple shirts and white shorts, go through their warm-ups. Some of them look like decent players, but some of them have the gawky and ill-formed strokes of beginners.

Eventually, just before the teams assemble and pair off for their singles matches, James sees his mother climb into the set of bleachers on the north side of the courts, socializing already with the other parents, including Tyler's mom and dad, who both wear sunglasses and pastels. James had told her she could go to Anniston with Dad to watch Alex, that he didn't need an audience, but she stayed, like it was her duty as a parent. Alex took off the night before with the team, picked up by Coach Runyon in the clunky white team van.

Today, James's opponent is a tall, lanky guy with a shock of black hair named Jonathan. He is a decent player, with a solid serve and deep groundstrokes. But he makes a lot of errors. James's biggest strength has always been his consistency. His teammates call him a backboard—someone who will hit back almost anything you feed him. It drives people nuts. He also has a strong, hard serve, and today he fires off powerful serve after powerful serve, which Jonathan has trouble returning. James makes quick work of him—6–2, 6–3—without expending too much energy.

Tyler, meanwhile, struggles with a lesser player whose groundstrokes float high in the air before landing deep in the court—a pusher, they call this type of player. The rest of his teammates all win their matches, so it's already a 5–0 rout when Tyler finally pulls out his match. He storms off the court, frustrated that it took him so long.

League regulations require them to go ahead with the doubles matches, even though the match is already clinched. Doubles is much the same story, but it takes James and Tyler the longest to dispatch their opponents, mainly because Tyler is sucking big-time today, spraying his forehand well past the baseline, sinking easy volleys into the net. James has to play shrink on court: "It's okay, Tyler. Calm down. Focus. Just hit your shots."

Eventually, he says, "Okay, just focus on getting the ball back in play. Stop trying to be fancy." He tries to mask the irritation in his voice.

The rest of the team is assembled on the sidelines, clapping and cheering them on along with the scattering of parents and family and friends. In the last game, James serves the match out, hitting two aces and two other well-angled serves. He hasn't played this well in a long time. When they win, Tyler gives him a high five and says, "Thanks for carrying my ass, dude." They shake hands with their opponents and gather their stuff and join the team on the sidelines. The Walker team doesn't waste much time piling into their vans, deflated and defeated and facing an hour's drive home.

"Great match, guys," Coach says. "I see some things that need improvement, but we'll deal with that on Monday. Enjoy the rest of your weekend."

Mom walks over and pats James on the shoulder. "Great playing, sweetie. Wow. You were on fire today," she says.

"Thanks."

Tyler's parents have already jetted off, and he walks up to the two of them. "Hi, Mrs. Donaldson."

"Hello, Tyler," James's mom says without much enthusiasm. "Good playing."

"Thanks," he says.

"Well, I'll see you at home," she says, leaving the two of them there by James's Jeep.

"Man, I played like shit," Tyler says once they are in the Jeep.

"Well, we won at least. That's what matters in the end."

"Amen."

"Hey, you wanna grab some food?" James asks.

"Of course, dude."

"How about Burger King?"

"Fine with me."

So that's where James drives, to the one that isn't far from either of their neighborhoods. After they eat, it will be a quick drive to drop Tyler off, which is what James prefers.

Once they order and have their burgers and fries and sodas and are situated in a booth toward the back, James lets Tyler enjoy himself for a few minutes.

"I better not play like that against Vestavia Hills or Mountain Brook."

"You'll get better," James says. "You were just rusty. You'll get that match toughness back."

"Yeah, you're right."

James takes a few bites of his burger, then some fries, then a sip of his soda. And then he's ready. "So I guess Alex is probably finished with his cross-country meet by now."

"Oh yeah?" Tyler says, shoving some fries in his mouth, looking out the window, anywhere but at James.

"He's gotten really good, really fast."

Tyler sips his drink and nods.

"He's doing better, too," James says.

Again, Tyler busies himself with eating. James had expected Tyler to say something surly, insulting. He didn't expect him to clench up in awkward silence.

"Nathen's been a good friend to him," James says.

"Yeah," Tyler says. "I *bet* he has."

There it is—the tone he was expecting. The knowing, smart-alecky tone. It's just what James needs. "So, listen, Tyler. I know what you're up to."

243

"What?"

"I know you're putting those notes in my brother's locker."

"What?" he says again.

"Don't deny it."

"Deny what?"

James stares at him silently. His dislike for Tyler only intensifies as he sits there, watching him squirm in denial. "He's my brother, Tyler. *My brother.*"

"What's your point, dude? I'm not doing anything. And so what if I was?" Tyler hesitates a moment, sips his soda. "Your brother's a fag. A *fag.* Doesn't that bother you, having a brother like that? A fucking faggot for a brother?" He shakes his head.

"Don't ever talk about him like that again," James says, more calmly than he intends. Because inside he is raging. He wants to reach over and clobber Tyler's face. He wants to punch him the same way he punched Greer a few weeks back. This despite the fact that he has never been a violent person. He got in one fight as a kid, on the playground in fifth grade. Jared Potter was picking on him and James finally got sick of it and pulled his hair and clocked him. But ever since then, he's never needed to get physical. He's never really even wanted to, until lately. Until now.

"Or what?" Tyler says, though not with much confidence.

He wants to say, *Or I'll beat your face in.* But he has a stronger weapon, he thinks. "I'll tell everyone how you were staring at me in the locker room when you were naked. And then everyone will start calling *you* a fag."

Tyler narrows his eyes at him. "Dude, they'd know you were lying," he says, trying to sound calm. But James can hear the panic in his voice.

"But I wouldn't be lying. You did do that, just the other day."

Tyler tries to laugh this off, but his laugh is weak. "Dude, you're nuts, just like your brother."

"Maybe. But I don't care. I just want you to leave Alex alone. Can't you fucking do that, huh? Just leave him alone."

Tyler shrugs and tries to laugh it off. "Whatever."

"I'm serious, Tyler."

"Okay, dude! I get it. Can we leave now?" he stands, his meal unfinished.

"When I finish," James says, calmly picking up his burger again. He feels a rush, like he can do anything he wants. He knows it will fade, and he knows this hasn't solved the world's— or even Alex's—problems. But it's something.

Tyler continues to stand there, like a bratty kid. But James is going to make him wait.

When they finally leave, they are quiet the entire way. As he gets closer to Tyler's house, James says, "You know, Tyler. I don't hate you or anything. We still have to play doubles together. I don't want it to be weird."

"Okay," Tyler says, quietly, sounding flattened and shell-shocked.

"But if you bother Alex anymore, you'll regret it. I swear." He could be in a movie, saying these words. He knows a lot of it is for dramatic effect, but it feels good because, at heart, he means it. And he thinks Tyler knows this.

11

Alex

The course in Anniston is in a hilly park on the outskirts of town. Luckily, the weather is nearly perfect—clear sky, light breeze, temperatures in the sixties. Alex stands with his teammates at the starting line, all of them wearing their gray shorts and red running shirts, their numbers pinned to the fronts of their shirts. He glances over and spots his father on the patch of grass that slopes down from the parking lot. So he did make it, Alex thinks, feeling a twinge of comfort and gratitude. His father spots him and waves like a goofball, holds up his thumb. He's wearing sunglasses and talking with Mr. Blume, Jake's dad, and Coach Runyon. Nearby are other parents from other schools, waiting and watching, shouting last-minute encouragements.

Nathen pats him on the back. "You ready?"

Alex breathes in. "Yep." He smiles.

"Try and stick close to me for the first mile."

"I don't wanna hold you back," Alex says.

"I won't let you." Nathen winks.

"These hills are going to be tough," Jake says. He's bouncing on his toes.

"No, I *love* the hills," Joseph says. He's tall and dark and always smiling, like all of this is just a piece of cake for him. Which, as the best runner on the team, it probably is. "You have to attack them, these hills."

"Runners, take your places," a big muscled guy shouts through a small megaphone.

Again Alex takes a deep breath, and before the big guy blows the whistle for them to go, he hears Pete say, "Good luck, Rookie."

Then they're off, the big herd of them, over a hundred boys running like dogs finally freed from their backyards. And it feels good, running in the jumble of everyone, collectively bound in the task of making it to the finish line. The run is a 5K, just over three miles. Normally that would be easy, but today Alex is a competitor, dodging other runners, negotiating hills, and trying to run as fast as possible without losing steam too early. He manages to stick by Nathen for the first mile, but then Nathen kicks it in and vanishes with the top runners, including Joseph and Jed, rounding a thicket and heading up a steep hill. Alex steals a brief glance behind him and sees plenty of runners. This spurs him on. Soon, he catches Jake and a few other guys from other schools. Jake looks over and smiles, quickly, then turns forward again to focus on the race. When they reach the crest of the hill, they are halfway done and begin circling back. Racing down the hill, he sees Nathen, chugging along, well behind the main pack of leaders, but still way ahead of the middle pack, where Alex still finds himself.

He pushes and pushes, even though it hurts, even though it feels like he's never run this fast in his life. Some runners pass him, but then Alex passes other runners, guys who started out too quickly. As he approaches the finish line—Jake has sped on ahead, but Alex still thinks he's in front of a few of his other teammates—he sees his father clapping his hands, shouting his name, cheering him on from the sidelines.

At the finish line there is a large digital clock set up on a pedestal, and when he passes it, the time reads 17:23. A record time for him, even with the hills. He slows his jog and starts the process of catching his breath, and before he knows it, Nathen has come up behind him. "You did it, Lex!"

Alex is still trying to catch his breath, practicing the cool-down exercises Coach taught them. He wipes his sweaty brow, then smiles. "I can't believe it. It felt awesome," he says.

"We're doing well," Nathen says. "Joseph finished second. And Jed wasn't too far behind him."

The two of them walk to the time-reporting table, and as they do, Pete and Jake and all the others gather around them and congratulate Alex, the Rookie.

After Alex signs the roster to report his unofficial time, he sees Coach Runyon walking toward him with his clipboard. Coach holds out his hand. "Well done, Mr. Donaldson," he says.

"Thanks," Alex says, smiling because the moment feels so damn good. Sure, he didn't finish near the top, but it's not about that for him. And then he sees his dad, walking over with Mr. Blume, holding a bottle of chilled Gatorade.

"Way to go, buddy!" he says, handing him the bottle and pulling him in for a hug, even though Alex is sweaty and gross. Alex fights the urge to break away, fights his embarrassment, because it actually feels good. His dad squeezes him tighter and, finally, Alex gives in and squeezes him back.

When they finally pull apart, Alex guzzles the Gatorade and listens to the chatter all around him. He'd want to collapse on the ground in exhaustion, if he didn't feel so charged. Now he feels like he could run the whole course all over again.

Alex sleeps till noon on Sunday, which is very late for him. But the night before, he was exhausted—from the week of practice, from the cross-country meet itself. He had ridden home with the team in the van that Coach Runyon drove, rather than with his father, because that's what teammates did—stuck together. On the ride back, they were rowdy and stupid and mostly jubilant because they placed second out of twelve schools. Not bad. "Last year we finished fifth," Nathen said. By the time Coach dropped Alex off at home, it was late in the afternoon, and he was totally worn out.

But the practices and the meet and the drive home were not the only things that had exhausted him. There was also the stress of the notes that Tyler had left in his locker. His locker, once again, had become a menacing little corner of the school. This set of worries dragged him down all week, even after his talk with James. He was able to put it out of his mind when he was in

Anniston, competing. But the minute they drove back into Tuscaloosa, a nervous, sinking feeling attached itself to him like a heavy animal.

This morning, lying in his bed, slowly rousing himself, he tries not to let those worries creep back in. After all, hadn't James reassured him? Hadn't he told him not to worry? Not to worry, in particular, about Tyler? Alex wants to believe him. He wants to believe that James can make everything okay. But after months of awkwardness between them, James's offer of protection seems too good to be true. Besides, what can *he* do? Alex wonders. And it's not like Alex can talk to Dr. Richardson about this. There would be too much to explain—stuff he's not *ready* to explain. Not to an adult anyway.

Nathen is flipping out, too. Alex had debated not even telling him about the notes in the first place, but he did. He didn't want to be alone in this.

"Holy shit," Nathen had said as they chatted after school in Nathen's Jeep earlier in the week. Then, after Alex told him he thought it was Tyler, Nathen said, "That little fucker."

"What do we do?" Alex had asked.

"Let me think." What Nathen ultimately decided was that they should play "wait and see," to see if Tyler was just playing some prank, to see if he was trying to smoke them out.

So that is what they had done, even after the second note. And then James came into the picture, which Alex revealed to Nathen on the phone the night before they left for Anniston. He'd worried about Nathen's reaction, but he also didn't want to lie to him.

"You told James about us?" Nathen asked, his usual calm dissolving.

"Not exactly. I mean, not in so many words. I guess I implied it."

"How did he react?"

"Mostly he was mad at Tyler. I don't think he really cares. Or maybe he just doesn't want to acknowledge it yet. Anyway, he's on our side."

"Okay," Nathen says, his voice calming.

"I'm sorry," Alex says.

"Don't be sorry, Lex. You did what you had to do. I'm the one who's sorry. I should kick Tyler's ass."

"Let's just ignore him," Alex said. "Please?"

Nathen had reluctantly agreed, but Alex knows that ignoring Tyler will be hard.

There is a knock at his door. "You awake in there?" Mom asks.

"Yeah, I'm up," he says.

She comes in wearing her gardening attire—white shorts, a hat, and a ratty pink T-shirt. "Dad got doughnuts this morning, but we decided to let you sleep. We saved you a few." She smiles, beaming.

"Thanks," he says. "I'm starving."

"Well, I'm gonna be outside in the garden."

"Okay."

Before she leaves, she says, "Oh, I almost forgot: Henry came by for you earlier. I told him you were still sleeping. Then he came again, around eleven?" She chuckles and says, "He seemed a little agitated that you weren't up yet. He may come by again soon, just so you know." Then she leaves.

Alex climbs out of bed and walks to the window. He lifts a blind and peers out. And sure enough, there is Henry, walking along the curb of his yard, fidgeting and twitching his hands. The beat-up dictionary rests on the walkway, like an old friend.

Henry is still out there after Alex showers and dresses, so he goes outside. He walks across the street, and Henry stares at him without greeting.

"You sure slept a long time," Henry says, sounding put out.

"I was tired from the meet yesterday."

"Did you win?"

"We came in second, which is pretty good. Anyway, Mom says you came by to see me."

Henry walks along the curb, nodding his head. "I did."

He wants to ask, What for? But he figures that might sound rude or mean.

"Mom's inside packing boxes."

"Oh," Alex says. "So you're really moving?"

"I dunno. Maybe, maybe not. Every day she changes her mind."

"Why move now?" Alex asks. "It's April. Can't she wait until the school year ends?" Isn't that what most adults would consider? What most *normal* adults would consider?

Henry stops his curb walking and turns and looks at Alex. Then he looks down at his feet. "She's mad at me."

"Why?"

"Because I asked her something that made her mad."

"What?"

"I asked her if that man was my father."

Alex knows right away that he is talking about Jack Pembroke. What other man could there be? Alex hasn't seen any boyfriends in weeks, maybe months. Still, he plays dumb. "What man?"

"That old man. Mr. Pembroke," Henry says. "He's always over here. They're always whispering and looking at me funny. She thinks I'm stupid. Just because I'm ten, it doesn't mean I'm stupid."

"Maybe he's just a friend." But do grown women have grown men as friends? It doesn't seem likely or possible.

Henry starts to pace again. "I didn't mean to snoop in Mom's desk. I just needed a pencil, because mine broke and I forgot my pencil sharpener at school and I had math to do. And I found this folder under some other papers. It had all these things cut out from the newspaper. Stories about Mr. Pembroke. Even a wedding announcement for Mr. Pembroke's son, from ten years ago."

Alex continues to listen, because he is stunned. Of course, he and James had thought the exact thing. But he can't believe Henry has figured it out. Henry seems older now, not like a kid.

"Then I kept looking at Mr. Pembroke's picture, and he kind of looks like me. I mean, I kind of look like him."

Alex has no idea if this is true, because right now he can't get a good grasp of what Mr. Pembroke looks like, besides the dark gray hair on his balding head and the ruddy face. "So you asked your mom?"

"Yes."

"And what did she say?"

"She got mad and started crying, telling me what she'd always said, that my father was gone." Henry's voice sounds like a kid's again, full of resentment and hurt. "She said I was stupid for asking such a question."

"Henry, I'm sorry. I'm sure she didn't mean it."

"She asked me why I always want to ruin everything," Henry says before he sits down on the curb and grabs his dictionary.

Alex wants to do something for Henry, wants to help him, comfort him. But all he can think to offer is his company. "You can come over to my house," Alex says. "You want to? We can swing and stuff. Watch TV. Look up new words. We have doughnuts."

"I guess so." Henry stares up at him now, his expression a look of blank resignation. But Alex recognizes the sadness underneath it. Sadness about his mother, about whoever his father is. And he knows that Henry doesn't want to go away again. He knows that even though Tuscaloosa isn't the paradise or new start that Henry may have hoped for, he is tired of being unsettled.

Since the day is nice, they end up on the swings in the backyard, after gorging on the remaining doughnuts. Dad is in his workshop off the garage, banging his tools around. James is in his room, with the stereo blasting, doing who knows what; they haven't really chatted since he got back from Anniston—not about Nathen, not about Tyler.

Mom, meanwhile, is still in the garden at the back of the yard, and when she spots them she waves.

"Your mom is nice," Henry says.

"Yeah, she is," Alex says. "But sometimes she can get in bad moods and stuff. Everyone does."

They swing for a bit, the spring air rushing and retracting against their faces. It feels good to float like this, his legs sticking out.

"I always had a picture of my father in my head," Henry says. "I never told my mom that. But I thought about him, about what he looked like and stuff. He was tall and had blond hair, and brown eyes, just like mine. He was real handsome and a good athlete, and he'd show me how to play sports and stuff. I mean, I don't really like sports. I'm no good at them. But I thought if my father could show me how, then I'd be good."

"You could still be good at sports," Alex says. "I just started running. And you're a lot younger than I am."

Henry doesn't respond to this, he just keeps on talking: "Sometimes I'd fall asleep thinking that when I woke up, he'd be there. Back from wherever he was. Maybe even back from the dead. . . . I know that's stupid."

"No, it's not."

"And then Mom would be happy again, all the time."

Alex nods. But he wants to tell Henry that no one can be happy all the time. That being happy all the time might even be boring.

"I can't believe my dad is Mr. Pembroke."

"Well, he might not be. But even if he is . . ." Alex stops because he doesn't know what to say.

That's when they hear Henry's mother calling his name. "Henry! Henry?"

Henry looks at him. "I should make her think I ran away."

Alex doesn't disagree with this, but he can see his own mother looking over at them, as if making sure they heard, too.

"That would really show her," Henry says. And for the first time that day he smiles. But instead of hiding or sitting still, Henry hops off the swing, picks up his dictionary in the grass, and starts walking toward the gate, slowly but with purpose. "I'll see you later, Alex," he says.

Mom orders pizza for dinner, and they sit in the den eating and watching TV. A Sunday-night movie is on, something hokey that Mom picked out. When a commercial comes on, Alex says, "You know, Henry told me his mom is making them move again."

Mom is sitting on the other end of the couch, a magazine folded on her lap. She is filing her nails—even during idle time, she is always doing multiple things. "Yeah, Laura mentioned that to me. She said she may have a good job offer in Charlotte."

"I bet that's a lie," he says, feeling bold and angry.

James, who's plopped on the other end of the couch, turns and looks at him with raised eyebrows.

"What makes you say that?" Mom says, stopping her filing.

"Well, I think she's leaving because Henry's starting to figure out who his father is."

Dad, who has been reading the paper in his chair, folds it down and looks over at his mother, then at him.

"And who might that be?" Mom asks.

"Don't you know?"

"No, I don't. It's none of our business," she says.

"Yeah right," Alex says. Because in this town, everything is everyone's business, whether you like it or not.

"Your mother's right, Alex. It's none of our business," Dad says, then lifts his paper again.

Alex wonders how much his parents truly know. Would Henry's mother have confided in them, or have they only heard through gossip?

"Well, I think it's shitty," Alex says.

"Alex," his Dad says, "watch your language."

"But it's true. Moving Henry near the end of the school year? Never staying put? Did you know that she told Henry his dad is dead? And we all know that's not true."

The movie comes back on, and they all stare at the TV for a moment.

"I agree with Alex," James finally says, nodding at him. "I feel sorry for that kid."

"Boys, I know Henry's your friend," Mom says. "But it really is none of our business."

Alex knows she's about to make some grand speech about how the world isn't fair, and so on and so on, so he gets up and storms up the stairs. He slams his door so hard that some of the pictures on his wall rattle.

A few minutes later someone knocks. Alex doesn't say anything, and after a bit of silence on both sides of the door, James creeps in.

"What brought all that on?" he asks.

"Henry told me that he thinks Mr. Pembroke is his father," Alex says.

"Really? Just like we thought?" James sits down at Alex's desk chair, turning it to face Alex, who sits on the bed.

"Yeah. He's a smart kid." Alex tells him about the folder, the clippings, and everything else.

"That's fucked up," he says.

"So, should we do something?"

"Like what?"

"I don't know. Something." He feels a sudden helplessness, but also a sort of rage. He'd love to do something rash. Maybe storm into Mrs. Burns's house and demand the truth from her. He might even smash a glass or lamp in the process. Or go to Mr. Pembroke's house—his mansion, really—and throw eggs at his window.

"Why would she move here and then move away again?" James asks.

"I don't know. None of it makes sense."

"Maybe he isn't Henry's father, not really."

"Maybe."

The thought gives him a glimmer of hope. Alex thinks about Henry's imagined father, the blond man with brown eyes. He thinks how great it would be if that were true, if such a man existed. What if he magically appeared one day to rescue Henry?

But he can't picture it. All Alex can picture is Mr. Pembroke and his grumpy face and disapproving stare. He wishes James had the answer, but he just sits there.

"Anyway," Alex says.

When James stands to go, Alex says, "So, um. You talked with Tyler."

James pauses and nods. "Yeah, I did."

"Okay."

Alex has so many questions. He wants to know what James said, what he did—but he also thinks it might be better to remain in the dark. He feels a sense of relief bathe over him, and that's enough for now.

"He won't bother you anymore."

"Thanks," Alex says.

James offers a sheepish smile and leaves the room.

On Monday morning, Alex wakes up feeling rested. But he dreads the week ahead—on Saturday, he has to take the SAT. Four hours of analogies and twisted logic and math problems and tricky multiple-choice questions. Four hours of sitting in a dead-silent room, sitting at uncomfortable desks with other high schoolers, their future academic lives hanging in the balance. James has always been good at these tests, but not Alex. He always thinks that the questions could have two or three possible answers, and so a lot of the time he feels like every oval he fills in is a big fat guess.

At his locker that morning he opens the door with only a slight feeling of nervousness in his gut. He doesn't see a note, and so he breathes easily.

During lunch with Pete and Jake, all they do is talk obsessively about the meet.

"I thought you were going to pass me," Jake says to Alex. "I couldn't let that happen, man." He smiles and sips his orange juice.

"My time sucked," Pete says, even though he beat both Alex and Jake. "Those motherfucking hills."

As they continue to talk, Alex glances around the room, cautiously, as if he's just taking in the scene and not trying to find Tyler in the crowd. When he does find Tyler, at his usual table, he looks the same. He is talking and cutting up, smiling his cocky grin, like an unchanged man. But what did Alex expect? The next time Alex steals a glance, Tyler is looking right at him. Alex holds the stare, but Tyler quickly looks away.

"Hopefully Coach will take it easy on us today," Jake says, just before the bell rings.

But no such luck: Cross-country practice continues full force all week long, even though there is no meet this weekend. Afterward Alex heads straight home (and of course, to therapy on Wednesday), shuts his door, and studies for the SAT, neglecting his regular homework, which manages to pile up.

Nathen calls him each night. "You sure you don't want help?"

"No. I'm cool."

"Okay," he says, sounding both disappointed and amused. Neither of them mention Tyler, as if not talking about him can keep the situation at bay.

Every evening when he gets home, Alex checks to see if Henry is outside. He doesn't forget about him, not completely. But the SAT doesn't allow much extra room in his brain. Besides, whenever he looks out there, he doesn't see Henry. Maybe no news is good news. Maybe silence is a good thing.

On Friday afternoon, Coach gives them the afternoon off. Alex is mentally and physically worn out, so he heads home to rest and empty his brain out before the big day. Plus, he wants to get a good night's sleep. He has to be at Comer Hall on the university campus, where the test will be administered, by eight the next morning.

During dinner—again gathered around the TV, with pasta and buttery French bread and a salad—the phone rings.

"I'll get it," Mom says, since she's closest to the kitchen.

Alex, James, and Dad continue to watch the TV—a wildlife documentary on PBS about gorillas. Mom said it was gross to watch gorillas while eating, but she seemed as interested as the rest of them.

"Alex?" she says a few seconds later, standing in the kitchen doorway with the phone cord stretched. "Have you seen Henry today?"

He shakes his head. "I haven't seen him all week. Not since Sunday."

"Alex says he hasn't seen him," she says into the phone, her eyes still focused on Alex. She listens for a few seconds. "Well, have you tried any other neighbors? . . . Uh-huh. Okay. . . . What about friends' houses? . . . Hmmm. Well, I'm sure he'll turn up any second." Mom pulls back into the kitchen and continues the conversation. On-screen, one of the gorillas is on his haunches, scratching herself while eating a big leaf.

A few minutes later Mom comes back to the den. "That was Laura Burns. She says Henry is missing. Well, she says he wasn't there when she got home today, around four. And he hasn't shown up yet." It is a little after seven o'clock now. "You swear you haven't seen him?"

"No," Alex says.

"Me neither," James says.

"Maybe he's at a friend's house and just forgot to tell his mother," she says, trying to sound reassured.

But Alex can see the worry on her face. And so he starts to worry a little, too. Where could Henry be? It's not like he can drive away in a car. And Alex doubts he is at a friend's house. Henry never talked about any friends, for one thing.

"I told Laura to call me when he turns up," Mom says, sitting down again to her meal.

Both he and James clean their plates and then head upstairs.

"Where do you think Henry is?" James says.

"I don't know. But I'm sure he'll be home soon," Alex says, though he's not sure if his optimism is merited.

James nods and goes into his room. Alex shuts his own door and crashes on the bed. He tries to close his eyes, but he can't stop thinking about all the information crammed in his head for the SAT. And he has a nervous feeling about Henry.

When the phone rings again a half hour later, he sits up and leaves his room and stands at the top of the stairs, listening. He can hear his mother talking, but he can't make out what she is saying over the TV. So Alex makes his way downstairs, reaching the kitchen just as Mom hangs up the phone.

"Was that Mrs. Burns?" he says.

"Yes. She says there's still no sign of Henry." She glances at her watch. "I'm going over there to keep her company. She's a nervous wreck, understandably."

Dad walks in. "Everything okay?"

"No, he's still missing."

Dad looks pensive, but not worried. "I guess the police can't do anything."

"She spoke to the police already."

"The police?" James asks, suddenly appearing from upstairs to join the fray. He trades somber glances with Alex.

"I'm sure he's fine," she says. "He'll turn up."

Alex thinks back to Sunday afternoon, when Henry said something about running away. He figured it was a joke of sorts. He thinks about telling his parents, but Mom is out the door and halfway down the front walk before he has a chance. From the foyer, Dad yells to her, "Call us if you hear anything, if we need to do anything."

When Alex was little, he ran away twice, but only for a few hours. One time he hid in the woods behind his house, in a ditch, but he got hot and sweaty and swarmed by mosquitoes and came home. The other time he simply hid behind a chair in the living room. His parents must have known he was there, sulking about something, because they pretended to call the police and then Alex rushed out of hiding, feeling both guilty and vindicated. He can't remember the reasons he ran away. They were probably silly, childish. But Alex knows that if Henry ran away, his reasons are anything but silly.

"I'm going over there, too," Alex says, and his dad just nods his approval.

"I'll come with you," James says.

On the short walk across the street, they are both silent. They don't bother to knock, since their mother just let herself in. Inside, the front living room is messy. Cardboard boxes are stacked here and there, and the heavy furniture is covered with folded and unfolded clothes, bags, and a few suitcases. The house came furnished, he knew from his mom, who was there the day Mrs.

Burns and Henry drove up with just a bunch of boxes and suit-cases, nothing else. The furniture is grand and bulky, but looks odd and out of place because of the disarray that surrounds it. He hears his mother and Mrs. Burns in the kitchen. He and James walk in there and find them sitting at a round kitchen table. There is an open bottle of wine, next to an empty wine-glass.

"Oh, hi, boys," Mrs. Burns says, forcing a smile. Her face is puffy and red, from worrying or crying or drinking, maybe all three. But she is still pretty, and Alex's anger at her softens in per-son. She has the face of someone sweet, if a little ditzy and needy. "Where could he be?" she says to them.

"Do you have any ideas, honey?" his mother says to Alex. He stands and leans against the counter and shrugs.

Then, looking at James, she asks, "Did you see him?"

"No," James says, sounding disappointed he can't offer up a miracle solution.

"He was upset with me," Laura says, to no one in particular. "But I had no idea he would . . ."

"He doesn't want to move," Alex says.

Laura looks at him, and then she nods. She forces a smile and then sniffles and wipes at her tears. "I know," she says. "I don't want to move, either."

"Then why do it?"

"Alex," his mother says, warning him.

She sniffles again. "It's for the best, believe me."

"Of course it is," his mother says in a reassuring tone, clasp-ing Laura's hands.

"Maybe for you," Alex says.

"But not for Henry," James says.

"Boys!"

"No, it's okay," Laura says.

Alex feels emboldened, especially with James standing next to him. "He thinks that Mr. Pembroke is his father."

"I know," she says softly.

"Alex, honey," Mom says, sounding scolding and exhausted.

"It's okay," Laura says.

"Is he?" James asks. "His father?"

"No," she says. She looks at Alex, then at James. "He's his grandfather."

Alex exhales some air, and he can hear his mother do the same. James just stands there, blank-faced.

"His father is Jack's son," Laura says. "Danny Pembroke. We met in college in Virginia. Well, I had dropped out of the small school I was going to. I wasn't doing that well and it was hard to make ends meet because I was paying my own way. Danny was in the law school at UVA, and he came into the restaurant where I waited tables. There was a bar there, too, where a lot of the law students came after a long week. And when I'd finish my shift, Danny would be there. He flirted with me, bought me drinks. He was a real charmer. And sweet, believe it or not." She sounds peaceful, nostalgic, like she is relating a fond memory of childhood.

"Well, I was just a college-dropout waitress, so I should have known better. Danny was a rich boy, I knew. Way out of my league. But I still fell for him. Turns out he was already engaged. To his current wife. She was an undergrad at Alabama, a high school sweetheart. But I didn't find out about her until I was pregnant.

"It was an accident, even if Danny didn't believe me." She pauses, and Alex thinks she may start crying, but she doesn't. "We had a fight. It was awful. I kept thinking it was all a bad joke. Or a bad dream. And I'd wake up and not be pregnant and could start over. Well, anyway. Danny told me he'd help me take care of it. Those were his words—*'take care of it.'* At first I thought, *No way.* But then I realized how hard it would be, you know, having the baby, with Danny already engaged. I certainly knew he wasn't going to marry *me.* An impossible situation.

"He gave me the money. I found out later that Jack gave it to him. And I made an appointment and got the required counseling. I even went so far as to drive to the clinic and sit in the waiting room. Danny had offered to come with me, but I could tell he was relieved when I said I wanted to go alone. So there I was. And, I don't know. I realized I couldn't do it. I just couldn't."

She starts to cry now—not sobbing, but a gentle release of tears. Mom scoots closer to her and embraces her. "It's okay," she says. "It's okay."

Alex remains frozen at the counter, trying to take in this new information. He has a hard time attaching it to Henry. He looks over at James, who is narrowing his eyes at Mrs. Burns, as if he can't grasp what she's telling them, either.

Laura finally pulls away and says she is fine. She wipes her eyes with her fingers and laughs a little, as if she had been crying about something trivial. "Goodness," she says. Mom grabs her a Kleenex to blow her nose. Then she resumes the story, about how she went home and told Danny she'd done it, and he said he was sorry and that he'd see her around.

"As far as he knew, it was all over," she says.

"Oh, Laura, I'm so sorry."

She nods. "I decided right then that I had to leave. Had to get away from there—away from Danny and the restaurant, away from my family even, who'd never accept me being pregnant out of wedlock."

Out of wedlock. The phrase sounds so old-fashioned to Alex, so ridiculous.

"So I packed up my car and headed for Nashville. I had the money that Danny had given me. I didn't feel bad about using it to get away." She tells them about the friend she moved in with, who was waitressing and trying to be a country singer. The whole story, to Alex, almost seems like a country song, full of heartache and bad luck, dramatic gestures.

"I waited tables, too, almost up until Henry was born."

"You were all alone," his mother says.

"Mostly. All through the pregnancy I thought about calling Danny, telling him the truth. I even almost called my parents. But I didn't. Each month I was more determined than ever. I was gonna make it on my own." She laughs now and smiles. "I was young and stupid and hardheaded."

She goes on talking, and they all listen with rapt attention. Eventually, she says that she met a man when Henry was two years old, and then moved with him to Atlanta. That lasted about a year, then it was over and she was desperate.

"I had a three-year-old to feed. Bills to pay. So I did something crazy," she says. "I called Jack Pembroke." She says she found his number in a phone book at the public library. She knew Danny was married now, had set up a practice in Richmond, and even had a daughter. "I didn't want to disrupt his life.

So I called Jack. I'm ashamed to admit it, but I knew he was rich, and I needed money."

"You did what you had to do," Alex's mother says.

"I told him everything. And he surprised me. He asked me how much I needed. He asked me my address, my phone number. He told me he wouldn't tell Danny. He agreed that it was best not to."

She looks over at Alex, then bows her head. "I knew one day I'd have to tell Henry the truth. But I kept putting it off. And as more time went by, it got harder. Jack kept sending money every month. We talked on the phone sometimes. I guess we became close. Friends. And he got it in his head that I should move here. He had a job for me. A house. I thought maybe he'd want to meet Henry. His grandson." She stops here and exhales, as if she's just run up some stairs. "So we came here. But Jack and I both got scared about telling Henry. We were afraid he might look Danny up, cause some trouble."

Alex wonders if Henry would do such a thing. Yes, he thinks. Probably. But isn't that his right? He stares at Laura with a stoic expression. She may have had it rough, but it also seems like she has made one bad decision after another. Alex wonders what his mother thinks of all this. She sits there, holding Laura's hand, looking sympathetic, but is she silently judging her?

"Jack finally told Danny about Henry. About me and Henry," Laura says. "This was in October."

"How did he take it?" Mom asks.

"He flipped out, of course. Well, at first he did. He's a big deal in Richmond now. A big-time lawyer. May even run for office. So, you can imagine."

"It must have been quite a shock."

"It was. But after the shock wore off, he cooled down. He still doesn't want Henry to know. He's not ready for all that. But over Christmas, he came by. I guess curiosity got the better of him."

"So he met Henry?" Alex asks, recalling the mystery man who had parked outside of their house in December. The man with reddish hair. Alex looks at James, who must be thinking the same thing, because he stares back and nods.

"Well, no, he didn't meet him. But he saw him from afar." Laura looks at her watch. "God, it's almost nine-thirty." She looks out the back window, as if Henry might magically appear.

That's when they all hear the car, a noisy engine that shuts off right out front. Laura dashes out of her seat. Alex, James, and their mother follow her to the front door. When Laura opens it, there is Jack Pembroke standing next to Henry.

Laura kneels down to Henry and pulls him close to her. She starts crying, not saying anything, hugging Henry close, like she never wants to let go again. And Henry sets his head on her shoulder and closes his eyes.

Jack Pembroke just stands there, looking down at the two of them. Not smiling, exactly, but with a warm, peaceful expression.

"We should go, boys," Mom says, and so they all ease out the door to let them work things out on their own.

Inside the house, Dad says, "Is everything okay?"

"Yeah," she says. "I'll tell you about it in the den." She eyes both of them, motioning for them to leave the adults alone.

Without protest, Alex and James head upstairs, walking together to Alex's room.

"Wow," James says, standing there.

"I know." Alex plops down on his bed. James sits down with him.

"I wonder if they're telling Henry the truth," James says.

"I hope so," Alex says. He feels relieved for Henry, but also sad. Because the mystery is over. Henry's real dad is suddenly in his life, and that imagined father, the man Henry has dreamed about, has been swept away for good.

The next day, Alex rises early, feeling groggy and famished. Mom has sliced strawberries for him and made him biscuits and bacon, all of which he devours. No one else is up this early, just the two of them.

"You okay?" she asks, sitting at the table with him.

He nods. "I just want the SAT to be over with."

Neither of them talks about the night before, but he feels the topic floating out there between them.

After breakfast Alex drives himself to the campus and finds parking, miraculously, not far from Comer Hall, along the quadrangle. He has his driver's license for ID, his No. 2 pencils. He is ready, as ready as he'll ever be.

He recognizes a number of kids from his class as they all mill about in the lobby and hallways before the test starts. Everyone looks shy and tense. Then he sees Jake and Pete, sauntering down the hallway toward him.

"Hey, Rookie," Pete says, slapping his hand, which Jake does, too.

"Hey, we'll probably be in the same room because they divide us alphabetically," Jake says. "We should sit by each other."

"Sounds cool," Alex says.

"Just don't cheat off him," Pete says, "unless you want to get, like, an 870."

Alex laughs and then sees Tyler down the hall. Tyler looks toward them, but then looks away quickly, staring at some bulletin board.

"Hey, we should go get pizza after this," Jake says. "You wanna?"

"Sure," Alex says, still staring at Tyler, almost daring him to look his way. And then all the classroom doors open. The test proctors stand in the doorways, motioning them all in.

"Here we go," Pete says. "Let the games begin."

Alex sits at his desk, closes his eyes, and breathes deeply. Once the test is set down in front of him—its thickness makes a slapping sound on the desktop—he is ready. He bubbles in his name and other personal information and then listens to the proctor—a middle-aged lady wearing a jarringly bright pink sweater—read out the instructions. The test begins and he answers all of the questions, in all sections. He thinks he does okay. Good enough, probably. And he can always take it again in September, if he has to.

He and Jake and Pete gather out front after they have been dismissed, going over certain questions, comparing answers, feeling relieved when they concur, groaning or questioning themselves when they don't.

"Okay, let's head to Mr. Gatti's," Pete says. "That all-you-can-eat buffet is calling my name."

Pete and Jake head to their cars in the opposite direction. Alex cuts diagonally through the quad, where undergrads are tossing Frisbees or lying on blankets soaking up the rays. Dog owners are tossing tennis balls for their pets to chase.

Alex hears someone walking in the grass behind him, and he turns and sees that it is Tyler.

"How did you do on the test?" Tyler asks, coming up beside him.

"Okay, I guess," Alex says, his heartbeat quickening.

"Yeah, me too, though verbal is a bitch. What the fuck does *froward* mean anyway?"

"I said it meant, like, stubborn."

"Damn. I missed that one."

"I may be wrong," he says, though he is pretty sure he isn't.

They continue to walk side by side, but Alex doesn't know what to say to him. Tyler is all of a sudden acting like they are still friends, comrades who have just survived a battle.

"You wanna go to Subway?" Tyler asks.

Alex can barely believe his ears. He almost stops in his tracks, because he is so taken aback, but he keeps going, Tyler keeping up with him the whole way. "I can't. I'm meeting Jake and Pete for pizza," he says. He fights to suppress a smile, because it feels good to tell him he already has plans, like it is some sort of small victory.

"Oh. Okay."

And then Alex is at his car. A safe haven.

Tyler stares at him a moment, and Alex can tell he is about to say something, or that he wants to say something. "Um . . . Okay, well, I guess I'll see you at school."

"Okay," Alex says.

Tyler nods and walks away.

Alex sits in his car, feeling baffled and relieved. But he also feels regret. He should have said something to Tyler. He should have told him to go fuck himself. He should have asked him where he was in August and ever since. Where was he when he needed a friend? Why did he leave those notes? What is his deal?

Now Alex doesn't need or want his apologies, his explanations. Alex starts laughing to himself. Someone looking in the car might think he is crazy, but he doesn't care. And that's just it: he didn't say anything to Tyler because he doesn't care about him or the other people who still shun him, who probably talk behind his back, who think he's a loser, a nutcase, maybe even a fag. They have no power over him anymore. He feels like he is encased in protective armor. And even if this feeling is temporary— and he knows it will be—it feels good, because he has never, ever felt this way before.

Later, after lunch with Pete and Jake, Alex drives home. He feels stuffed from all the pizza, but otherwise he feels as light as a single sheet of scratch paper. When he pulls up, he sees that Mrs. Burns's car isn't in the driveway, and neither is Jack Pembroke's Mercedes. No sign of Henry.

Inside, Mom and Dad grill him about the test.

"I think I did decently," he says, setting his bag down in the kitchen. "Better on the verbal probably."

"How soon will you know your scores?" Dad asks.

"I think in a month or so."

"I'm sure they'll be great," Mom says.

"Did you see Mrs. Burns today?" Alex asks.

"No, I haven't seen her, actually. I thought I'd give her some breathing room," Mom says.

"Yeah, I guess that's a good idea." He heads up to his room to take a much-needed nap. He's about to pull his blinds shut when he sees Henry outside, sitting on his front steps. His nap will have to wait.

He passes James's door on his way out, so he knocks. When James opens the door, he looks rumpled, wearing shorts and a wrinkled T-shirt, his hair messy, like he hasn't showered yet. "I'm going to chat with Henry," Alex says. "You wanna come?"

"Sure," he says, rubbing his eyes.

Henry waves gently when he sees them coming. "Hi, James and Alex," he says with his usual mirthful voice.

"How are you doing?" Alex asks, sitting down next to him.

"I'm fine."

"You sure?" Alex asks.

"I'm sure."

"You want to talk about it?" Alex says.

"Yeah, you can talk to us," James offers.

"I'm kind of sick of talking," Henry says.

James laughs. "Tell me about it."

A light breeze picks up and musses James's already ruffled hair. A few neighbors drive by slowly. "So what happens now?" Alex says.

"Mom says we're moving to Charlotte."

"That's too bad," James says.

"No, it's okay," Henry says. "We're not leaving till school is out."

"Why Charlotte?" Alex asks.

"Mr. Pembroke found mom a job there. At a bank. Plus, we'll be closer to Virginia."

"Oh," Alex says. "Closer to your dad?"

Henry nods. "Yeah." His red hair glimmers in the sunlight.

"That's good," James says. "Right?"

"Yeah. Mom says he wants to meet me." Henry shrugs and picks a scab at his knee.

"Of course he does," James says.

Alex smiles up at James, and James smiles back.

"It's funny," Henry says, still staring down, now scratching his leg.

"What is?" Alex asks.

"I have a dad. I feel different now."

"Yeah," James says. "Of course you feel different. It's kind of like you woke up to a new life or something."

"Yeah," Henry says, looking up finally, nodding and smiling. "Do you think he'll like me?"

He and James trade glances. How could either of them know? Maybe his dad is a big fat jerk. Maybe he will think Henry is odd. But before Alex can reply, James says, with his usual assurance, "Of course he will."

"Yeah," Alex says. "He's going to love you."

After school and practice on Wednesday, Alex drives to his appointment with Dr. Richardson. For months, these once-a-week sessions have been—to Alex, at least—nothing more than dutiful appearances. He goes because his parents want him to, and all he really talks about is school and how he feels fine or okay. He suspects even Dr. Richardson knows that Alex is just going through the motions. But today he feels a nervous twitch of excitement, even a sense of worthwhile purpose.

"Alex. Right on time as usual," Dr. Richardson says when he opens the front door.

Alex steps inside the foyer, and then off to the side, to his office. He sits on the lumpy couch.

Dr. Richardson sits on the love seat to his right, his pad of paper resting on his knee. "So, how's your week been?"

"It's been good." He tells him about cross-country, about his teammates. He talks about the SAT and how he thinks he did pretty good. He tells him a little about Henry. "I mean, I'll be sad to see him go. But this will be good for him, so he can finally meet his father." Dr. Richardson nods and smiles. Then they both sit there, quiet for a moment.

"Is there something else, Alex?"

"Not really." He looks over at the bookshelves, filled with heavy psychological tomes and rows of paperbound journals of various hues. "What we talk about? It stays between us, right?"

"Yes, it does, Alex. Just between us. I've told you that."

"Good," Alex says.

"Is everything okay?"

Alex clears his throat. "Yeah. I've never felt happier."

Dr. Richardson nods. "I can tell." He pauses, then asks, "Why do you feel happier? Can you talk about it?"

Alex can feel the butterflies in his belly, like they are fluttering around, desperate for escape. Finally he says, "I have a new friend."

"That's good."

"He's been my friend for a while now," Alex continues. "I guess you could say he's more than a friend."

"Okay," Dr. Richardson says.

There is no going back now, Alex realizes, but it's okay. He feels like he is getting lighter and lighter. He smiles, then says, "His name is Nathen."

12

James

Graduation takes place at the end of May, when the heat of summer is sneaking in, day by day, before it takes over completely. The ceremony is held on a Friday night in Coleman Coliseum on the university campus, where Alabama plays its basketball games. A fraction of the seats are filled with rowdy and proud family members and friends of Central High graduates.

James has no idea where his parents and brother are up in that crowd. But he knows they are probably there already, on time—Dad with his camera, of course, and Mom with her tissues. Right now James and the other seniors are milling about on the coliseum basketball court, which has been covered with a red carpet for this occasion. Rows of folding chairs, with an aisle down the middle, face the stage that has been erected. Everyone is wearing the red caps and gowns—a shimmery red, like something a superhero might use for his cape. Most of the boys wear shirts and ties and slacks underneath, while the girls wear dresses.

James manages to find Nathen in the gathering throng, and the two hug each other with exaggerated force. Things between them, surprisingly enough to James, haven't been weird. Sure, there is that underlying secret about him and Alex, but as each day goes by, James cares less and less. Maybe it should bother him, but it doesn't. Nathen is still the same Nathen—laid back, cocky, fun, and kind. And Alex is still Alex, but better. He seems happier, more confident.

"So the big night has arrived," Nathen says.

"Yep. At last."

"Man, this year flew by," Nathen says.

Normally James would agree, but the year has also felt slow at times, like it would never come to a close. Still, the past two months did speed along, a whir of school days and weekends packed with tennis matches (the team got third at State this year), parties, homework, papers, the prom (he took Clare, "as friends"), and final exams.

Preston soon finds them in the crowd and slaps them both on the back in greeting. His bushy hair pokes out from under his cap, which looks like it might fall off at any second. "Don't we look like assholes in these things?" he says.

"Hey, I thought they flunked you," Nathen jokes.

Greer approaches and mockingly hugs all three of them, fake-crying and saying, "Boo hoo hoo. These were the best years of our lives! I can't go on!"

And even though for weeks, months even, James has felt a

growing distance between him and Preston and Greer—actually, between him and the entire school—he feels a tinge of sadness right now. They all look like an army of dorks clad in red, with their pointy caps like helmets perched precariously on their heads. James is happy to be with them.

He looks around for Clare, and for Alice, but they are lost in the crowd. Alice still has to finish some classes in summer school, but she's allowed to march in the ceremony this evening.

"Am I still picking you up later for the party?" Nathen asks James.

"Yeah, man." The unofficial blowout graduation party is later that night, this time at Hank Plott's house. James is sick of parties, but this one will be bearable. It's the last one of his entire high school existence, after all. He can't very well skip it.

Soon they hear Mrs. Lackey—the physics teacher and one of the faculty members in charge of organizing the graduation ceremony—shouting at everyone to take their seats. They all have a numbered chair assigned to them, alphabetically ordered. James finds himself sitting in the third row, between Kim Donald, a majorette, and Jeff Donnelly, a freckled, pudgy guy who James has barely said two words to. But now all three of them chitchat like they are best friends, until Principal Willis marches onstage to get things rolling. Some other faculty members are sitting up there on the stage, dressed in suits and dresses, and the two covaledictorians—Cliff Wetzel and Valerie Towson—are given their prized seats, though neither will give a speech. James is pretty proud that one of the valedictorians is going to Duke, too, even though he hardly knows Valerie. Maybe that will change now. James himself is one of twelve salutatorians—the consolation prize—but none of them gets any special placement tonight.

As Principal Willis starts yammering on about how proud he is of them and how they have great futures ahead, James thinks about next year. Next year at this time, he'll have finished his first year at Duke. Next year Alex will be the one graduating, the one on his way to college. A year is a long time—it seems impossibly far away. And to think, Alex could have altered everything. This year, next year, all the years to follow—all would be unimaginably different because of one irrational moment. James shudders inside, realizing like never before how lucky they are—how lucky he is—to have avoided such a calamity.

Snap out of it, he thinks. *You're at your graduation. Everything is fine now.* And James can see it clear as day: Next year Alex will be sitting here, in one of these uncomfortable chairs, wearing one of these ridiculous red gowns. He sighs, as if releasing a bubble of air that has been trapped inside him.

Before he knows it Principal Willis is calling every student to the stage to receive the diplomas, name by name. There are more than five hundred seniors, but Principal Willis moves the list along at a decent clip. Each time a name is called, people in the crowd cheer and hoot and holler. He watches Clare, one of the first on the stage, march to receive her diploma, walking gracefully. James lets out a holler of appreciation.

Soon Mrs. Lackey motions for his row to stand. Then they march single file to the stage. The line moves forward and eventually he climbs the steps. He sees Clare back in the first row, sitting now with her diploma encased in its red faux-leather pouch, and she winks at him.

"James Donaldson, salutatorian, graduating with honors," Willis announces into the microphone. It seems insanely loud, but James walks and grabs his diploma. And he is so eager to get off the stage without disaster that he barely hears the applause and the hoots from his friends and the cheers from his family, somewhere up there.

After the ceremony, in the twilight outside the coliseum, Dad makes them pose for countless photos—James and Alex, James and Mom, James and Nathen, James and Nathen and Preston and Greer, James and Clare, the whole family together. Afterward the family has dinner together at Cypress Inn, on the river. Just the four of them.

The restaurant is paneled with blond wood, the tables set with stiff white cloths. Their table overlooks the Black Warrior River, which shimmers peacefully in the moonlight, a contrast to the busyness and hectic activity around them.

"Well, how does it feel, Mr. Graduate?" Dad says, putting down his menu.

"It feels pretty good," James says.

"Free at last," Alex says.

"This will be you next year," James says.

Alex nods and looks down, as if embarrassed.

"So where is this party you're going to later?" Mom asks.

"Hank Plott's house," he says.

"And Nate is picking you up?"

"Yeah."

"Good," Mom says. "He looked so handsome tonight."

James looks at Alex, who is focusing intently on his menu. Even in the dim light of the restaurant, James thinks he can detect a blush.

They spend the rest of dinner talking about summer plans. James will be a runner at a law firm, which basically means he will be an errand boy, a messenger. He may want to be a lawyer one day—he's not sure—so it can't hurt to work in such an office. Alex will take a few classes at the university and mow some yards here and there. He'll also be running and training with his friends Pete and Jake, and maybe Nathen, before Nathen leaves for NYU. They'll also go to Gulf Shores a few times for vacation. Nathen is coming along for the second trip, in July.

"Well," Dad says, "I want to make a toast."

James and Alex smile at each other, because they're just drinking Cokes.

Mom holds up her glass of wine. James can tell that she is flush with emotion, dewy-eyed.

"To my two sons," Dad says, clinking his glass against their mother's.

Alex and James hold up their sweaty glasses. "To us," James says, looking right at Alex as their glasses clink.

At Clare's pool party the next day, the sky is cloudless and the sun is strong. They wear shades and glob on sunblock and keep cool by jumping into the pool, where the water is almost icy cold at first. It is a small gathering—James, Clare, Alex, Suzy, Nathen, and Alice—meant to celebrate the end of school and the beginning of summer. It is also, unofficially, a celebration of their future lives, which will take most of them away from Tuscaloosa. In the fall, Clare is heading to Davidson, a small liberal arts school in North Carolina, not far from Duke, actually. Nathen will be in New York, where he wants to study film. Suzy, meanwhile, is going to the University of Texas. James isn't sure of Alice's plans, but he expects she'll be staying in town, just like Alex.

James is holding on to the side in the deep end of the pool. Nathen is on the diving board, continuing his run of daredevil dives and flips, making the water explode over the edge of the pool. Suzy is floating on her back on a raft in the shallow end, her eyes closed, her heavily lotioned body shining like a new coin.

Alex and Alice are reclining and talking on two of the plastic reclining lounge chairs. Alex is smiling, looking at ease. And Alice is, too. He hears her laughing—her sharp, boisterous cackle that he used to find annoying now sounds appealing and welcome. Her hair is back to its natural color, a light brown, cut shorter, making her look, somehow, more mature. She wears a navy blue one-piece, which contrasts with her pale skin. Alex is tanner, from all the running—though it's a farmer's tan, so his chest is pale—and his body has a healthy leanness.

Clare comes out from inside, carrying another pitcher of sweetened iced tea, which she sets on a table that is covered by an umbrella. Then Clare jumps into the deep end. When she comes up for air, she perches next to James.

Nathen does a cannonball and water splatters in every direction.

"He's a nut," Clare says, laughing.

Nathen swims all the way to the shallow end and climbs out. His dripping trunks are hanging precariously on his hips before he yanks them up. He heads for the table without drying off and pours himself some tea.

"This is nice, isn't it?" Clare says. Her wet hair is the color of hay and clings to her head like a helmet.

"It's great."

Nathen brings his iced tea to a chair next to Alex. Soon, Alice gets up and wades into the shallow end. She dips underwater and swims toward them.

"Alex has really come out of his shell," Clare says, glancing over at him and Nathen.

"You could say that," James says.

Alice swims up next to them and treads water. "He's gonna break some hearts next year," she says.

"Maybe," James says. He can't help himself from smiling at this. He looks at Clare and she smiles knowingly at him, like she is holding in a secret. And maybe she is.

Mr. Ashford comes outside then, carrying a Tupperware container of hamburger meat and hot dogs. "You kids hungry yet?" he shouts.

"Yes, sir!" Nathen shouts back. The others mutter their yeses as well.

"I better go see if he needs help," Clare says, and climbs out of the pool.

"So, you must be psyched to be done," Alice says, still treading water.

"I guess so. You'll be done, too, soon enough."

"Yeah. Summer school won't be so bad, I guess."

"And then what?"

"I may take the first semester off, work. Save a little money. My stepfather says he'll help me with tuition at Alabama now. So I'll probably start in January."

"That's awesome," James says.

"Yeah, it's pretty cool."

"I like you with brown hair. You look good."

Alice giggles. "Oh, James," she says, pulling up alongside him by the ladder of the deep end. She splashes him.

He splashes her back. "I just meant that . . . I mean, you look happy."

Alice grins and looks away. "Thanks. I'm feeling okay." She ducks underwater, as if she wants to hide from him. When she comes up, she is still smiling. "Your brother is a doll by the way," she says. "We're going to hang out when you leave us for Duke."

"You are?"

"Why not?"

"Why not," James agrees.

She shoots him a suspicious look, her eyes slanted.

"I mean it," he says. "He'll need some friends."

"Hey, we all need some friends."

"That's true," he says. In September, he'll have to start over. He'll meet new people, make new friends, date new girls. The world he knows now will recede and a new one will open up.

"Besides," Alice says, "Alex and I . . . I don't know. I barely know him, but I feel like he's a kindred spirit. I know that sounds stupid. I mean, we both thought we hated this town, and all those assholes here. But we like it, too. I mean, it's what we're stuck with, you know? This town. This school. The people. It's not all bad. You can learn to live with it."

James nods. He glances over at Alex and Nathen, talking together quietly. "Yeah," he says. "I know what you mean."

"People can surprise you."

He looks at Alice, searching her face for any scars from her accident. But he can't see any. It's like the car accident never happened. But he knows it did. "They sure can," he replies.

"Food's almost ready!" Mr. Ashford shouts.

"Guess we better get out," James says.

"Good, I'm starving," Alice says.

They both climb out of the pool, and Alice tiptoes across the hot cement and over to the grill to pick her burger. James walks to the lounge chair where his towel rests in the sun. He starts to dry off and he freezes there, taking in the scene: Alice holding her paper plate, somehow at ease around these people who used to be strangers; Nathen, standing with his hands on his hips, a towel draped around his neck; Suzy, running her hands through her sun-baked hair; Clare in her red bikini, standing by her father with a fork, trying to be the helpful hostess; and Alex, his arms clasped across his chest, looking at Nathen with what James can only describe as affection.

Later, as the sun starts to set, Nathen drives the two of them home. They listen to the radio without talking, feeling content but also zapped of energy by the long day in the sun.

"Call me later," Nathen says to both of them when he drops them at their curb. The three of them have plans to watch a movie together tonight. He honks his horn as he drives off.

James checks the mailbox—he's expecting some summer orientation packets from Duke—but it's empty, meaning Mom or Dad must have gotten it already. Before walking to the door, he notices Alex stealing a glance across the street. Henry and his mother left over a week ago, packing their car with boxes and suitcases and anything else that would fit. He and Alex waved to Henry as they drove down the street, out of a sight.

"I keep expecting to see Henry sitting on the curb," Alex says.

"I know," James says.

"They should be in Charlotte by now."

"Probably."

They both pause, taking in the sight of Henry's empty house, the yard that is sprouting summer weeds. There is no For Sale or For Rent sign posted yet. Maybe it will remain empty for a while.

"I hope he meets some new friends," Alex says.

"I'm sure he will," James says. After all, he thinks, Henry met Alex, he met me. They were friends, weren't they? "He'll be fine."

The two of them continue standing there. It's nearly dark now. He listens to the heavy chirping of crickets, seemingly everywhere, making their music. A few lightning bugs fly around the yard, creating little explosions of yellow. He and Alex used to spend summer nights chasing them around the yard barefoot, cupping them in their hands and then putting them in a jar, the top punctured with holes to allow them to breathe. They used to compete, to see who could capture the most. As if he is having the same exact memory, Alex starts chasing one of the bugs around, his hands cupped in preparation.

James closes his eyes. He thinks of the summer ahead. All year long, he has been impatient to start a new life, to get away from here. But now, he wishes he could slow things down. Suddenly, he's in no rush to go anywhere.

Acknowledgments

Even though writing is mostly a solitary pursuit, this novel would not have been possible without the help, encouragement, and support of many people through the years.

I owe a huge thanks to a great writer and teacher, A. Manette Ansay. Thanks for sharing your wisdom and for believing in me from the very beginning. I also want to thank a few other wonderful teachers who inspired and nourished my love for the written word: Janice Winokur, Tim Richardson, Bill Engel, and the late Nancy Walker.

Thanks to the creative writing department at the University of Florida for providing time and space when I was a young and clueless neophyte. Mike Magnuson, in particular, provided invaluable instruction—and quite a few laughs. I also thank Erin Page and Diane Zinna, immensely talented writers, for helping make the Gainsville years a lot brighter. Finally, much thanks to the Henfield Foundation for providing an early shot in the arm (as well as a few bucks).

My friends in Austin were always there to listen and talk (often over margaritas), to make me laugh, and to help keep my chin up. Thanks to all of you, especially Scott Landry, Taylor

Andrews, Richard Lewis, Becky Shore, Jason Morris, Melissa Tullos, and Maria Hong. Amanda Eyre Ward deserves a special call-out for years of pointed comments, kind words, and much-needed cheerleading. And lastly, thanks to Clay Smith for his friendship, for his support of the written word, and for giving me the guts to move to New York City.

In New York, I have been blessed to know so many talented and amazing people, all of whom have made finishing this novel much easier. A few people need to be singled out. Helen Ellis, fellow Tuscaloosan and novelist, has been a mentor from day one, always pushing me to productivity and waving me to the finish line. Amy Chozick is the best friend anyone could have—thanks for always being there, even when you were thousands of miles away; I can't wait for *your* novel. A heartfelt thanks to Ed Wintle for always inspiring me and for never failing to offer words of encouragement and generosity. Thanks to everyone at Vintage/Anchor for making the workplace feel like a second home—as well as a place that enriches and encourages creativity. Finally, as I wrote this novel, these friends shared their thoughtful, helpful, and much-appreciated comments and suggestions: Katie Freeman, Jenny Jackson, Kate Runde, Lisa Weinert, and Jason Wells.

Thanks to the brilliant and glamorous Rob Mandolene for so generously sharing his artistry. I'm thrilled to know you.

George Nicholson, my agent, is a dream come true. Thanks for taking me on and for teaching me so much along the way. I feel honored to be your client and your friend.

Jodi Keller at Delacorte Press has blown me away with her editorial brilliance. I can't thank her enough for her thorough and tireless attention to my manuscript—and for helping me make this book the best that it could be. Indeed, I want to thank the entire Delacorte Press/Random House team, especially Beverly Horowitz and Michelle Poploff, for standing behind this book, and Vikki Sheatsley, for her wonderful cover.

In the end, I'd be nowhere without the love and support of my family, especially Mom, Dad, Avery, Eric, Julie, and Ethan. I can't adequately express how much you all mean to me. All I know is that the world would be a much better place if every person grew up and lived his life surrounded by such love, support, tolerance, patience, and, yes, weirdness. You guys are amazing.

About the Author

MARTIN WILSON was born in Tuscaloosa, Alabama. He received a B.A. from Vanderbilt University and an MFA from the University of Florida, where one of his short stories won a Henfield/Transatlantic Review Award. He lives in New York City. This is his first novel.